DAUGHTER
of
SNOW *and*
SECRETS

KERRY CHAPUT

Black Rose Writing | Texas

ISBN: 978-1-68513-390-0
LIBRARY OF CONGRESS CONTROL NUMBER: 2023948132
PUBLISHED BY BLACK ROSE WRITING
www.blackrosewriting.com

Printed in the United States of America
Suggested Retail Price (SRP) $21.95

Daughter of Snow and Secrets is printed in Adobe Caslon Pro

*As a planet-friendly publisher, Black Rose Writing does its best to eliminate unnecessary waste to reduce paper usage and energy costs, while never compromising the reading experience. As a result, the final word count vs. page count may not meet common expectations.

To all the women who have ever felt forgotten by history.

DAUGHTER
of
SNOW *and*
SECRETS

CHAPTER ONE

Dauphiné, France, *1681*

I've started thinking about death. My death, to be specific. The years I spent with the Huron in Canada taught me to listen to my wandering thoughts that warn of danger. If my old friend Naira were here, I'd ask her if she's seen the moment I die, and if it's possible to have power in your last moments. But Naira isn't here, and I have a job to do.

I settle into controlled breathing. Narrowed eyes. Silent steps. Back in my familiar place in the shadows where the black night protects me. Through the window I watch the family of four rocking and crying. Eyes closed, I plunge my fear deep away from the moment.

Around them, three soldiers pace. *Dragoons.* At one time, my heart would have raced, and my mouth would have gone dry. Now, I'm as centered as a stone in the wind. Focused on my targets.

A young soldier, perhaps twenty, looks down. His superior shoves him forward toward the family sitting at their square wooden table. The pale soldier places his hand on the mother's shoulder. A tear leaks from her eye as her husband's lip quivers. The young dragoon knows he must prove his strength. He closes his eyes. Perhaps he'll do the right thing.

He grabs the woman's hair and shoves her head back. He kisses her. Forceful and sloppy. She doesn't fight. The children, twin boys around twelve, bury their faces in their hands. The father reaches for his wife, but the older dragoon slaps him hard enough to knock him to the floor.

I narrow my eyes and scan the room. Pot roasting over the fire. Hunting spear on the mantel. Broken glass jars on the floor that crackle under the dragoons' perfectly shined boots. The sickening twinkle in their eyes. These men aren't soldiers, they're savages.

The father pushes himself from the floor, but a portly dragoon shoves his heel into the small of his back and holds him flat. I step onto a teetering rock, which I know is dangerous, but not one tiny detail can slip past me. Not now.

I lean forward onto my toes, the rock shifting ever so slightly, my cheek pressed to the cool glass. Just as I position the perfect angle, the young dragoon pulls the wife from the chair and drags her toward the bedroom. I consider my options when my foot slips and the rock tumbles out from under me.

By the time I pop back up from hitting the ground, one of the dragoons has already bolted outside and grabbed me. I resist, but he pulls both my arms behind my back and throws me inside where I stumble over the threshold. I catch myself on the table.

The second dragoon yanks me up. "What do we have here? Another Protestant?"

"I'm a neighbor." That's all I get out when he shoves my cheek to the table, my hands bound behind my back.

"Naive girl thinks she can protect her friends," he says. He buries his nose in my hair and inhales deeply. "She smells ripe for the taking."

I lock gaze with the father as he struggles under the dragoon's boot. The soft skin around his eyes is swollen and purple with restrained tears. "Shh," I whisper to the man. "It will be all right."

The father shakes his head in sorrow.

"You will escape," I say with forced calm.

"How?" he whispers.

I wink with the hint of a smile. The dragoon's nose cracks when I knock my skull into his face. Arms free, I slam my fist into the man's elbow. When he falls forward, I crack my head back into his nose again. The sad excuse for a soldier takes a moment to cover his bloody face.

He underestimated me. *Grave mistake.*

I whip around and shove my boot into his groin and strike my elbow into his shoulder blades. The younger dragoon stares at his superior crumpled on the ground and stupidly decides to rush toward me. I pull a knife from my stocking and throw it with precision into his man's neck. "I almost believed you would be kind," I say.

He falls to his knees, blood rushing over his hands.

The portly man grabs a chair and throws it at me, releasing his boot from the father's back. I'm able to duck under the table to avoid the errant chair, and skid on my side while kicking my feet into his shins. The floor quakes when he thuds like a fallen pine. He grabs my ankle, but I shake him away like an ant. He still clutches me, so I yank my knife from the deceased dragoon's fleshy neck where it slides out with a pop. I toss it with the same trajectory as a tomahawk. I haven't seen one of those since Canada, but I imagine its power as the knife slices his bulbous abdomen like a ripe melon.

He grunts and holds his shaky hands over the knife. "The King will find out about this."

I grab linen and wipe blood splatter from my cheek. "Oh, I'm counting on it." My voice thrums in even, cool tones, but something about this man rattles my insides. He exudes darkness.

"You dare defy the Crown?" His face fades to ash. "You will pay."

"No, monsieur. We will survive. I'll make certain of it." After he wilts to the floor, I turn to the man who sniffed me. "And you? How would you prefer to die? I extract my knife from the man's belly. "Knife, spear, or blow to the head?"

His mouth puckers as he glances around for a weapon. "I have a family."

I motion to the cowering Protestants in the corner. "And what of this family? You were about to torture them." I step closer to the soldier, twirling the blood-splattered blade in my hand.

He lowers his gaze to my steady grip on the blade that just killed two of his men. "Simply following the King's orders, madame." He snarls at the word *madame*, seeming to realize I am not a lowly neighbor who happened upon this grisly scene.

No, I orchestrated every moment of this fight.

"Ah, the king's orders," I say. "Torture Protestants until they convert." I wipe my blade clean, taking my time, memorizing every detail of his face. Somewhere in middle age, like me, the corner of his eyes puckering into fine lines. A jagged scar across his cheek pulls one side of his mouth up in a twisted smile. He lowers his head like a territorial barn cat, prepared to pounce.

"When will you people understand? We don't have the choice to convert. We are chosen by God."

He sneers, a heavy twitch in one eye. "Who are you?"

"No one of consequence." I widen my stance. "Come for me. Take your shot. After all, I'm just a woman." A woman who can drain enough blood from his neck to kill him in sixty seconds.

He swipes the back of his hand across his crusty nose and hesitates. Maybe he knows I've made a vow to only kill who attacks me. Maybe he knows my faith keeps me grounded and prevents me from turning into a monster like him. Or maybe he senses the fire in my belly to protect Protestants by any measure.

He chooses wisely and backs away like the cornered rat he is. "You won't get away with this."

"I just did."

He growls, knowing a Protestant woman just outsmarted him. "I'll remember your face."

"I hope you do." I pull the hunting spear from the mantel. "Now, let's see how fast you can run."

He stumbles through the front door. I chase after him for fifty paces, until he disappears into the trees. A cold chill climbs my neck. Something I never feel anymore and don't dare to examine, so I allow him to fade into the night.

Back in the cabin, I collect any weapons I can find.

"Thank you," the mother says, arms wrapped around her sons.

"No need to thank me. Now come. We must leave."

"Leave?" the father asks.

"Unless you'd like to stay and see what happens when they find two dead dragoons in a pool of blood on your floor."

"We have nowhere to go," the mother says.

"Of course you do. You'll come with me." I step outside and wrap myself in the cape I left under the window. Snow flurries flutter from the clear, star-splashed sky.

One of the twins steps out to watch me. "You planned this. You wanted them to bring you inside."

"You're a smart boy."

"We could have outlasted the torture," he says. "We're prepared for our time."

"I know that's what you've been taught. I was once the same." I button my cape and help him tighten his jacket. "I don't believe we're meant for torture."

The rest of the family joins us. "We hoped they would leave once we refused to convert," the mother says.

"The dragoons are unruly. They'll hurt all of you, even the children, until the man of the house relents. If he doesn't, they eat your food, steal your money, and break everything from furniture to your skulls. If you do convert, they move onto the next home and the next family to torment."

The parents cover their mouths. Sometimes I forget how sheltered the mountain Protestants are. Growing up as I did in La Rochelle, torture was as routine as the sunrise.

"Why do they hate us?" The inquisitive boy asks, his upper lip stiff to ward off any tears.

"Hate runs deep in their core. They're taught from their earliest days that we are evil and should be sacrificed to support the will of our Catholic King."

"How do you know all this?" the father asks.

"About Catholics?" I shake a collection of snowflakes from my hair. "I used to be one." I motion for them to follow. "Hurry. To that tree line."

The family stumbles along, their breath wavering in the crisp air. "It's so dark," the mother says.

"That's how we will travel undetected," I say. I lead them to a thicket of trees where a wagon awaits. "There are blankets and food. Settle in. It will be a long night."

Out from the trees emerges Andre. We've been married ten years, yet his shining eyes still make my heart flutter. He slides his arm around my low back and pulls me close. He wipes the blood from my temple with his thumb. "Are you hurt?"

"No." I lean close to his lips. "I've never felt more alive."

The family glares at us from the wagon. "Who are you people?" the father asks.

I glance at Andre and back at them. "We are the resistance."

The mother pulls the boys close. "We weren't aware there was a Protestant resistance."

"And that's just how we like it," Andre says. He kisses me as firm and intense as the day we escaped France a decade ago. "Shall we take them home, Madame Boucher?"

"Yes."

"Where is home?" the boy asks.

"Geneva," I say with a smile. "You'll be very happy there."

Andre and I sit close together in the front of the wagon as he positions the reins. "How many did you kill?" he asks with a tilted head.

"Two."

He grips the reins tight. Adjusts in his seat. "You let one free?"

"You know my rules."

He nods. Andre long ago accepted my wild ways. "He'll report back to the king."

"I'm aware." I stare ahead and watch my breath turn into a white cloud in the misty air. The dragoon's hooded eyes looked dark enough to be black. They hover in my mind like heavy chunks of coal.

Andre takes in a breath of sharp, clear air. "Perhaps next time I'll—"

"No." I shoot him a firm look. "This is our arrangement. I fight. You carry us to safety."

Andre has many smiles. This one, closed and rigid, shows me there are words he refuses to say. Instead, he plants a soft kiss behind my ear. "As Madame wishes."

"Time to move."

Andre handles the horses, and we roll through the night at the onset of a long journey heading east. Off in the trees, I glimpse two shining, glossy lights. I think they're a deer, but I soon realize they're the darkened, soulless eyes of the man I let run free. He watches us. My head spins to follow the orbs of black and white. Andre, attuned to my every twitch, places his hand on my thigh. "Something wrong?"

"No." I force myself to stare forward, my stomach tightening like a fist. "We saved four more Protestants. Right now, that's all that matters."

I lean my cheek on Andre's shoulder and soften into his protective presence, but inside, worry tumbles fast and erratic like a stone down a mountain. That dragoon will report me. He will remember me. And he will not relent until he slices me in two.

CHAPTER TWO

Wrapped in a swath of bear fur, I stand outside our two-room cabin as snowflakes gather on my cheeks. Snow, like magic, settles my restless heart.

Andre steps outside and envelops me in his strong arms. I lean my head to his chest as we watch the beauty of Geneva unfold before us. Powdery white treetops against a marigold sunrise.

"Do you ever imagine a day when this view will be enough?" Andre asks.

I lift my head, puzzled. "Why would you ask me that?"

"Isabelle, I understand who you are. I accept that I love a fighter who is meant to change the world. I would never stand in your way."

"But?"

"I just wonder if you do this because it's your calling or because you're punishing yourself."

With a firm hand to his sternum, I push myself away from the heat of his body. "Does it matter?" Perhaps it's both.

A subtle tightening of his jaw gives me pause, but then he kisses my temple. "I will fight alongside you forever, my love."

I wait for the remainder of his thoughts to tumble out, the tangle of fear and hope he carries that always seems to snag at my heart. I hear nothing but birdsong and creaking spruce limbs under the weight of snow piles. Once again, Andre communicates in the words he does not say.

"Do you worry about me when I'm out there?"

Without hesitation, he says, "The only thing I worry about is that you sleep soundly, knowing you have done everything you could."

He's right. My nightmares stopped years ago, but I still wander the cabin at night, dreaming up new paths for the resistance, conjuring the moment I might die in battle. Every Huguenot I save reminds me there are thousands more.

"Are you two done?" Elizabeth steps outside, her hair a frizzled mess.

"You should be happy your parents love each other so much," Andre says.

"Yes, well. I don't plan on falling in love." She sniffs ever so subtly. "It makes people soft."

I extend my arm and pull her into our embrace. Our trio of safety replenishes my will to carry on. "The more you fight it, the harder it pulls you under."

Elizabeth is all fire, and I couldn't be prouder. She hasn't known an easy life, having lost her mother years ago, but I'm grateful that she has never known persecution. I'll make sure she never does.

"Isabelle, what will we work on today?"

Although Elizabeth isn't my birth daughter, I told her years ago she could call me mother. She prefers my first name, and I quite like it. I've been a Colette, a Beaumont, and now a Boucher. But Isabelle has always been the real me. "Perhaps we should take a day of rest and read by the fire."

"And sew?" Elizabeth says with a laugh.

After a pause, we both burst into laughter. Andre rolls his eyes. "My sweet girls. You both terrify me." He kisses Elizabeth on the forehead and rubs my cheek. "Don't come home with any broken bones."

Elizabeth winks. "Not unless they're someone else's."

· · ·

The snow covers the morning in a blanket of quiet, except for the crunch under our boots. Elizabeth, brave girl that she is, insists on walking in front of me. She carries a stick found in the forest, just as I taught her.

"Isabelle, when will you tell me more about your time in France?"

"I've told you everything you need to know," I say.

"All I know is that you were once a Catholic and Papa loved you from the moment he saw you."

A whirl of wind picks up flakes of snow ahead of us. "As I said, you know everything of importance."

"I'm fifteen. I know three languages. You've taught me to live off the forest and how to track footprints at night. And yet, you continue to treat me like a fragile child." She whacks the stick against a tree and a clump of snow falls from a branch onto her head. She turns to me and shakes the snow from her dark hair.

"You are not a child, Elizabeth." I brush her shoulders dry. "You are a brave, cunning young woman who can handle anything in front of her."

"Why teach me to fight and shelter me at the same time?"

A mass of gray wool flies through the air and takes Elizabeth to the ground. Elizabeth grunts when her back hits the snow, but she becomes a fighter in an instant, kicking her attacker away. Elizabeth jumps to her feet and blocks hit after hit with the ease of a warrior. Jab, block. Punch, block. Slap, block. They tussle and roll as Elizabeth grows impatient and throws her attacker against a tree, grabs her stick, and shoves it against the attacker's chest.

Hands up, the attacker removes their hood as blond locks tumble to her shoulders.

"Aunt Charlotte, give me a challenge next time," Elizabeth says.

"You're fast, Elizabeth." She catches her breath while shooting a glance at me. "You taught her well."

She helps Charlotte up with a firm hand. "You've both have."

"Well done, Elizabeth." I throw her stick aside. "My turn."

I ready my stance, hands up. Elizabeth matches my position, and we circle each other.

Charlotte provides directions. "Patience. Outlast her with focus. Always listen behind and above you for another attack. Feel your environment. The snow under your feet. The whistle of the cold wind. The faraway trickle of a frozen stream."

Elizabeth looks up to a bird soaring overhead. I pause. "Cricket, pay attention! Do not get distract—"

Before I can finish, Elizabeth has bent over and shoved her shoulders into my stomach with such force, she knocks the breath from my chest. Her knee is braced against my neck.

Charlotte steps up to us. "What is the most important lesson?"

She releases me with a smile. "Attack when they least expect it." She helps me up. "I told you, I pay attention. I'm not a child."

"You're an excellent student," I say.

"Come," Charlotte says. "Let's climb trees until our hands bleed." She seeks the most difficult tree to climb while we follow leisurely.

"You never answered my question, Isabelle."

I shrug one shoulder. "What question is that?"

"Why make me a fighter but protect me in this sheltered village and tell me nothing of your past?"

I wrap my arm around her shoulder. "I teach you these skills and provide a life where you will never need to use them."

"I don't understand the purpose of that."

"If I have learned anything in my life, it's that peace is never everlasting. One must always be prepared."

She softens against my arm. "Were you always a fighter?"

"Every day of my life."

.   .   .

Elizabeth and I return home sore, scratched, and laughing. Andre has supper prepared and a roaring fire to warm up next to.

"What trouble did Isabelle and Charlotte get you into today?" Andre asks.

"The usual," she says with a smile. "Maybe someday you'll bring me on one of your secret trips."

Andre scratches his neck. "What we do is very dangerous."

"I'm a great fighter now," she says. "Just ask Isabelle."

I clear our bowls and try to avoid her questions, which is growing more difficult by the day.

"I can help. I want to help."

Andre leads her to the fire and points to the carved wolf on the mantel. "This is Isabelle.

Her life has made her into a fierce fighter who vows to protect her pack." I listen to his view of me, but I don't meet his eyes. "We have cause to fight. They've killed everyone we cared about and forced us from our homes."

"They killed my family too, Papa."

"Your mother died of sickness."

"I know. I meant your parents. Isabelle's friends. Charlotte's sister. Don't you always tell me all Protestants are a family whether we have met or not?"

"Yes," he says with a proud smile.

"Then let me join the cause. I want to help you save them."

I turn to look directly at Andre and shake my head slowly. Andre hugs her, still looking at me over Elizabeth's shoulder. "Perhaps someday."

"I love you very much, Papa. But you can't keep me here forever." She kisses his cheek and walks toward her bedroom. She grabs her dress in her fists while keeping her elbows straight.

"Whether or not you ever engage in battle, you will always be a fighter," I tell her.

"What did you expect? I was raised by the two of you." She shuts her door and Andre and I exhale a sigh of relief.

Andre leads me to the bedroom and as we get dressed for bed, he whispers, "She wants to be like you. I don't blame her. You are quite magnificent."

I slip on my nightdress and braid my hair by the warmth of the fire. "She looks so much like Louise, with her dark hair and big brown eyes."

"But her person is all you," Andre says. "She is us."

I stare at the silver moon dangling low in the sky. "I don't want to put her in danger."

Andre wraps his arms around my waist and rests his chin on my shoulder as we both watch the moon. "I'm grateful she's never known the torture of living as a Huguenot. Here in Geneva, we are simply Protestants and townsfolk."

I lean my cheek to his soft hair. "Who sneak into France and kill Catholic soldiers."

"We save Huguenots," he says.

I turn to face him. The years have only made him stronger, more handsome, and wiser. "The day I met you at the abbey, I felt something."

"That was a very long time ago." He glides my plait softly over my shoulder.

"I think deep down, I felt our shared past. Our mutual desire for freedom. I felt you before I knew you."

"We were both hiding but found our way here. And I'm thankful every day that we never gave up." He pulls me into a kiss, soft but firm. He slides my shift down my arm and kisses my shoulder.

"I want Elizabeth to feel that same kind of love."

Andre cups my cheeks in his hands. "I want that for her too."

"We can't put her in danger, but she's pushing so hard."

He grazes my neck with the back of his fingers. "She's growing up. I suspect this is just the beginning."

"We can keep her safe, just a bit longer. Can't we?"

"Yes, my love. We can." Andre lifts my leg around his low back and presses me into his bare chest. He lifts me like I'm a feather and carries me to bed. As he removes my shift and kisses my chest, I forget every worry. All I feel is Andre's lips. His touch. I become a woman in the arms of the man I love. Nothing more. Nothing less.

The fighter in me can rest because his touch softens me like nothing else in life. Andre's intense eyes don't leave mine as we share bodies and kisses and the joy of our peaceful home.

I curl into his chest as his quiet breath warms my neck. I wait for him to drift to sleep and remember all those nights I dreamt of his touch and now, after adventures and rescues, and poisons and beatings, we are now two Protestants sharing a life.

"Isabelle," he whispers.

"Yes?"

"I love how you love us."

I settle into his embrace and try to sleep, but all I see when I shut my eyes are that dragoon's eyes in the forest, and I wonder how long until the king sends his soldiers to kill me.

CHAPTER THREE

The next day as Charlotte and I make bread, our daughters talk of the town gossip by the fire.

"Clémentine has started to speak of marriage," Charlotte says with a grimace.

I mix flour, yeast, and salt with my fingertips. "Is that so bad?"

"How did Henri and I manage to raise a daughter who only thinks of men?" She punches her fist into the center of soft dough.

Charlotte and Henri, the most cunning people I know, who still thrive on driving a knife through a Catholic's heart, have raised a lovely, quiet daughter uninterested in the Protestant fight in France.

"She's just like your sister." Memories of my days in La Rochelle don't burn the way they used to. Perhaps it is age, or maybe I'm a different person, but I don't blame myself the way I once did. Charlotte's sister Clémentine died trying to be brave like me.

"She even looks like her," Charlotte says with a smile that quickly fades. "That was so long ago."

"With our trips to France, it might be good for Clémentine to settle down and start her own family here in Geneva."

Charlotte sighs and shakes her head. "If only we could convince her to follow in the family business."

"Smuggling Protestants into Geneva and killing Catholics?"

"Exactly," she says. We smile, remembering how far we've come. I can't help but envy that her daughter desires a safe home, far away from struggle.

Charlotte's weapon of choice is poison. She likes to watch them suffer. I can't say I blame her, though I prefer swift and necessary. Blades, or a swift knock to the temple.

"What about Elizabeth?" she asks. "She's got a fire in her eyes, that one."

"That fire is what scares me. She's desperate to come to France with us."

She cocks her head. "What does Andre say?"

"We both want to protect her." I place the dough in a bowl and cover it with linen. "I didn't realize this until I had a daughter, but life made me this way. Would I have preferred to live a quiet life in a cottage with Andre. growing old in peace?" I shrug. "I'll never know who I might have been."

"If there is one thing I know, it's that you would have become the resistance even if you never knew struggle. It's in your heart, Isabelle. Putting good in the world is who you are."

I grasp her hand. Henri emerges from his slumber at midday, his hair in a mess of black waves. He wraps his arms around Charlotte and nibbles her neck. "Smells delicious, my love."

She swats him away, but her childlike smile around him has never faded.

"Good morning, girls," he says.

"Good morning, Papa," Clémentine wraps her father in a hug.

"Monsieur Reynard," Elizabeth says with a nod. "Nice of you to join us today."

Henri looks over his shoulder at me. "She is far too much like you, Isabelle."

"That's a good thing." Charlotte winks.

"All right." Henri smooths back his hair. "Time to chop wood."

"I'll help you," I say. "I could use some fresh air."

"Go on, you two. I'll watch over the bread and the laughing girls." Charlotte throws a linen towel over her shoulder.

"Come on, old friend." Henri throws on his jacket and hat. He hands me an ax and we walk into the woods, as I tow a wagon.

"What troubles you?" he asks.

"How do you know something troubles me?"

"Please, Isabelle. I've known you my entire life. You're shrewd and always looking for the next attack, but beneath that hard exterior I still see the girl who stole food with me. You may be able to hide it from Andre, but I see the fear in your eyes."

I set the wagon down and we begin work on the trees. "I made a choice on our last trip to France. It might come back to ruin us."

A snarl tugs at Henri's lip. "I've never understood your rules."

"Yes you have, you simply live by different ones."

He slings the ax, focused on his task for the day. "Somehow, after all the Catholics have done to us, you don't want to see them burn like I do. You still care about being a good person, something that escaped me long ago."

I place my hand on his arm. His muscles tighten and twist, pulsing under my touch. "You and Charlotte have made a wonderful life here."

He looks to the sky then shuts his eyes. "I lay awake at night and remember every kill in detail. The way their blood pools and their eyes go hollow."

"How do you feel when you think of them dying? Does it make you happy?"

"No." He lets the ax fall to the snowy ground. "I remember my father, burning in front of us. I'd rather focus on their blood than my father's screams."

"While you think of their pain, I think of the Huguenots that are still in that hell. And I tell myself that I'll do anything I can to save them." I take my turn cutting branches while Henri leans against a nearby trunk.

"What happened on your last rescue?" he asks.

"I saved a family of four and killed two dragoons."

"And?"

I swing the ax again and again. "I let one free."

Henri forces a stoic look. "Did he get a good look at you?"

I wipe my shoulder to my cool cheek. "Yes."

"What does Andre say?"

"He knows I let a dragoon live, but he doesn't know he watched us through the forest as we rode away."

He kicks off the tree. "We have two options. We keep you here and safe until time has passed." I take a rest while Henri picks up his ax. "Or, we find that man and kill him."

"I won't kill anyone unless they attack me."

With an eye roll, he says, "Your rules. Fine, I'll do it."

He hits the trunk with one hard crack and pulls me back as we watch the cedar teeter and fall with a thud into the forest.

.   .   .

Years ago, Andre and I held hands in a candlelit barn to pray in secret. Now, though we may pray in daylight, we still meet in a barn to plan our rescues.

Andre and I stand on one side of a map of France, and Henri and Charlotte on the other.

"We'll all go," Henri says. "Isabelle can find him, and I'll do the honors."

"He might not even be in Dauphiné anymore," I say. "Maybe he's returned to Paris and reported a Protestant resistance to the king."

Charlotte rests her hand on Henri's arm. "This is why it's best for the women to kill. No one will believe a woman could fight off dragoons and save an entire family."

"There must be other areas we can help and still keep Isabelle safe," Andre says. "They're killing Huguenots all over France."

"These bastards are taking advantage of fear. Poitou is the only place they've officially initiated the Dragonnades," Charlotte says.

I stare across the table at her. "So far."

Andre lifts his hand. His instincts are as sharp as ever. We pause and listen. Silence. Andre slides his knife from his sheath and nods to Henri. They stand at the door and wait. When they hear snow crunch,

Andre nods. They burst the door open and grab whoever is listening and drag them inside.

"Elizabeth?" Andre drops his weapon. "What are you doing?"

"I want to help. Let me come with you to France."

Her eager eyes prove she isn't ready to assist in this fight.

"Elizabeth, we need you to stay with Clémentine while we travel. You have a very important job," Charlotte says.

"I'm old enough now." She steps to me. "Isabelle, please. You know I can do this."

I glance at the others and remember myself at her age. Running from dragoons. Beaten, branded, tortured. "No."

Her eyes well with tears. "You don't think I'm strong enough?"

A twinge shoots through my heart. "I think you're stronger than I ever was." I pull her in for a hug and Andre and I look at each other. "I'd like to keep it that way."

Andre leads Elizabeth to the door. "We're done here for the night. Let's all go home."

We drag a disappointed Elizabeth out of the barn. Charlotte whispers to me. "What will you decide?"

"Andre and I need to stay close to home for a while."

Charlotte, ever the impatient woman, grabs my arm. "You can't give up now. There are dozens more houses being taken over by these monsters."

My insides are pulled in two, shredded between the desire to save them all, and a need to protect Elizabeth. "What would you do to save Clémentine?"

"If my daughter held any desire to fight, and trained the way Elizabeth does, I would bring her into the resistance. If we don't keep the cause alive, it dies with us."

The patter of rain onto snowmelt grounds me to this place. I've learned to listen and breathe, so memories of France don't destroy me. Memories that live in my body and threaten to explode.

I imagine Elizabeth in France as a Protestant. She has no idea the suffering she would risk. "Elizabeth will not carry my burdens."

. . .

As I comb and braid Elizabeth's hair for bed, I struggle with what words might explain how I feel. I can't find them, so I work in silence.

"I just want to be like you," she says.

My fingers freeze. That's what Charlotte's sister once told me. Before they killed her. I tie a ribbon to Elizabeth's thick, dark plait and turn her to face me.

"You're brave and strong and you've saved hundreds of people." She swallows a quivering voice and finds her strength. "I've never met anyone as formidable as you."

"The Isabelle you know was born of necessity. Life forced me into impossible situations, the likes of which I hope you never see. I am brave because I have lived in unimaginable fear."

"Don't you understand? I'm already in it because you raised me."

I brace my arms next to my sides as my trunk goes weak. "What?"

"Yours and Uncle Henri's brandings. Papa's whip marks. Charlotte's thirst for killing. You never have to tell me how awful it was. I see it, and I feel it."

"We try to protect you from our terrible past."

She lays her hand on mine. "All that did was make me want to save people even more."

That connection we all have to our past, our ancestors. The people who barely survived, and the ones who were lost long ago. I forget how strong that bond is. I think we can feel their pain in our bones.

"I know my mother was weak," she says.

"Louise was kind and loving. She had a different life than Papa and I."

"Do you think because I am half her that I don't deserve to join the fight? The Catholic part of me doesn't understand the sacrifices of the Protestant part?"

I want to show her that she's one of us. She will always be one of us. But again, words escape me. I think carefully about how to express to her all that she means to us. "Elizabeth, you're as good as anyone I've ever met, Catholic or Protestant. I want to keep that heart whole. The things we've seen have damaged us, and I don't want that for you."

"I should be doing more," she says with tightened lips.

"You do more by living. And I would never think differently of you because your mother was Catholic. I hope you know that."

"I don't remember her. I've been raised by you and Papa, and I want to be part of your world. You both hold me at a distance when all I want is to join your cause. The cause *you* taught me to be proud of."

"When you have your own children, you will understand." I kiss her temple and walk away, afraid that she'll mistake sympathy for softening on my stance.

She attempts to speak, but the words deflate to an exasperated sigh.

Before closing the door, I tap my fingers on the latch, searching for something to calm her worry. I have none. "Good night, Cricket."

Back in my bedroom, Andre reads by candlelight. "That went well."

I settle in bed next to him. "You're not helping."

He sets down his book and turns to me. "She's looking for you to approve of her. Ask her to join us."

"She's spirited. Always has been. I'm trying to protect her."

"Sounds like someone else I know. And her mother tried to protect her too."

"Monsieur Boucher, if you have something to say, I suggest you say it plainly."

Andre smiles and tucks my wayward curl behind my ear. "Your mother's attempt to protect you only made you fight harder. I see that in Elizabeth."

"Aren't you scared of what will happen to her?"

"Terrified. But I learned long ago to let the women in my life be who they wish. I worry every day that you won't come back to me. That you'll not survive one of the rescues." He rubs my cheek softly.

"You don't share that with me." Though I've always seen it in his eyes.

"Because if you ever stop fighting, you'll lose everything that makes you the woman I fell in love with. And you'd already be gone."

I kiss him, his soft lips and strong jaw as delicious as ever. I climb atop him and stare into his eyes. "Do you think she's ready?"

"I think there are ways to keep her safe and allow her to be part of this thing we've started."

I press my forehead to his and growl. "I've never known another man like you, Andre. So strong, yet so soft."

He sits up and pulls me to him with a thrust which takes my breath away. He slides his hand up my thigh and between my legs. "I'm soft only in heart." He throws me to my back and pins my wrists to the bed. His mouth barely touching mine, he says. "And rough when you need me to be." He sucks on my neck. Softly bites my ear as my body pulses with heat.

He lifts my leg over his shoulder and grips my hips tight enough to make me gasp.

For all my fight, nothing gives me a rush like melting in his arms.

CHAPTER FOUR

When Elizabeth wakes the next morning, Andre and I are hard at work at the table with a map between us.

"What are you doing?" she asks with sleepy eyes.

"Checking the route for our next rescue," Andre says. "Would you like to see?"

A smile tugs at her lips, almost afraid to pull too wide. "Really?"

I nod, still uneasy but resigned to this decision. Andre's right. Better to allow her in under our control than to risk her doing something foolish.

Elizabeth sits at the table and Andre points to Geneva. "We're here." He slides his finger west along the mountains to Grenoble. "This is where we need to be."

"There are so many mountains. Isn't it dangerous to travel?"

We've long traversed these trails and villages made up of sympathizers and protectors of Huguenots. "We know where to stay. There are kind people who help the refugees."

"Are they part of the resistance?"

"Yes," I say. "Everyone plays their role."

"Who are we rescuing?" Her eyes light up with excitement.

"We'll find a family who's had dragoons take over their home, and we will watch and wait," I say. "Then we strike."

She grows excited while I bite back my worry. "What will I do?"

"You have much to learn, Cricket," Andre says.

"Papa, you're going to have to find another name for me. Cricket isn't very tough."

My memory fills with warm, soft, happy memories of Naira, who gave Elizabeth that nickname. Sometimes I miss her so much I have to brace myself until the wave of sadness passes. With no one to guide me, I must rely on her teachings from years ago, still fresh and clear in my mind.

Andre must sense I'm thinking of Naira, so he brushes my cheek with the back of his hand.

"Elizabeth, you'll need to learn these trails before you can join us. You'll stay with friends while we complete our rescue."

She practically bounces out of her chair. "How can I help?"

"Watch and learn," I say. "We leave at midday."

Her face lights with excitement. "I'm going to tell Clémentine." She kisses Andre's cheek. "Thank you."

Once the door shuts, Andre pulls me to sit on his lap. "We can protect her."

"She's so young and wild."

He clasps his hands together around my waist. "Just like you were."

"Exactly. I ran into so many awful things believing I could save everyone."

He runs his fingers through my curls. "Darling, you do save everyone."

I glance at the map and remember those black marble eyes. "Do you think I was foolish to let that Dragoon free?"

"You haven't allowed your pain to turn you dark. There's nothing foolish about that."

I kiss his cheek and inhale his scent. Pine and smoke and winter air. "He knew what he was doing. He didn't fight me because he wanted to track us. He'll let us lead him back to the resistance."

"I sense my love has ideas brewing."

"He wants us to lead him, so that is what we'll do." Andre kisses my neck as I formulate a plan. "We'll lure a group of dragoons right where we want them. Then we'll attack."

Andre runs his tongue along my throat and chin and wraps my legs around his waist. "As Madame wishes," he says.

Something about the threat of every rescue makes me hungry for him. "Take me to bed."

He stands, carrying me to our bedroom with ease, where he tears off my clothes and moves me like a symphony. In our bed, I have no fight. Only pleasure.

. . .

The trail from Geneva to Grenoble is filled with sad memories for so many. Thousands have left their homeland and escaped unimaginable torture. But on these worn trails, I also feel hope. Protestants helping refugees and protecting secrets. A network of kindness and love. The long road winds along ridges and over rocky mountains that lead them to safety, just as it did for us years ago. Today, we walk in reverse as the trail leads us to Elizabeth's first look at the resistance.

"You'll encounter refugees on the trail," Andre tells her. "Direct them to the closest friendly house and offer a bite of food if you have it."

"How long do they travel to get out of France?"

"Days. Weeks. Months." Andre looks up to check the horizon. "Routes in all directions can lead them to safer places."

"Is it difficult for you to go back to France, after everything that happened there?" she asks.

Andre looks at me with a soft smile. "When you've seen all that we have, you realize that home is a feeling, not a place."

We traverse the rocks and peaks, using farmhouses to guide us through the muddy landscape. As winter fades, the sun melts the snow during the day and hardens it to ice at night. Conditions are not ideal for long treks. We each carry a sack with minimal food, wine, fur, and personal items. I've worked with Elizabeth to prepare her for long journeys, though I hoped she'd never be on one.

Elizabeth grabs my wrist. "Thank you. I know you didn't want to bring me."

"You're capable of fighting just as hard as we do. Possibly even more. I was simply trying to protect you."

"You've protected me by teaching me." She nods. "I'm ready for this."

"One thing at a time, Cricket." We stand at a peak and stare down into a rolling valley of green and white and a cluster of farmhouses with smoke trails from their chimneys. "Learn our route. Hear our stories."

We scrabble down the hillside after Andre to the house at the edge of the valley. As the sun sets in a warm glow, we knock on the front door of this small white house.

Madame Durand creaks open the door. "Hello, friends. Lovely day for a walk."

She opens her arms and pulls Andre into an embrace, followed by myself, and she stares in awe at Elizabeth. "Certainly, this isn't your Elizabeth."

Elizabeth smiles. "Yes. I'm happy to be here, madame."

Madame puts her arm around her and guides her inside. "Come, dear. I have so many stories for you." She whispers to me, "How much should I tell her?"

I shake my head, exasperated. "Enough. Perhaps a dose of fear will temper her eagerness."

While Madame prepares a meal and begins her education to our newest recruit, Andre reaches for me. He tilts his head and smiles as he tucks a curl behind my ear. "I know you're happiest on the trail. I see it in your face."

"I'm happy every time we rescue another Huguenot."

"I think the chase might give you a thrill too, my love."

I expect a smile or a wink, but his face falls flat before turning toward the fire.

We help Madame Durand prepare dinner, and we sit for hours telling stories, both funny and sad, so Elizabeth can understand the world she's about to join.

"Aunt Charlotte has told me some terrifying things from La Rochelle," she says. "I can't understand how the Catholics hate us so much."

Madame nods. "It's hard for us all to understand."

"Isabelle and Uncle Henri have brandings from their childhood. Brandings! As if they were cattle."

Fear wiggles through me. Our heartache need not be displayed as a flag of the resistance. It belongs locked inside, far, far away, fueling us with its angry heat.

Andre must notice my face because he squeezes my hand under the table. "Cricket, it's time to sleep. Up the ladder there's a loft with a nice warm bed."

Elizabeth nods, her eyes lit with excitement. "Goodnight."

She climbs the ladder and Madame leads us to our usual room in this two-bedroom cottage. Madame's husband died years ago, and I think her guests keep her from feeling lonely. "Settle in," she says.

"Thank you, as always," I say.

"You are always welcome here." She hesitates. Glances behind to make sure Elizabeth hasn't climbed down. "The village has received word. The dragoons have expanded their program."

"More towns?"

"More towns. More billeted soldiers." Her breathe hitches. "More torture."

My body clenches as the old familiar feeling of defeat clamps its fists over my heart.

"One house at a time," Andre says. "That's all we can do."

Madame's eye twitches. "What else haven't you told us?" I ask.

She wrings her hands together, obviously trying to avoid this conversation. "They speak of a woman, a French fighter who attacks soldiers."

"I've made an impression it seems," I say.

She lifts her eyebrows. "You don't seem worried."

"I'm not. Let them fear me. It will work to my advantage." There's an odd comfort in being the hunted. A familiarity of unease that I've always known somehow centers me in a way that calm never does.

"They've started to look for you. The woman with the red curls."

I shake out my curls. "My hair is auburn."

Andre, ever the quiet force, bows his head. "Thank you, Madame." He waits until Madame Durand has settled in near the fire. He closes the door and stares at me.

"I don't want to hear your rational thoughts, Andre." I rub my temples to quell the incoming ache. "I can tell from your expression that you're about to hold me back."

"Let me do the next rescue. It's too dangerous for you."

"No." I sit on the bed and watch the flames dance in the fireplace. "If I'm here, I fight."

Andre lowers to the bed next to me, staring at the amber flames flickering high then low. I glance at his twitching muscles under his cheekbones, poorly hiding his clenched jaw. "Andre, do you fight because I do? Do I make you live this life?"

Andre rubs his neck until it reddens. "Yes."

I want to collapse in his arms and beg for forgiveness. I've known this, of course, but he's never uttered a word of this to me. He's spent ten years fighting alongside me without a drop of hesitation. At least not out loud. "I'm so sorry."

"It's not that simple." He rises, pacing the room, choosing his words carefully. "I do this for you and only you."

"It sounds simple. I've forced you to risk your life, and now I've recruited your daughter." I collapse to the bed, my face buried in my hands. "Take her back to Geneva. I can't do this."

Andre kneels before me, his warm hands around mine. "I have to do this because I love you. If I allow myself to fight for the rage I carry, I'll become a monster."

My hands drop though my mind screams to keep them over my eyes and go back to where my pain doesn't bleed into his. "What does your rage feel like?" I ask.

"Like a seething, hateful boil about to pop. I've fought it because I don't want to be that person. I want to be a good father and husband."

I kiss his hands. "You are good. That's why I kill the soldiers. Let me do the hateful things." It's where I feel most powerful.

"You only kill who attacks you," he says. "That's your line to keep you doing this for the right reasons. If I tell myself I only do this for you, that keeps me from dipping into the depths of somewhere I do not want to go."

"We will always hate them for what they've done." I trace the wood grain of the floor with my toe. "But I don't want you to hate me."

He guides my chin toward him with the tip of his finger. "I could never."

"My choices force you somewhere you don't want to go."

"When I look at Elizabeth, I think of the thousands of children who'll be hurt by France's lowliest soldiers. I want to save them all, but I also want the dragoons to burn, and I can't tolerate myself when I think that. So I follow you and support you."

I pull him to bed and lie on his chest. His heart thumps against my cheek. "I use my hate to remind me never to give up. As long as there is a breath in my chest, I will fight."

Andre pulls back my sleeve and kisses my wrist branding. "Does it still burn?" he asks.

"No. I can't remember that pain. Or I won't."

"This fight will only grow more dangerous," he says with a controlled sigh. "I'm afraid we'll need to adjust our approach."

I lean to kiss his neck and bury my face in his rough skin. "They're looking for me. That's just where I want them." Something stirs inside me. A split down my center into two halves. One side hungers to kill. The other desires a lifetime with Andre.

Now comes the impossible task of living with two parts in a battle toward death. If my dreams mean anything, that end will arrive sooner than anyone anticipates.

CHAPTER FIVE

I wake with all senses alert. A hand on my arm. A whisper in my ear. It's still dark. I grab the offending hand and throw them to the ground until I can get my bearings.

"Isabelle!" Elizabeth says, her face muffled by the floor.

I roll off her and catch my breath. "I told you never to surprise me like that. I can control myself during waking hours, but once I'm asleep, you take your chances."

Hardly affected, Elizabeth rolls to her stomach and smiles widely. "I'm alright."

"Why have you woken me up so early?"

"Training, obviously." She jumps to her feet.

I flop my arm over my eyes. "We aren't at home, Elizabeth. Let me sleep."

She removes my arm and overlooks my scowl. "Do warriors sleep? No. They prepare."

"She's right." Andre is peering over the bed at us, a silly smile on his face.

I groan. "I've trained her too well."

Andre throws my cape over my head. "The resistance waits for no one."

I toss my cape aside and prop on my elbows. "What about you Monsieur Boucher?"

"You're the fighter, remember? I'm here for emotional support."

He buries himself under a pile of fur and Elizabeth tugs on my arm. "Come on, we only have an hour before daylight."

"Fine." My weary legs cry for a reprieve, but my mind knows they will be stronger for it.

We trek through the clear, crisp morning, weapons in our hands, on our backs, and tucked in our boots. "You introduced me to the quiet of the mountain mornings," she says, a wisp of haze in her breath. "How the snow speaks to us."

"It is special." I stop and eye a target. A birch tree fifty paces away and a clear shot. Narrow trunk and thinned branches. I reach back for my arrow and lift my bow. A swift pull back to my temple and one second to aim. Release. It spirals into the center of the tree, splitting the bark in the trunk's center. "Your turn."

Elizabeth takes the bow and an arrow from my quiver. She closes one eye, positions her shoulders, and narrows her focus. She takes an extra second and releases. Her arrow lands within a finger's width of mine.

"Well done, Cricket."

"Can I not be something more fierce?"

"Not yet, my dear."

"Have you always been this good at archery?"

I can't stop myself from laughing. "No." I remember Naira, her teachings and her expectations. All the bruises and sore muscles she left me with, and how I learned to find my warrior. "We all have challenges, but those things simply require more attention."

"Ah, like a needy friend or an itchy rash."

A bubble of laughter climbs through my throat but I catch it with a tight smile. "Yes, just like that."

Elizabeth looks up. "Should we climb trees now?"

A shiver trickles down my neck. Noises. Subtle but noticeable. I lower her to a crouch and motion for her silence. I nod to her boot, and she removes her blade.

"Sheepherder?" she whispers.

I shake no. The cadence is off. No staff tapping the ground. Unconcerned footsteps tromp along the trail. I motion for her to follow as we creep toward the noise.

In the distance, I glimpse movement. Through the shadows, a young man. I can tell by his shoulders and his posture. His long, billowing limbs like haricot verts on a vine. Elizabeth hides behind one tree and I jump to the other side of the trail to hide behind another.

I lift my hand to remind her—*seek patience*. I can hear her breathing from here. Our wild child is too eager. I peer behind the trunk to get a glimpse of him. Young, as I suspected. Clean shaven. French military dress. *Merde.*

He's a dragoon.

They shouldn't be on this side of the border. I look back at Elizabeth, eyes wide. She tries to read my expression, shifting to the other side of the trunk to view my face. The papery bark tears under her hands and she falls to the ground.

The dragoon reacts swiftly, lifting her and wrapping his arm around her neck.

"Who are you?" he asks. "What do you want?"

I close my eyes and pray she's listened to everything I've taught her.

"I'm just a girl, monsieur," she says with a quivering voice.

"A girl?" He considers releasing her but pulls her close again, scanning every direction, his knife in hand. "Who are you with?"

"No one."

"A child out here in the dark on a refugee trail by yourself? I don't believe you."

"I'm not a child. I'm a young woman. Now let me go." She wiggles and bucks, but he holds tight. I can't attack and risk him slicing her. Too much at stake. *You can do this, Elizabeth.*

"Not until you tell me who you're with and where you're going."

Elizabeth settles, closes her eyes. Good girl. "Monsieur, you need not worry about me. I ran from my mother, wicked woman that she is. I've lost my way and I simply want to get home." She begins to shiver. He's smart, not taken by a girl in distress. Next tactic.

"Perhaps you could escort me home? My father could provide you with a meal."

Good. He must be hungry. What is he doing out here?

He grunts. After another look around, his arm softens. Just as it does, Elizabeth slams the back of her head to his chin. Without hesitation, I jump from behind and twist his wrist while Elizabeth throws him face-first to the ground, her knee between his shoulder blades.

"Get off me, woman!" he yells.

"What's a dragoon doing in these mountains?" I ask. I keep his face pressed to the icy dirt, so he doesn't see my face.

"Looking for someone."

Elizabeth grabs his hair and pulls. "Who?"

I see why she frightens Andre. Her intensity goes deeper than either of ours, and for no reason other than to make the world a better place. No panic-inducing memories or bubbling revenge to hold her back.

He tries to fight but we anticipate his moves and hold him firm to the cold ground. Elizabeth holds the tip of the blade to his cheek. "Who are you looking for?" He doesn't speak, only grunts. Elizabeth grazes the blade across his cheek as blood springs to through his pale skin.

"A woman," he blurts.

"Anyone in particular? Or just any conquest for a soldier who thinks everything is his property?" She presses the blade to his temple.

"A woman fighter. Red curls."

Elizabeth glances at me. "I have black hair, if you didn't notice," she says. "Although I can protect myself."

"This woman has killed over a dozen soldiers to rescue Huguenots. I've set out to find her."

I withhold my boot from crushing his neck. "Why are you out here, in the dark?" I ask.

"If I were a Huguenot, I would flee France. I want to catch her and present her to my Lieutenant. I'd be a hero."

"They haven't sent you here?" I ask.

He tries to move again, but we don't budge. "No."

"Why does your lieutenant want her?" Elizabeth asks. He resists and attempts to kick me, but Elizabeth makes a small nick in his ear with the tip of her blade. "Tell me, or I'll slice this ear off and feed it to the pigs as slop." I nearly tear up with pride.

"She's a menace." He growls. "They call her the Red Fox."

I roll him to his back. "I am a wolf, not a fox." I slam the handle of my blade into his temple and wipe the sweat from my upper lip.

We stand and stare at this young soldier, stupid enough to believe women are harmless. "Feed his ear to the pigs?"

She shrugs. "Seemed appropriate. What do we do with him?"

"Leave him here. That blow to his head will keep him black for a few hours."

She nudges him with the toe of her boot. "What now?"

"Back to the cottage. Time to change routes. And plans."

·   ·   ·

Andre examines a map, a painted red rock bouncing in his palm. We use it to mark our next stop. Elizabeth paces behind me. "The soldier said he went alone," she says.

"Which means there will be more of them," I say.

"They want to kill you," Elizabeth says with sudden realization.

"It isn't the first time someone has wanted that."

Andre sighs. "I'm sorry, Isabelle. We need to return to Geneva."

"No. There are a dozen more routes." I move the painted red rock to different points on the map. "Here and here. I have options."

"They're all on the lookout for a Huguenot with red curls." His pitying glare ignites the side of me hungry to slash through dragoon flesh.

I lean close to Andre's ear so Elizabeth can't hear me. "Take her home. Let me carry on."

"I'm not going home." Elizabeth crosses her arms. "I don't need to hear your words to know what you're talking about."

"It's too dangerous." I point to the position of the next cottage on the route. "Another eight hour walk to get to our wagon."

"You can't stop." She begs Andre with giant eyes. "I keep telling you I'm ready."

Andre's eyes bore into me, so I toss the pebble back to the map. "There could be dozens more searching for us."

"No," she says. "They're searching for *you*."

The door clicks open, halting our family disagreement for the moment. Madame steps in with a young girl. Perhaps twelve. She's ragged and pale.

Andre rushes to help her near the fire. The girl trembles. Blood trickles down her temple to her chin. Elizabeth stares at me, eyes large and panicked.

Madame wraps a blanket over her shoulders and removes her soggy shoes. She hands her a bowl of warmed broth from over the fire. The girl sips, but her hands shake so violently she spills on her chin.

Elizabeth dots her chin with a cloth. She sits next to her. "What happened to you?"

The girl remains silent for several minutes. She wipes her face and examines her bony fingers caked with dried blood. "I escaped."

I kneel in front of her. "Can you tell me more?"

She swallows with a painful wince. "Dragoons took over our village. They lived in our houses." Tears flood her eyes. "They broke my mother's arm. Beat my father so he'd convert."

"Did he?"

"No. They beat him for hours while blood pooled on the floor. My father's last words were, 'Never.'"

I reach for her hands. "What's your name?"

"Anne."

I force a smile to calm her frantic eyes. "How did you escape, Anne?"

"Mother and I slept on the floor after they took our beds. She told me to follow the trail from Rhone to Geneva. There would be friends along the way."

"Why didn't she come with you?"

"They had broken her legs."

Everyone looks down, these stories all too familiar. "She sacrificed herself to save you," I say.

"I escaped in the dark after the dragoons drank all our wine. We've seen in other homes how the abuse gets worse after the food and drink are gone."

"We're glad you're here." Her hands remain frozen, even cupped around a warm bowl of broth, save for a few jerks and jolts.

"My sister and her new husband lived next door. I begged her to come with me, but she wouldn't leave her home."

"Why not?" I keep my voice steady and barely above a whisper.

"She's pregnant. And frightened." Anne's trembling hands cause her arms to shake, then her neck and head. She spills the broth on her lap. Elizabeth takes the bowl and I lift Anne gently in a hug. "It's alright. We're here." I hold her while her body weight collapses, and she cries into my chest.

Elizabeth makes a face I've never seen on her. Anger, determination, and something new. A twinge of disgust. Watching her begin to see these atrocities makes me ill. I turn away, holding the girl until her sobs lighten. A long, painful ten minutes pass while she whimpers and wails.

Madame helps her exhausted body to bed where she cleans her skin and rubs her forehead until she falls asleep.

"Did you hear that?" Elizabeth whispers. "We can't let them kill her village."

"They probably already have," I say.

"No." She shakes her head. "We should fight. For her. For her sister and their unborn baby."

Andre places his hand on Elizabeth's shoulder. "We can't fight every battle."

Elizabeth throws his hand away. "You want to turn around now? Her village is right along the Rhône. We can make it in two days."

"We could," I say. "And they could be waiting to attack us."

Elizabeth grits her teeth. "You were my age once, Isabelle. You fought without fear of consequences. You saved your family and friends and people you didn't know."

How pure my hate once was. Resist. Fight. Kill. Accept death as inevitable. Now my focus is muddled, tinged with worry for those I love. "I'm smarter now, and I won't march you into danger. Neither will your father."

"She's right, Cricket." Andre seems relieved, especially to place the blame on me. "We should escort the girl back to Geneva where she'll be safe. We'll make a new plan at home."

"We just give up?" Her eyes well with tears.

"No." I step in front of her and square my shoulders. "We make good decisions so we can save more. We're no good to the resistance if we're dead."

"Aunt Charlotte was right. You're too careful." She trudges up the ladder to the loft.

"Aunt Charlotte was just as wild as her." I throw my hands up. "You aren't firm enough with her."

Andre pulls me into his chest. "I'm glad Elizabeth is wild. She learned from you."

I resist the urge to push him away and scream that he should try harder. Resist louder. Protect her like I am.

Instead, I bury my cheek to his warm neck, tired and broken by Anne's tears. "I'd be foolish to stay on this trail with a sixteen-year-old matching my every step."

"Our plan was to introduce her to the trail and the dangers. We've done that." He kisses my temple and situates a pile of straw and fur near the fire.

Shadows bounce across the stone cottage in time to the flames. "I've made a critical error."

He lifts a fur blanket and motions for me to join him. "What's that?"

"I was wild and free and angry a very long time ago. I've since forgotten how powerful youth can be. The freedom of only having yourself to risk."

Andre and I fit together like vines growing free in the forest. I tuck near his chest where I'm warm and safe.

"She'll learn patience," Andre says with a yawn.

Patience is impossible when you're sixteen and staring at the world's worst injustices. Memories of my childhood in La Rochelle grip me like fingernails. I remember the helplessness. The anger. The feeling that I was the only one who wanted to fight. That desperation drove me into the arms of my first husband. James Beaumont was a weak man, but he taught me to find strength. Every choice I've made with Elizabeth spins through my mind in a cloud of doubt.

Andre's words come back to me. If I don't allow her to be herself, she will travel by the wrong guideposts. I listen to his breaths steady, grateful he's never held me back but wishing he'd find more fire buried deep inside him.

·   ·   ·

The bright morning sun beats through the tiny window. I wake to the sound of laughter. Andre and Madame sit at the table, drinking wine and sharing bread.

"What's all the laughter about?" I ask.

"We're telling stories, dear," Madame says.

"Please, share."

Andre kisses me good morning. "There's a look in your eyes the moment before you attack. The wolf in you bleeds out through your skin. Naira would be proud."

"Why is this funny?"

"Because you're fiercer than any man and dragoon that has ever lived."

"And you were raised in La Rochelle where Protestants are instructed to be passive and quiet." Madame hands me a hunk of bread. "You broke convention, my dear."

"The dragoon in the forest called me the Red Fox."

"Fox?" Madame cocks her head.

"A menace with red curls."

"Well, I can't disagree with him there," Andre says with a smile.

Anne walks from the bedroom, face washed, and hair braided. "Good morning."

"Good morning." I reach my arm for her. "How are you?"

She places her hand on her swollen eye and forces out a word. "Fine."

"The Bouchers are kind enough to take you home with them, Anne," Madame says. "You'll be leaving as soon as you fill your belly."

Her brow tightens. "Leave France?"

"You can't ever return," I say. "But you'll be safe with us." We find it's best to speak plainly in these situations.

Andre stands. "Our child certainly can sleep." He stands on the bottom rung. "Cricket!" He climbs the rungs and peers into the loft. When he turns to me, his eyes pull giant. He shakes his head with closed eyes as sickness roils through me.

"No." I run to the table and see a red pebble sitting at the village on the Rhône.

"That's my village," Anne says. "I woke early. It was too difficult to sleep. Elizabeth asked me about my home. We whispered so we wouldn't wake anyone."

"She's gone," I say to Andre. "She thinks she can battle a company of dragoons all on her own."

The wild girl wins this time, and the protective mother has no choice but to track her footsteps. Damn her.

CHAPTER SIX

Two days climbing and watching. My feet have never pounded the earth so fast. Andre and I have barely spoken, both overwhelmed with thoughts of Elizabeth on her own, eager to prove herself to a resistance she has no experience with. Both angry and scared—at the world and each other.

"When we find her, I'm going to hug her tighter than I ever have," I say. "And then I'm going to lock her in our house for eternity."

Andre doesn't respond.

We hurry along the last stretch of trail before the first friendly farmhouse, where we hope Elizabeth has stayed put. "What was she thinking? Map study and practice fights with me in the woods are not the same as meeting a group of drunken dragoons at a remote village."

Andre still says nothing, and his silence irritates me like an itch. "Are you going to speak, or just let me go on?"

"I thought I might let you fatigue yourself," he says.

I straighten my arms and march forward, but he reaches for my hand. "I know you blame me for this. I blame me too."

I soften, having forgotten how Andre gets quiet when frightened. I get angry. "I just want to find her and bring her home, where she's safe."

"Our last night in Geneva, she asked about your past. I told her how you broke Henri from the Bastille, and how you poisoned your first husband."

"You shouldn't have told her so much." I pick up a rock and toss it sideways, gritting my teeth together. "Do you forget she is so wild she thinks she can take on the entire country on her own?"

He stops walking. "I did not forget. I just don't believe lying to her will protect anyone but you."

Unable to tolerate another step, I halt in a cool shadow as chills climb up my arms. "I'm not lying, Andre. I understand her in a way you refuse to. She needs guidance and I seem to be the only one giving it to her."

He kicks at the soil and walks a slow circle. "You want her to see you as powerful, knowing, and strong. I want her to see how broken we are."

"How could that help anybody?" My voice is no longer calm or steady. It's shrill.

"You could stand to see your broken parts a little more clearly, Isabelle."

If gazes could level someone to the ground, he'd be face first in a pile of dirt. "Why? You seem to point out my faults enough for both of us."

My neck tightens in the cold shade of the trees.

"I'm sorry," he says. "Let me try this again." He exhales long and slow as he reaches for my hand. "Elizabeth wants to be brave like you. I want her to see that bravery comes with consequences."

"What is bravery other than a refusal to die?" I yank my hand away and catch my breath. "We are only brave when forced into the impossible. Something I've tried to keep her away from."

"I understand why you've never been upset that we didn't have a child together." I won't look at him. "I've seen how big you love Elizabeth. You worry about yourself in a way you were afraid to before."

Tears rush to my eyes. "I just want a better life for her. Safe and happy."

"Yes, and she wants a better life for others, just as you do." He smiles and gently tucks back my unruly curl over my left eye. "Keeping her from that will only make her want it more."

"She's so much like you, Andre. Strong in a way I could never be. Gentle and good."

His face hardens. "But unlike me, she never questions her right to fight."

"Perhaps she's the best of both of us," I say.

"Yes," he says with a slow nod.

I swallow, trying to move past the things we've said to each other. We're frightened and we love her. I long for his touch but I can't yet reach for him.

We arrive at the farmhouse. Andre throws the barn door open. Empty and dark. "The wagon is gone," he says.

We turn to find the owner of the house approaching. "Bonjour, friends. Elizabeth said to tell you she will meet you at the village."

"She can be sure of it," I say.

"I was hesitant to let her go without you, but she insisted Isabelle wanted her to go ahead. I've only ever heard stories of her from you both. She's beautiful. And intense."

Andre rubs his eyes. "That's her."

"Monsieur, may we borrow a horse?" I ask.

"Of course," he says. "She left a few hours ago. You can still catch her before sundown." He hands us a satchel of supplies for the road and prepares a horse for us. Andre jumps up and reaches for me as he's done for years. I mount the horse in front of him and we say farewell to our friend.

We gallop through meadows where wildflowers peek into the sunshine, under a cloudless, breezy blue afternoon. Andre's chest against my back, his breath on my neck, this is where I usually feel most free. But the worry in my heart slowly tears a gaping hole in any sense of freedom.

Still not speaking, our bodies seem to speak in heat and tension, bouncing against one another along the uneven terrain. Thankful for flat, lush land, we ride for hours. As we move closer to Anne's village, smoke climbs into the sky. Small trails from smoldering fires around the village and giant fires from wood cottages.

"If she isn't here—" I can't bring myself to finish the thought.

Andre pulls the horse to a stop as we survey the morbid scene. Bleeding, broken bodies. Houses burnt to ash. A man dangling from a tree branch spinning ever so slowly by the creaking rope around his neck. I've seen all the tragedy this world has to offer, but Elizabeth hasn't. She isn't ready for this.

We walk through the remnants of a town that once thrived with Huguenots. A cross hammered into the earth where Huguenots once prayed. A red cravat dangling from a stick where their communal oven stood.

"Please let her have missed this," I say. Numbness spreads through me at the thought that she could have tried to fight an army of dragoons. Or worse, that her heart is irrevocably damaged from the horrors she should never have witnessed.

We step through the remains of Protestant life, the smell of burnt, rotting flesh stifling the air. Blackened logs that once were a home crackle and split with gasps of smoke.

We hear crying. "Hurry." I lift my skirts and run toward the sound. I maneuver around a deceased family, huddled together, frozen in time and blood. Sitting at the feet of a dead body, is Elizabeth, weeping.

We rush to her, grateful to see her intact and unharmed. Tears streak her reddened face. I kneel to her and notice what she cries over. A pregnant woman, cold and blue, hand still grasping her swollen belly.

"This is Anne's sister," Elizabeth says. "I was too late. They killed them all."

I want to grab Elizabeth and drag her away from this horror, but Andre removes his Geneva Bible he so bravely carries against his chest. He kneels beside her, and they hold the book together. All the hurt I carried with me today slides from my body and I kneel with them.

Faith alone should carry us through grace. A lovely principle to live by, though its practice has left me with many questions. My beliefs tell me I've already been gifted God's grace, yet I make choices every minute of every day in contrast to this. Something in me will not let me sit in our torture. That part of me has been scarred by this impossible life and isn't guided by faith. That part is guided by control.

Surrounded by the ashes of our people, we hold hands, and we pray, reminded once again that our fight may never be over.

.   .   .

Huddled around a fire off the main trail, we pass around a jug of wine and wait for someone to speak.

"I can still smell their burning bodies." Elizabeth stares at the fire in disbelief.

I nod, knowing I can say nothing to alleviate her pain. She imagines herself in those dead bodies. Her family hanging from a tree. I know it because I've spent a lifetime living it.

"How can they be so evil?" she asks.

Andre stokes the fire solemnly. "Power makes people do horrific things." Restrained and rigid, his body doesn't match his tone.

"Papa?"

"You could have been killed, Cricket." He slams the stick into the fire. "I trusted you with a bit of freedom, and this is how you repay me? This is how you prove you're strong?"

Elizabeth wipes tears from her eyes. "I needed to try. I'm sorry."

"You acted brash and selfish." Andre's voice quivers, which I rarely hear. He punches a tree trunk which causes us both to jump. He walks into the night to calm himself while Elizabeth weeps into her palms.

"He's just frightened. He'll calm soon enough," I say. "We'll leave at daybreak." I rest my hand on her shoulder.

"No." She pulls away from me. "I'm eager to move forward. To find the monsters who did this."

I stare, unsure what to say. "You heard your father. You betrayed us."

"I did. And you can take me home, but I'll just find my way out here again." Her knee bounces as she stares at the fire. "I'll be better prepared next time."

"Have you heard nothing we've said to you tonight?" I wonder if we're having the same conversation.

She turns to me, eyes wide, gripping my arms tightly. "You've kept me from this horror. I understand why." I nod, grateful she understands. Her face flattens. "I'm part of the resistance now. I'm ready to kill."

She stares in my eyes for a long minute, then smiles and buries herself in fur, where she falls soundly to sleep. Numb, I wait for Andre to return. He does, knuckles bruised but finally breathing steady.

"She's decided she will fight at any cost." I try not to bore my stare through him as if to suggest this is his fault. It's both of ours. Neither of us knew how to control the untamed wilds of this girl's heart.

"I was wrong," he says. "She's not like either of us."

"No," I say looking down at her tear-streaked face. "She's a new kind of fighter." I stare at her in awe, unsure whether to be proud—or terrified.

· · ·

Our return to Madame Durand's house is uneventful and very silent. We stare at the door, hesitant to step inside.

"I want to tell her," Elizabeth says. "I want her to know I tried." Without waiting for our response, she steps inside.

Madame welcomes us in. "We've been waiting for you."

Anne looks stronger. Possibly ready to trek to Geneva. She stands with a smile. "I'm happy to see you all safe."

Elizabeth swallows and steps forward. "I have something to tell you."

Anne glances at Madame in worry. "What is it?"

Elizabeth holds Anne's hands. "I tried to save your sister, but I was too late. I'm so sorry."

Her cheeks redden. "You went back to my village?"

"Yes."

The girls stare at each other for an intense, quiet minute. One who lived through the horror, and another who's been through it only in stories. Until today. Anne gently hugs Elizabeth, tears pooled in her blue eyes. She rests her cheek on Elizabeth's shoulder.

"I couldn't save her," Elizabeth says. "She had already died. Your village is gone."

Anne pulls away. "I know. But I've never seen anyone try to save us."

Elizabeth shakes her head. "I don't understand."

I step forward and place my arm around Anne. "You've been raised in a free Protestant community, Elizabeth. One where both parents taught you that life shouldn't be about suffering."

"What did your parents teach you?" she asks Anne.

"What they all teach us. Suffering brings us closer to God. We are to stay strong in our moment of torture."

Something switches in Elizabeth's eyes. An understanding of a world we've tried so hard to shelter her from. "You don't fight back?"

Anne shakes her head.

"We are a lonely group of failed Protestants, Cricket." I rub the side of my thigh. "The ones who wouldn't listen to instructions to die in silence."

Andre joins the tense circle. "Anne, do you need a moment alone?"

Anne nods and I wrap a blanket around her. I kiss her forehead. Nothing will ever be the same for her, a sentiment I try to convey to Elizabeth through my sorrowful gaze.

Madame leads her to the bedroom and shuts the door.

"I'm sorry you couldn't save them," Madame says.

"None of you seem upset," she says. "I don't understand how you aren't outraged."

Andre holds her hands. "We've accepted that we can't stop these atrocities. All we can do is save one person at a time."

"The killings will continue? The torture, the pain?" Her face twists, fighting off tears.

"Yes," I say. "At some point, you accept pain and let it feed your will to fight."

Elizabeth raises her eyes. "I'm sorry I hurt you both, but I'd do it a thousand times over for a chance to stop this madness."

Andre hugs her tight, nearly squeezing tears from her eyes. "None of it would mean anything if we lost you," he says.

"I'd like to go to sleep now." He releases her hesitantly. She climbs the ladder to the loft, but we can still hear her quiet sobs.

Andre rubs my fingers with his thumb. We exchange smiles, a truce.

"It's good for her to understand what she's walking into," Madame says. "Now, I have news."

We follow her to the map. "There are three new villages taken over by dragoons. Possibly more, but this is what the most recent message said. "Here, here, and here." She places three pebbles around Rouen.

"They're next to each other," Andre says. "That's new."

"Word has spread about the resistance. They're instructed to search for the Red Fox."

"A fox is difficult to catch," I say. "Wiley and fast, they love to hide in the shadows."

"This is different," Andre says. "It isn't a house we need to take on, it's hundreds of dragoons, all waiting for you."

"And we will use that to our advantage." I examine the placement of the pebbles. "We can outsmart them."

"How?" Andre asks. "You won't kill anyone who doesn't attack you."

"No, but Charlotte will."

CHAPTER SEVEN

Two Months Later

Entire villages of Protestants have been wiped out. Some by murder, others by recanting and fleeing the country. No one wants to convert because when they do, the dragoons simply pick up and drop their evil on the next Protestant home. Charlotte, Elizabeth, and I gather at a home in Rouen after months resting and plotting. A friend, unnamed and absent, has left her home for our use while we prepare. The men will join us later. This mission requires a woman's touch.

"Tell me again how we lure them?" Elizabeth asks.

"I told you," I say. "They will think we're Catholic."

"I understand that, but how? We wear plain gray wool. Not a stitch of silk or embellishments on us."

Charlotte ignores our conversation and unfolds her collection of bottles. She's spent years curating and perfecting her potions. She can kill a dozen men without lifting more than a smile. "We lie," Charlotte says without looking up.

"They'll be searching for a redhead Protestant, not a Catholic family," I say.

Elizabeth stands next to Charlotte and examines the bottles. "These are all different kinds of poisons?"

Charlotte points to each one. "Belladonna, arsenic, cyanide. And this one is our old friend, antimony." She holds it up to the light. "Just ask Isabelle how well this works."

"That's enough, Charlotte."

"Is this how you poisoned your first husband?" Elizabeth asks. "Beaumont, right?"

I hope my forced cough will show how much I want Elizabeth to stop her inquisition. "We must plan." I lift a letter from the box in the mantel. "Madame says she left us a gift." Inside the letter is a skinny brass key. I hold it to the light. "Come."

The girls follow me to an armoire in the bedroom. The key slides in the lock perfectly. When I open the doors, we find a dozen gorgeous gowns with matching shoes. Elizabeth pushes past me to run her fingers over the material. "They're so colorful."

"Where did she get these?" Charlotte asks.

"You don't want to know."

Charlotte laughs once and hard. "That sounds dangerous, and I'd actually love to know."

Both Charlotte and Elizabeth stare at me expectantly.

"A member of the resistance takes them from dead bodies in and around Rouen."

"And how does a Protestant have access to dead Catholic women?" Charlotte asks with a smirk.

"I said nothing about Protestants." I step up and grab a gown. "Now, let's search the area."

The slide of soft fabric should feel luxurious, but once again, the clothing synonymous with Catholic life steals the air from my chest.

Elizabeth gasps when Charlotte tightens her stay. "Look at my waist!" She glides her hands down the layers of petticoats, tilting her head to the side. "I could conquer France in this finery."

"They're made to keep you restrained and lightheaded," I snap. "Lest you gain any ideas or allow any opinions slip from your mouth."

Elizabeth grimaces. "This is all nonsense. I know that." She lifts her skirts and twirls. "But killing Catholics is much more fun in fancy clothing. Can we keep them?"

"No," we say together.

Dressed in stolen clothes, we stroll through the nearest village, one of three on the map. I take note of every house. Every set of eyes we pass. Dragoons linger around the tavern, unbothered by the cries that screech from the house at the end of the row. Elizabeth gasps but I loop my arm through hers. "Don't react," I whisper.

"We need to save her. She's hurt."

Charlotte hooks her other arm. "Keep walking, Elizabeth. Don't forget your teaching."

Ten dragoons. Two more at the house in the center. I pretend to drop my basket as I sneak a glance through the window of the house with the screams. Three torturers. There must be at least two dozen in this village. Too many.

Heat shoots through my center like a fire scorching my insides. There, inside the home is the man I let free months ago. I recognize the eyes. The scar twisting his cheek. The hate in his gaze. He doesn't see me—yet.

"Good day."

The smell of ale hits me like a whack to the face. I stand slowly to find a young, handsome soldier waiting for us to clear his path.

I bow my head. "Pardon."

"Certainly you wouldn't be snooping, would you, Madame?" His expression is difficult to read, in part due to his obvious inebriation.

"I simply stumbled," I say.

The young man's cheeks flush red. He sways side to side.

Elizabeth steps forward. "She's lying." Charlotte and I lock our eyes on her. "Tell him the truth, Maman." She nods toward the soldier. When I say nothing, Elizabeth places her hands on her hips. "My mother is secretly searching for a suitor for me. Hiding it poorly, I might add."

My neck tightens, furious at her for her impulsivity. "We live in a nearby village, and we've heard of the good work you're doing here."

The young man extends his arm then bows. "I assure you, there is no one more unappealing than yours truly." His eyes linger on Elizabeth and all I can think of is myself at that age falling for a handsome Catholic soldier. Charlotte knocks her hip into me.

"I'm simply a mother who wants the best for her family."

He turns back to Elizabeth. "I am certain your future is meant for more than a lowly soldier with a taste for ale." His arm waves into the air at nothing in particular. "What is your name, girl?"

He sways backward and turns away. "Beaumont," she says, a little too eagerly.

I could kill her. Using my first husband's name.

"Well, related to nobility? I doubt you need a match from one of these ruffians. Best to visit the Beaumonts in Paris to find a—" He burps without covering his mouth. "Husband."

Elizabeth tilts her head to gather her thoughts. Foolish girl. "You know of my family?"

"Of course. Lieutenant Beaumont has made quite a name for himself, dashing bastard that he is."

I might faint.

"What relation are you?" he asks.

"I am his…" Elizabeth pauses, leaning closer with a smile to disarm the soldier. "Niece."

Charlotte, sensing my motherly instincts to slap Elizabeth back to sense, pulls Elizabeth away. "We've taken enough of your time, monsieur."

"Time, time, perhaps I'll discover a rhyme." He holds a smile on Elizabeth who raises her eyebrows at his nonsense. "With a squeeze of lime." He laughs to himself. "What were we saying?"

It's not often all three of us are stunned into silence. "Good day, monsieur."

Charlotte and I drag her out of sight while the soldier stares into the sun until his eyes water.

"What were you thinking?"

Elizabeth straightens her shoulders. "That you needed time to count soldiers. Did you?"

"No. I was too busy controlling your ridiculous behavior. Using my first marriage? Have you listened to nothing we've told you?"

"I see how young men look at me. I was using my beauty to my advantage. That fool didn't seem to see me at all." She pulls her hair away from her face. "Usually my smile makes them flustered and stupid."

She does have her mother's boisterous voice and dangerously flirtatious smile. "That soldier was an odd creature. Speaking in rhymes? As if life is at all humorous."

Charlotte exhales as if to say, *not for Isabelle*. "Elizabeth, I was just like you. Eager and strong, and unwilling to sit back and wait."

"And now?"

"Now I understand what Isabelle taught me. What Naira taught her. Patience. Listen. You control the attack."

"While you were watching me, I looked inside that window," Elizabeth says. "That old man burned her. Her husband wrapped her arm in cloth. I don't know how she isn't still screaming."

"A burn is a small sacrifice to save the entire village." I turn away, too angry to look at her. We march back to the farmhouse on the edge of town, the cool evening air doing little to soften the anger that pounds through me.

Back at the farmhouse, Elizabeth sulks into the bedroom. "I'm sorry." She shuts the door.

"She's just young and eager," Charlotte says.

"Impatient and impulsive."

"Not everyone has your focus, Isabelle. Remember myself ten years ago?"

"I'm shocked I kept you around ten years ago." We sit in front of the fire and sip wine. "I admire Elizabeth. I really do. I'm just so worried she'll get hurt."

"I remember Naira teaching you bow and arrow. How frustrated you'd get."

"Yes."

Charlotte rolls her goblet in her fingers. "What would Naira tell you about Elizabeth if she was here right now?"

I smile at the thought of her. Sometimes I miss her so much my chest aches. "That

Cricket is special. Wild, like me. But strong and smart. She would tell me she has gifts I don't and that I was always meant to raise her."

"That's… specific."

"Naira sometimes whispers to me in my dreams. She came to me a few nights ago. I was standing in the forest on a misty night, trying to find something. I never see her, but I hear her." I slump in my chair and blow my wayward curl from my eye. "Naira's voice is a lot more pleasant than the dreams I used to have of blood on the walls in La Rochelle."

"I still dream of bits of flesh in those blood streams." Charlotte stares at the fire. "Only now, it's the blood of the dragoons."

For the first time in years, my forearm pulses hot. I scratch my branded H, wincing when my fingernails scrape along the sensitive scar. Screams jolt through me, haunting memories of that man holding me down, laughing.

Charlotte notices me. "Henri still scratches at his branding too."

I tighten my hand into a fist and squeeze my forearm tight enough to hurt. "It was that moment that changed me. Not when I was branded, but watching Henri, knowing I couldn't save him."

"Our people have endured such torture." Charlotte's eyes well with tears. Rare for her. "Hundreds of years of senseless abuse and death. We fight, flee, convert. But they don't stop."

I nod in understanding. Helplessness settles in our souls and guides our choices forever. It's why I won't kill unless attacked. Revenge puts me under the control of my memories, and I never want to live there.

"So, James is in Paris?" Charlotte wipes her eyes and refocuses.

"Apparently."

"I wish the poison would have killed him." She sniffs. "He deserved to die."

I glance at her from the corner of my eyes. "He's no longer a concern of ours."

"Until Elizabeth used his name."

"He's nobility now. He wants nothing to do with the Protestant he was once married to, and all the trouble we cause."

"You know that's not true."

Tightness grips my throat. "What do you mean?"

Charlotte leans forward on her knees. "James Beaumont wanted to own you. Control you. He only walked away ten years ago because we would have killed him if he didn't. If he finds you anywhere near Paris, you'll have the King's royal circle to contend with."

"I didn't know he was still alive." We turn to find Elizabeth, hand over her mouth, and we both sit up straight. "I assumed he was dead by how you spoke of him. Papa told me you poisoned him."

"I did. But not enough to kill him," I say. "He's dead to me." I stand and open my arms to her. "It's time you heard my story. From me."

She curls into my arms in a weepy embrace. "I'm ready."

We sit by the fire, and I tell her everything. Dancing all night for the dragoons until my feet bled. Hearing Etienne murdered. Saving Charlotte's sister only to have her arrested after I left La Rochelle. The exile, becoming a King's Daughter in Canada. Meeting her father. Marrying James and using him for secrets. Rescuing Henri from the Bastille and killing my sworn enemy. Living the life of my dreams with Andre and keeping her from experiencing all that has hurt me.

Elizabeth listens intently, a seriousness settling into her eyes. "I'm glad you told me."

Charlotte sighs. "I craft poisons and Henri abducts Catholics who harm people. Sometimes he harms them back. We want revenge for our families. But your parents only care about saving Huguenots. They're good people."

The tears I've choked back to tell her my memories find their way to my lower lids, turning my vision hazy.

"I promise to listen, Isabelle." Elizabeth swipes her knuckle softly under my eyes to wipe away my tears. "I'm ready to learn from you both."

"Do you remember Naira?" I ask.

"No," she says with a smile. "But she speaks to me too. Sometimes in my dreams."

Naira is part of us. I'm not surprised in the least. "What does she say?"

"That I'm starting a journey and you're the only one who can take me to the end."

Charlotte takes a deep breath. "Sounds to me like the Red Fox is about to cause some mischief."

I want to grab Elizabeth in my arms and run home with her. I want to lock her in a room where she can be safe. But I find myself staring into her dark amber eyes, and I hear Naira whisper, *her turn.*

"You will listen to everything I teach you."

Elizabeth bites back a grin. "I promise."

"You're already a fighter, but you haven't yet learned the most important lesson."

"What's that?" she asks.

"Embrace the reason you fight. It's the only thing you can truly rely on.

CHAPTER EIGHT

Andre and Henri arrived this morning with the wagon and horses. We've encountered the strange dragoon several times and, lucky for us, he's usually drunk and full of information. We've spent the last three days watching the village, taking notes, teaching Elizabeth a plan to remove one family in the night. We must stagger the rescues to limit the chances of something going wrong.

"Have the ladies caused any trouble we'll have to fix?" Henri asks with his usual swagger.

"Please," Charlotte says. "I'm constantly cleaning up your messes." Henri grabs her and kisses her, long enough to make Elizabeth roll her eyes.

"It's a good thing Clémentine isn't here to see you swoon," Elizabeth says. "How you two ended up with the most careful, pious girl, I'll never know."

"She's just like her namesake," Charlotte says. "My sister was kind and sweet and didn't understand my calculated nature. If my daughter wants to stay in Geneva and start a family, then I'm glad she has no interest in this life."

Andre wraps his arm around me. "Do we have a plan?"

"I've missed you."

His cheek tugs at a half-smile. "I always miss you."

Elizabeth growls in frustration. "Here." She positions rocks on the table to resemble the configuration of houses in the village. "We start with this house."

Henri peeks over Charlotte's shoulder. "Why that one?"

"A woman was burned the other day. She's the grown daughter of an older couple. She offers herself for abuse, so they leave her parents alone."

Andre touches her hand. "Cricket, I know you want to help, but we can't choose people based on—"

Elizabeth clamps onto his wrist and drags his hand to the simulated field behind the houses. "A trail leads to the trees behind their house. Only two dragoons are stationed there who leave for the tavern every night at the same time. One of them has a bad leg and can't run."

"Oh." Andre seems impressed. "How do you know about the dragoon's leg?"

Elizabeth clears her throat. "We've befriended someone. A young man."

"A dragoon?" Andre's face doesn't move a twitch, but his neck flushes red.

"Yes."

Charlotte and Henri back away. "We'll give you some privacy." Henri leads Charlotte to the bedroom.

Andre turns to me. "This isn't what we discussed. No interactions. She's still learning."

"Ask her what he thinks her name is."

Elizabeth bites her bottom lip. She mumbles into her shoulder.

"What?"

"Beaumont. Elizabeth Beaumont." She looks to me for reassurance and I nod to encourage her to tell the truth. "I thought James Beaumont was dead but he's living as nobility in Paris. The young dragoon thinks I'm Monsieur Beamont's niece."

Few things rattle Andre's calm, but that shakes his entire body.

"How was I to know Isabelle didn't kill him with that poison years ago? I'm sorry, Papa. I made a mistake. But I've learned and I'm listening to Isabelle and Aunt Charlotte now. I promise."

Andre lifts his hands then balls them into fists. "We will plan for this rescue tomorrow. Now please, go to sleep."

Elizabeth hangs her head and climbs the ladder to her loft.

Andre turns from me. "James is nobility. Elizabeth is friendly with a dragoon and goes by the name Elizabeth Beaumont. What exactly went wrong here?"

"Andre, she doesn't understand patience. Containing her is like holding fire in your hands." I wrap my arms around his waist and lean my lips to his neck. "There's no stopping her blaze now."

Andre lifts my wrist to his lips and kisses gently along my scar. "A scorching H on an eight-year-old. They branded you and Henri. These men are monsters. All of them."

"The worst part of that was the one who charred my flesh was not much older than I. A child himself, he learned hate from the evil men around him."

A protective anger rises to the surface of Andre's usually calm demeanor. An intense need for carnage that I rarely see. He imagines Elizabeth branded as an eight-year-old, I'm certain. This is why he fights for me, because if he fought for himself, he would slash every one of their throats and bathe in their blood.

.   .   .

It's a thirty-minute walk from the cottage to the village. We will only have a few hours before the dragoons return and find their occupants missing. Charlotte waits in the trees with her bow and arrow, and I watch the house from the dark shadows, waiting for the evil beasts to finish their nightly harassment.

Andre, Henri, and Elizabeth remain at the cottage to plan an escape route and prepare food for the journey. Elizabeth forced herself to comply, though she did so through tightened lips and a growl.

I creep closer to the window where the firelight flickers against the dragoon's face. I force down the disgust that rises in my throat. I've been her, too many times to count.

"Get up," he says to the woman on the floor.

"I can't." I can't see her, but I imagine her so clearly huddled on the ground, weak and fragile.

"Get up and pour me wine." The hate that seethes through his bared fangs and his sallow, downturned eyes feels so familiar. So many memories of these men occupy my nightmares, they all look the same to me. This one is older. He's sat in his anger for decades, I can tell. Under the wrinkled cheeks and ungroomed beard, there is something wicked. Liquid evil thick as oil.

"Please, monsieur. I need to rest." Her thready voice nearly ruins me.

He holds his pistol and slams the butt into her arm. She screams, wild and desperate. I lower my head, trying to control myself from jumping inside and setting his beard on fire. A fight will cause a commotion and with houses this close, I can't risk it. But the dragoon's snarl fills me with such vile hate, I understand my group's hunger for murder. At least in this moment.

I hold back tears while he beats her. I glimpse Charlotte's glassy eyes hidden in the trees, her tears glowing. The woman's screams turn to whimpers while I bury my head in my arm, breathless and aching.

"Are you prepared to convert?" he asks. She doesn't respond, so he steps over her limp body and retrieves his hat. "To the tavern, then. We'll be back for more, mademoiselle." He throws a glance at the younger dragoon who also steps over her, kicking her with his boot.

I imagine wrapping my fists around his neck to watch his eyes pop until his final breath escapes his body. Once they leave the house, Charlotte joins me. "I hate them."

"What I feel is worse than hate. And I'm terrified of the part of me that feels it." I've often wondered who I'd be without the darkness that slithers through my soul. I need it, like air and blood.

We climb through the window into the bedroom where the woman trembles on the floor, a gash dripping from her temple down her pale, wet face. She stares ahead, unaware we stand over her.

I reach for her hand. "We're here to help, madame."

She doesn't flinch.

Charlotte gathers the older couple who pray, eyes closed, near the fire in the main room. "Come now. We must get you to safety."

The couple stares at Charlotte in disbelief. "We have nowhere to go. This is our home."

"It's no longer your home. We need to save your daughter."

I lift the woman's lanky body, her neck uselessly flopping her head around. Charlotte helps, a gentle embrace around her most likely broken arm. The woman grimaces. That's good. There's life left in her.

We sneak out the door, on the lookout for eyes, but find only the sounds of drunk soldiers and boisterous songs from the tavern. The couple follows us, tears streaming down their faces. "Will she live?" the mother asks.

Charlotte and I know better than to answer that question.

What seems like hours later, our exhausted group arrives at the cottage. The woman dragged her feet as we moved through the trees, but her body once again falls limp as soon as we cross the threshold. Andre and Henri lift her to the bed and Charlotte tends to her wounds. "I'll make her a poultice for the burn." Charlotte's focus has returned. "She's feverish and turning red."

Elizabeth rests her hand on my back as I crouch in front of the fire. "Was it awful?"

"It's always awful."

She glances over her shoulder with a long pause. "Will that woman live?"

"I don't know."

"She has a chance now because of you. That's amazing."

With a slow head shake, I sit in the feeling of being too angry and devastated to cry. All I feel is empty, as rage trickles through the cracks in my heart.

Elizabeth sits with me in silence, into the night as the group tends to the woman and her worried parents. Henri places his hand on my shoulder. "She's gone, Isabelle."

Though I knew those words were coming, they don't land any less painfully.

"There's something you need to see."

Elizabeth follows me into the bedroom, where the grieving parents sob over her lifeless body. Charlotte and Andre both stare at me with concern.

"What is it?"

Henri leads me to her body where a bubbling burn mars her shoulder. Henri pulls back a sheet to reveal the blackened, seared flesh on her chest. "Is that?"

"Yes, Charlotte says. "A branded H."

CHAPTER NINE

Henri and Andre escort the grieving couple to the next stop on the trail while the women remain in Rouen, finalizing our plan to rescue another family from the village. We've taken a risk, but that woman's skin did something to us. Without words, we all acknowledged what must be done.

We huddle in the trees, watching the tavern, counting dragoons and noting their movements. "Seems unfair to only rescue one more," Elizabeth says. "Isabelle, I know you're ready to do something drastic. I can feel it."

If Elizabeth weren't here, I'd have already killed every one of these men. With her close, I force restraint. But she's right, I am ready for drastic. It's as if the world is spinning faster and activating evil to rise to the surface and I have no choice but to match its fury.

"Can we each take two homes, and escort the families to the woods while they drink the night away?" Elizabeth asks.

"It's possible," I say. "But too much can go wrong."

Charlotte glares at the tavern window. "What do you think, mistress of poison?" I ask her.

She rubs her knuckle on her chin back and forth as she considers her options. "Is it really possible that the man who branded you and Henri is here now?"

I've told myself it would be impossible, but deep down, I know the truth. I saw the wicked in his eyes. "It's been over thirty years."

"He was a young man. Several of these soldiers fit the age."

"Maybe many of them practice that now," I say. I won't listen. I won't imagine the man that threatened me with a knife to my throat and burned my skin could have spent the last three decades inflicting the same torture on countless other Huguenots. And now he's within my reach.

"Don't you want to kill him?" Elizabeth asks.

The truth is that yes, I do want to kill him. I want to watch the life drain from his eyes. I want to burn his flesh the way he burned mine. "There's no point. Not unless he attacks one of us." My words sound hollow. Like a bite with no teeth.

"You can want to kill him, Isabelle," Elizabeth says. "I want to kill him."

"As do I." Charlotte doesn't flinch. She thirsts for the same things I do—but feels no guilt.

The young soldier we met the other day tumbles out of the tavern, alone and drunk.

"Do you trust me?" Elizabeth asks. Before I can answer, she leaps forward.

I want to grab her, but Charlotte holds my arm. "Let her go. We're right here."

Elizabeth approaches him with a curtsy. "Bonsoir."

The soldier turns, realizes it's her, and attempts to slick back his hair. "Mademoiselle Beaumont."

The sound of that name makes me want to scream.

"Bonsoir." She tilts her head and smiles. "I only have a few minutes."

"You shouldn't be out here alone." Everything sways, from his hips to his eyes. "I'd take my chances in the forest if I were you."

"I'm not alone." She steps closer and lifts her eyes to him. "Are you in charge of this operation?"

"Me? No. I'd rather be climbing the walls at my mansion."

She tilts her head. "Why would you climb the walls?"

"To let the cats chase me. Obviously." The man has a habit of fiddling with his hands near his face, holding his fluttering fingers near his ear. "My father forced me here." He straightens his arms to his sides. "Well, never mind about that."

"I don't even know your name."

He flutters his fingers once more to complete some sort of tune, then pauses while he clears his throat. "Monsieur Tremblay, cadet."

"You seem to be having a grand time tonight, monsieur." She peers behind him into the tavern window.

He rubs his eyes until they're red and swollen. "Me, as my family's biggest disappointment, doesn't belong anywhere near this village."

Elizabeth straightens her spine. "Why not?"

"These soldiers are imbeciles. Not a speck of art or humanity in their hardened hearts."

I look at Charlotte, surprised to hear sympathy from anyone in a dragoon uniform.

"The screams are horrific," she says. "Do you hurt the villagers too?"

He shakes his head, eyes closed. "No." He plays another short tune with his fingers at his ear. "I don't understand how this helps France."

"I heard a man brands the Huguenots with an H. Is that true?"

Tremblay pulls Elizabeth into a dark shadow. "You should leave. Once they return from the tavern, they begin hurting the Huguenots. Especially the women. Trust me, the inhuman sounds will turn you savage, ready to claw your way out of this hellish village."

Elizabeth doesn't flinch. "Has anyone converted?"

"Not one."

"Then why continue?"

"Those feral beasts enjoy it." He braces his hands on his knees to catch his breath. "I shouldn't be telling you this."

"But here you are."

Tremblay covers his ears and sings to himself while marching in place. Finally, he stands tall and nods to himself. "Lieutenant Louvois. He's been branding women and children with hot iron for years."

"Why be so cruel?" she asks.

"He says Huguenots are dirty liars who deserve to be treated like cattle. He started it in his youth and has carried on the sick tradition, like his signature. Why he can't sculpt a slab of marble or turn paint and canvas to something beautiful, I do not know."

Elizabeth's shoulders sink but she regains composure. "What do you think?"

"I don't think anyone deserves that. The ale from this place is the only escape I have from the horrors of what we do. Tomorrow will be another day and next week another village. More death. More screams." He rocks back and forth, biting back a grimace.

Men laugh at the door to the tavern, celebrating the broken bones they've inflicted this week. Tremblay turns away. "Take me back to the filthy streets of Paris where the world makes sense."

"I should go. But I'm glad I spoke with you."

"Are you?" He laughs uncomfortably. "Why?"

"I thought you all enjoyed hurting these people. You've surprised me."

"I am but a useless man, singing to himself and playing an invisible violin in my mind, while drinking enough ale to kill a small boar."

Elizabeth places her hand on his and I force back a growl. "Just because you don't break their bones, doesn't mean you aren't complicit. You watch them and do nothing."

"What is she doing?" Charlotte whispers.

"Being Cricket." She's softening him with honesty. A powerful antidote to evil, but one

I've never felt strong enough to employ. I hide from too much.

"I don't have a choice," Tremblay says. "I have no power here."

"We all have a choice." She lifts her skirts and walks in the opposite direction from us into the trees. "Louvois. Where is he from?"

"La Rochelle," he says mid-burp. "Why?"

"Goodnight, monsieur."

Elizabeth doesn't speak the entire walk back to the cottage, but as soon as we step inside, she asks, "How do you feel, knowing it's him?"

My wrist scar warms with the thought, but I can't find the words.

"You were right near him and didn't murder him," Elizabeth says. "We have to go back and finish him off."

Charlotte steps between us. "She doesn't want to do that."

"Why not? He hurt you and Uncle Henri and probably hundreds of other kids. For *fun*. You could have killed your first husband but now he's loose in Paris feeding money to these thugs. I don't understand you!"

I've learned to harness my frustration with her. The louder she yells, the harder I lock down my feelings. "They're all monsters. Even your bumbling cadet. Our mission is to save Protestants, and that is what I will focus on."

"He isn't *my* cadet. Although yes, he is a bumbling fool."

Charlotte clears her throat. "We can do both. I have a plan."

"This sounds dangerous," I say.

"Everything we do is dangerous." She lifts her bag of poisons. "We use their bravado against them."

"How do we do that?" Elizabeth asks.

"We throw them a party."

. . .

The unruly dragoons set a house on fire in the village. Although the men haven't returned yet, we decide we can't wait, and Charlotte lays out her plan to kill two dozen drunk savages.

"You won't kill Louvois, but you won't stop Charlotte from doing it?" Elizabeth asks.

"That's correct. I never stop Henri either. I don't judge how anyone gets through this impossible life."

"The only way to get the villagers out is to kill every last one of those swine," Charlotte says. "Are we ready for tonight?"

I tuck blades into my boots and under my skirts. "They'll certainly be searching for the Red Fox after this."

"That means they fear you," Charlotte says.

"Red Fox is all of us. If they fear the resistance, then we're succeeding in what we came here to do." Knives and swords and spears disappear from the table as we hide them in our gorgeous Catholic clothing.

Elizabeth hands Charlotte her bag of poisons. She holds them up with an adoring smile, then tucks them in a basket looped around her arm. "I'm ready."

Elizabeth tracks my every move as I lift my basket of arrows, axes, and swords, and feel for the stolen pistol hidden under my skirts. "Let's go."

The long trek through the forest is quiet and heavy. Moonlit paths of silver cast night shadows around us like a nightmare. I remind myself that I'm the protection. Elizabeth is the distraction. *Charlotte will kill.*

Creeping through the outside of the village, we examine each cabin. We count dragoons and ignore screams and cries. "We have a job to do," I remind Elizabeth. She nods, forcing back tears.

"I counted five dragoons still in homes," Charlotte whispers. "Two roasting meat in the town center, and the rest in the tavern."

Elizabeth and I set up our weapons along the perimeter of the tavern, placed strategically for every step of our plan. "It's time."

My auburn hair tucked tightly under a linen wrap and a stolen Catholic cross necklace around my neck, I focus and breathe, as Naira taught me to do. *Attack when they least expect it.*

The first time I wore a Catholic cross was here in Rouen. I was a helpless servant to a wealthy family whose son tormented me. When I beat him bloody, it was the first taste of power I've ever truly felt. I've never looked back.

We enter the tavern with baskets of bread and salted meats and pickled cauliflower. Elizabeth steps ahead of us, hand on her hip. "Who are all these handsome soldiers?" The room turns to smile at the three ladies carrying food.

"They look hungry," I say.

Charlotte slaps the bar top and nods to the only Protestant in town not beaten—the brewer of wine and cider. "Barkeep, serve these fine men a round of drinks."

The dragoons, predictably, sit tall with grand smiles. Conceit is the easiest thing to manipulate in unintelligent men.

Elizabeth whispers to me through a forced smile. "I don't see him."

"No. We'll have to be patient and hope he shows."

Tremblay greets us with a bow. "Mademoiselle and Madame Beaumont." He forces a smile and through gritted teeth, whispers, "I believe you must be up to nothing good."

If he continues to call me Madame Beaumont it will be that much easier to leave them all for dead. "We're grateful neighbors and we want to offer our thanks for all you do." His usual glossed over eyes show a hint of mischief.

He nods to Elizabeth and motions for us to join his table. Charlotte drinks her own cider, certain to keep her mind straight, but she flirts and laughs with the men as easy as breathing.

"These men will lose their heads soon enough," Tremblay says. "You shouldn't stay long."

I ensure my head wrap is tight enough to conceal my hair. "You'd be surprised how strong we are, Cadet Tremblay."

"I have no doubt." He smirks as if he knows things.

"Where are you from, monsieur?" Elizabeth asks.

"Le Marais in Paris." He looks over his shoulder. "I am not like the rest of these ruffians."

I pinch my hand hard to keep myself from rolling my eyes. "How so?"

"Look at them." He scans the room with his light blue eyes. "None of them act like gentlemen. Uncontrolled and ill-mannered. Much like my pet monkey, rest his soul."

We collectively move past his monkey comment. With him, it appears we must choose which of his eccentricities we allow him to entertain. No time for childhood exotic pets.

Charlotte hands me a jug of wine. I refill his cup and slide it back to him. "But you aren't?"

"No! I am nobility. Educated and cultured. I don't belong here."

Elizabeth releases a laugh then covers her mouth.

"You don't believe me?" He props his hand on his hip.

"Nobility does not work, let alone as a lower-class soldier." I kick Elizabeth under the table to remind her that insulting the man is not the best way to handle him. To my surprise, that is exactly how to handle him.

"I agree." He straightens his jacket and lowers his voice to a whisper. "I do not take part in their activities because I cannot stomach the sound of screams of pain but also because I have no idea how to fight. I wouldn't want to mar these elegant fingers." His eyes widen as he laughs like a madman.

"Something you should have mentioned before joining the ranks of uncontrollable soldiers," Elizabeth says.

My instinct is to jump in, prevent her from walking into trouble. But she seems to read him well. She somehow understands that this man feels lost and appreciates a harsh tone.

"My father finds me childish. He would not grant my inheritance until I proved my worth. He is a Noble of the Sword and finds me useless with my violin and poetry."

Elizabeth nearly shakes her head in surprise. Oh no, don't believe he is any different, Cricket. They're all evil.

"Poetry?" she asks.

Watching my daughter's heart soften could be the most terrifying moment of my life. Warriors can trust no one. "Why enlist here and not fight one of the king's many wars?" I ask.

"Battle? With blood and swords and things? No. I was told I could be stationed in a village and help with the Huguenot problem. I believed I would be helping to convert them through vigorous conversation, not watch their bones break in front of me." He swallows with a hard blink as if it's painful. He catches himself and drinks more wine. "I shouldn't have told you all that. Please, forgive my recklessness. Father says I'm too emotional. I let my words tumble out without any thought to the consequences."

Best to silence him before he collapses into a pile of tears in our laps. "How does your commander feel about you?" I ask.

"The man despises me!" He rubs his neck until his skin flushes red. He suddenly looks like a boy with wide eyes and freckles.

No, Isabelle, no room for sympathy. "Is he the one with the scar?" I ask, voice steady.

"Yes. Louvois. Nasty man that he is, he brands children. Can you believe it?"

I will myself not to graze my wrist. "I can."

"Do you hate Huguenots?" he asks.

"No," Elizabeth says. "We do not hate them."

"Good. It would be just like me to say the very wrong thing. So few people share my views."

Charlotte laughs loud enough to rattle the walls. Charming and entertaining, she captivates men with jokes and stories, but catches my eye and in one flash of her gaze, the fighter beckons me. After all these years, we don't need to speak. Our eyes do all the talking.

I pour more wine and keep Tremblay talking. "Where will you go after this village is gone?"

His eyes hang heavy and unfocused. "Bergerac, Montauban and then Castres, the Rhône valley. Huguenots flee to the Swiss Confederacy." He burps. "Can't say I blame them."

I place my hand on Elizabeth's. "The crowd looks thirsty." She nods, acknowledging my instruction. I bring Charlotte's secret pouch to the counter where Charlotte laughs as though she is drunk and loose, much to the delight of the dragoons. These sorry soldiers have no idea what they're up against.

Elizabeth positions herself at the open window cooling her skin with the breeze.

"A round of wine for the soldiers?" I ask the innkeeper.

"Are you trying to get yourselves killed?" he whispers to me.

"We are simply peasants looking to thank these men for their service." I wink.

"I know who you are," he says. "I bet your hair is red, isn't it?"

I hand Charlotte the pouch of white powder and wink to the innkeeper. "Will you help us get them out?"

"Which family?" He looks around to prevent focus on our conversation for too long.

"All of them."

His breath hitches but he shakes off his worry and throws the linen rag over his shoulder.

He pours wine for all the dragoons. Charlotte joins him as I block the view, smiling and waving at several glossy-eyed soldiers. These bastards have no idea what's coming. And I can't wait to show them.

While Charlotte prepares the poison wine, I turn to face her. "Where is the commander?"

"At one of the homes." The innkeeper forces a smile. "Torturing one of the women, no doubt."

I conjure his scarred cheek. His vacant eyes. "I'll be ready for him."

Charlotte and I hand out wine to every man in the tavern. "To your good health," Charlotte says. "May you remain handsome forever!"

The men raise their glasses and drink. We watch the room, seconds dripping by like honey. Tremblay has not sipped his wine, as he has already passed out on the table. Elizabeth watches him closely.

A few men cough and clear their throats. Scratch at their necks. Faces swell and redden, brows bead with sweat. One man realizes what's happening and charges me. I reach to my ankle and remove two blades. He's desperate and doesn't stop, so I throw a knife into the center of his throat. With a gurgle, he falls to the ground in a heap.

Charlotte, her own blade in hand, steps behind a dragoon and slits his throat. Two men fall to the floor, choking and breathless. I step over them and another reaches for my neck. I slam my elbow to his cheek and knee his stomach. I leave him there for the poison to finish him off.

I move toward Elizabeth, who is poised, ax in hand outside the window. Charlotte makes quick work of the dragoons, slicing and stabbing as they fall into pools of blood. Tremblay, still drunk, reaches for his wine and Elizabeth panics. She drops the ax and rushes to him, slapping the drink from his hand. "Don't drink that!"

Another dragoon grabs Elizabeth's ankles and pulls her to the ground. She kicks his face and rolls out from under him but three more pile on top of her. No hesitation. I grab the ax and swing the flat part of the blade to one's skull. It rings like a bell and clunks to the wood floor. Several men fight with Elizabeth, desperate to hurt her in their last choking breaths.

I can fight anyone but watching them assault my daughter does something to me. One man grabs her by the hair and reaches into his uniform for a blade. I swing the ax to slice his ear off. I didn't try to kill him. That would have been humane. I wanted him to hurt. TO bleed and scream. Charlotte and I fight the mass of poisoned dragoons like a drunk battlefield, blood splattering the walls and dousing the dead men's hair.

Elizabeth frees herself and pulls a knife from her ankle. Without the slightest hesitation, she stabs a dragoon in the eye. Placing her foot on the man's chest, she pulls the knife from his flesh and attacks another, and another. They're all too drunk and choking to give much of a fight.

One dragoon still holding out aims a pistol at Elizabeth. I throw my knife to his face, but before the blade slices his cheek, a bullet rings out.

CHAPTER TEN

There are moments in life where you suspend into disbelief. Where time stops and you question everything you've ever known. Where your body goes numb, and the world disappears. Tonight was one of those times.

Some unknown time after the blast of that pistol, Andre and Henri arrive in the tavern, knives and pistols in hand. They find us standing over a pile of dead dragoons, Tremblay shaking in the corner, and Elizabeth bleeding from her arm.

"Cricket." Andre rushes to her side.

Henri steps inside. "We came to help you."

"It appears we didn't need your help," I say, finally able to speak after the scare of nearly losing my daughter.

"I should say not." He pulls Charlotte in for a hug.

Andre motions to the pale young Tremblay on the floor. "Why didn't you kill him?"

"He saved me," Elizabeth says. "Well, he shot me by accident. It grazed my arm and landed in that man's chest." She points to the dragoon shot at her feet, my blade wedged in his cheek.

I won't let the fear take hold. Our job is not yet done. "The commander is still out there, and I'm certain he heard the shot. We have dozens of families to rescue."

Andre steps toward me. "Are you alright? You look different."

"Just focusing." Barely grasping at control is more accurate, but I can't let him know how unsteady I feel. "What do we do with him?" I point to the violin-playing poet cadet.

Elizabeth grabs Andre's arm. "Please, Papa. Don't hurt him."

He kneels in front of the young man who is sweating and confused. "You saved my daughter?"

He nods, looking like he might faint. "Yes. She saved me too."

"Leave him here. He can watch his fellow dragoons bleed into the floor all night." He points a knife at his face. "If you stand in our way, I will carve out your eyeballs. Understand?"

His head shakes but nods something close to yes.

Andre grunts, his blade waving at the cadet. "What kind of dragoon are you?"

"A terrible one," Tremblay says.

Charlotte hands me the pilfered pistols now wiped clean of dragoon blood. "Phase two."

Andre makes sure Elizabeth's arm is wrapped. "I'm fine, Papa," she says. "You're not doing this without me."

One after another, we pour out of the tavern. The innkeeper doesn't look rattled. He motions to the house at the far end of the village. "He's there. He likes that house."

"You handle the villagers," I say to Andre.

"Do you want me to help you?" Andre loves to offer, knowing I'll never accept his help.

Between us, it's the ultimate language of love.

"No. Henri and I will take care of him."

Without questioning, Henri steps to my side and we rush through the dark night toward the eerie quiet at the edge of the village. Just like when we were children, we walk close, shoulder to shoulder. A common fight unspoken between us.

"Is he really the one who branded us?"

"I think so."

"Let me kill him." Henri's fury runs deep. He's never let go of that horrid memory. They killed his father and made him watch. He's waited his entire life for retribution. I want to tell him it won't bring his father back, but I think Henri needs justice like he needs air to breathe.

People scurry from their houses behind us, led by our secret resistance, but Henri and I remain focused on the last house where our first torturer still carries out his evil deeds. We approach the windows in the corner and glimpse the dragoon heating something in the fireplace, a husband and wife tied back to back in the center of the room.

"He takes his time, enjoying how his victims squeal and beg," Henri says, glaring through the window. "They aim to ruin us from the inside."

"They never ruined us," I whisper.

Henri reaches for my hand. He's backlit by the starry spring night, highlighting the youthful boy who still resides deep in his soul. "They took everything from me."

"Then let's take everything from them. We start with this sick bastard in here."

He nods and we creep to the front door. I point to Henri to indicate he'll make the first move. He kicks the door open and the dragoon spins to face us, branding iron flaming red. He bares his yellowed teeth as he rushes toward us. Henri lifts a chair and shoves the man against the wall. I kick the iron from his hand.

Henri battles with him as I untie the terrified couple. "Go outside. Find the others." Their weak legs barely carry them out the door.

The dragoon manages to grab his knife and slices Henri's arm. Remembering Naira's teachings, I take a deep breath and listen to the night. I hear the men grunt and fight, and I focus on the dragoon's eyes. His wicked smile. Blood saturates Henri's sleeve, but he doesn't back down.

I approach the dragoon from behind. I use my boot to kick him swiftly in the mid back. He falls to his knees. Without hesitation, I crack the handle of my blade into his temple. Not to knock him out. This time, I will end him.

He was attacking Henri, after all.

The man slumps to the ground. Henri wipes blood from his nose, his face pale and eyes unfocused. Henri paces a circle around his crumpled body. "Is he dead?"

His chest still flutters. "Not yet."

"I have to finish him off. But first," Henri steps over him and places the branding iron in the embers.

"What are you doing?"

"Giving him a proper sendoff." Henri kicks the dragoon in the stomach, but the man just shakes from the hit with no reaction.

I grab Henri's arm. "We don't torture, Henri. Kill him or leave him to suffer, but don't torture. We're better than them."

He stares at the glowing rod as he spins it in the fire. "I've never understood how you keep faith in people after all we've been through."

"It isn't people I have faith in." So many times I've held Henri at the brink of devastation, stopping him from ruin. It's like a dance where I lead, and he follows. After all our years, we know the steps by heart.

"What is it then?"

I hope I can stop him, though the hate in his eyes tells me it's useless. "I have faith that our ancestors who died left us a world that will improve. If we fight for it."

"I used to think so." His eyes redden and swell.

"When the blood drips down the wall, it's impossible to tell who it came from. Is it Protestant blood? Catholic? We bleed the same. We hurt the same, but we are not like them." I couldn't live with myself if we were.

"You kill too," Henri says.

"If my people are attacked, I protect them. I do not kill for sport."

"And this is why this man is here. You let him go to torture more villages. More innocent people."

Perhaps Henri has taken the lead tonight and I'm to follow. "Are you calling my mercy foolish?"

"Nothing about you is foolish." He spins the iron in the fire and lifts to examine its crudely formed H. Different from the one that seared our flesh all those years ago, but the glowing iron lit red from inside ignites my memories. "I'm the foolish one for believing I could escape this hell," he says. "All this time, you've known it was part of us. We'll always be the terrified kids in the shadows of La Rochelle."

"Except we're not." I reach for his arm. "We're part of the resistance. We save people."

"It isn't enough for me." He stares at the branding. "I wish I could be as strong as you, but I'm not." Henri shoves the brand to the unconscious man's cheek as it sizzles and smokes, forcing a whimper from Louvois's throat. Henri grits his teeth and grinds the hot iron into the dragoon's flesh. When he lifts the smoking iron, a black H covers the man's face from his jaw to his eye.

He grips the iron rod hard enough to cause his hands to shake. I reach for Henri and pull him into a hug. "I'm sorry we lost everything. I'm sorry your father died, and you were sent to the galleys. I'm sorry you were imprisoned. I'm sorry our lives changed the day the dragoons murdered Etienne."

A loud thud vibrates at my feet when the rod drops to the floor. Henri lays his cheek on my shoulder and hugs me back. "I love you, Isabelle."

"I love you too." My voice catches and it surprises me. Not much can summon my tears these days.

"You've been saving me for thirty years. I've never said thank you." He smiles.

"Come on, let's get you home to Charlotte." I hold his hand and lead him to the door. "Wait." I step over the unmoving Louvois toward the back of the cabin. On the table next to his long, pristine sword lays a note from the king's chief minister. I glance back at Henri. Standing in the front door, watching the night sky.

The note thanks a Lieutenant Louvois for his dedication to the French Army. He discusses the Huguenot problem and the Lieutenant's need for control over the unruly group of soldiers. Commitment to the Crown and a promise to uphold the standards of French royalty. He mentions the resistance. We have had reports of agitators. Namely, the Red Fox. *If it is true that a woman has killed many of our soldiers*, the minister writes, *we must find her and her accomplices, and burn them all.*

These words no longer fill me with fear. They indicate our resistance is working. "Henri, they're looking for me."

Henri turns around, smiling at me from the moonlit doorway. "They have no idea what they're up against."

"The letter is signed, your Cousin." I look up at Henri's fierce eyes. "He's related to the man leading the Dragonnades." I grasp the sword tight in my hand and take in the feeling of triumph. The dozens of Huguenots we saved, and the dozens of dragoons we have stopped. Henri feels it too. I see the calm in his eyes.

A loud bang cracks the silence like shattered glass.

Henri's chest blooms with blood. He looks at me shocked, as he coughs up more blood.

"Henri?"

Movement from Louvois. Without a thought, I rush to his shaking hand to stop him from shooting again. I stab his own sword through his hand and into the wood as the pistol slides across the floor. The dragoon tries to focus, staring at his splintered, severed palm nailed to the wood floor.

Henri has fallen to the ground, shaking in tremored jolts, coughing and spitting bright red blood. I slide on my knees and cusp his head in my hand. "Henri, no."

He stares at me shaking, but with no fear in his eyes. He's always known this would be his end. He smiles. "I burned him."

"Yes, friend. You did. You burned the hell out of him."

Resolved and unafraid, he says, "Tell Charlotte and Clémentine I love them."

My chest aches like I'm bleeding with him. Like the air is being stolen from us both. Like life has taken a desperate turn.

He falls limp in my arms. I run my hand through his wild black curls one last time. "Sleep well, Henri Reynard." He drifts away like the clouds, leaving a still body and empty eyes. He is gone.

My Henri is gone.

The dragoon grunts behind me and I rise to my feet, a new sense of hurt and anger taking over my body. My hands are no longer my own. "Where did you get a pistol?"

He rolls his head side to side but does not focus on me.

"You kept it hidden, didn't you?" I step closer as slow and calm as I've ever been. "You wanted to kill us when we least expected it. When we thought we'd won."

His eyes open but cannot focus. I kneel in front of him and examine his branding. "You'll thank me for what I'm about to do."

I look back at Henri and let fury rage through me. I remove my cap and let my locks fall around my shoulders and into my eyes. "I am the Red Fox."

He grows alert enough to widen his blurry eyes.

Then I smash my toe into the side of his head with the hardest kick I've ever managed. I wait for his chest to stop moving, and I step away. My hand trembles when I lay my palm on Henri's forehead. He's cold and rigid. What's left of him, anyway.

Louvois lies in a pool of his own blood, unmoving from the blow to his temple. His hand is severed, his face branded. What a way to die. I step back to his pale body. "It isn't enough for all you've done to hurt us. I should skin you and slice your fingers one by one. But you won't feel the pain, so what is the point?"

I almost wish he was alive still so I could watch him suffer at my hands. The darkness I've fought for so long unspools inside of me and seeps out my pores. It washes away my morality and all I can see is my dead friend, our years of pain, and the mangled body of our tormentor whose chest has stopped rising and falling.

I turn the blade in the firelight and ponder stabbing it through Louvois's eye socket, but Andre flashes into my mind. Like hands reaching toward hell and pulling my back to the light. Elizabeth needs guidance, and it can't be from a woman who desecrates a dead man. Even an evil one.

I turn from him, tears pressing into the backs of my eyes, and bend down to feel Henri's shockingly cold face. "I promise to fight for you, my friend. Always."

I walk out of the cabin, through a pool of blood, and out to the windy night. My hair free, I walk past a tavern of dead dragoons who can no longer hurt innocent people in the name of their king.

I stride with purpose back to our house, quietly, peacefully through the woods, vengeance on my mind. Tears streak my face, but they do not break me. They break something loose, something I can no longer hide.

. . .

One step through the door to our cottage on the Huguenot Trail, and everyone feels the news without me having to speak. Charlotte looks at the blood splatter on my dress and my puffy eyes and she knows.

"No," she whispers. "No."

I hang my head and Elizabeth catches Charlotte from falling to the floor. She holds her while Charlotte sobs and rocks. Andre steps toward me. "I'm so sorry, Isabelle."

I lay my head on Andre's chest and cry. Tomorrow, there will be no time to grieve as we escort the Huguenots to safety. But tonight, at this moment, I feel the pain in my heart from one of the greatest losses that has ever ripped through me.

Part of me is gone, left with Henri's soul into the afterlife where I know he breathes free.

We cry with our family and share a moment of grief that only Huguenots seem to understand—the inevitable, painful, ongoing cycle of hurt.

. . .

Two hours is all it took for Charlotte to drain herself of anger and grief before she asked me what happened. I explain every detail, biting back my own emotions to let her feel the loss.

"We have to bury him," she says.

I shake my hand. "It's dangerous to go back."

She stands with resolve, searching for her cape. "I don't care about danger. I'm getting his body and burying him properly. On the battlefield he's spent his life fighting."

"In a rescued Huguenot village."

"Yes." Her voice breaks but she remains strong, shaking away the emotion that twists her face.

Andre and Elizabeth offer to bring food and blankets to the Huguenots in the barn so Charlotte and I can make our way back to the village.

We don't speak, but creep through the night, sharing a purpose. The wind howls, a shrieking flutter through the trees. I think of Naira, as I always do in these moments. *Warriors need rest,* she would say. *They return stronger. Focused.*

Charlotte's tears have dried, her steps quickened. I follow behind her, bow and arrow in hand to protect her. We walk through the center of the abandoned, blood-stained village where screams and cries once filled the air. Where dragoons took it upon themselves to force conversion through any means necessary.

It is not the religion I fight, it is the minds of ignorant people.

I point to the last house where a fire still smolders. I stand back and give Charlotte time with Henri. Time to say goodbye. She whispers and cries, her grief filling the air like a windstorm. Her desperate voice eats away at my stern demeanor, taking chomps out of the armor I've crafted for decades. Unable to listen for one more second, I walk back to the tavern to look through the window at crumpled bodies and streams of blood on the walls. What is the point of it all?

Henri is with his father. He's with my mother and sisters, and with Etienne. His memory will remain with us, in our hearts. I must fight the urge to brand all the corpses with an H in memory of my closest friend and ally.

"Isabelle?" Charlotte is focused, her lone voice echoing through the desolate street.

The much too familiar smell of thickened blood and rotting flesh no longer makes me sick. It's simply another unimaginable night in the life of a Huguenot. "Are you ready?"

"Yes." The whites of her eyes web with veins, like little streaks of lightning forced out by tears. "Let's give him the burial he deserves."

I nod and prepare myself for another wave of grief as we step inside the cabin. But before I can let myself feel the loss again, I notice something.

"What is it?" Charlotte asks.

A severed hand lies mangled in a sea of dark blood. "Louvois. He's gone."

CHAPTER ELEVEN

We buried Henri in the woods behind the ruins of the Protestant village. Where once Huguenots prayed and sang, bodies of Catholic soldiers now rot, and Henri's memory will watch over them. A true symbol of sacrifice if there ever was one. Charlotte cried over his grave. We slept a few hours on the earth, unwilling to say goodbye. I couldn't summon tears as anger burned hot in my chest. This morning, it still smokes.

Andre joins me staring at the fire. He kisses my temple. "Travel will be difficult on little sleep."

I don't turn to look at him. "Nothing seems difficult right now."

"I'm going to miss him tremendously." Andre says. "But he was like a brother to you. I'm so sorry you had to see that."

"What I saw was a Huguenot fighting to the death to make sense of this world where there's so much pain."

"I think he died exactly how he would have wished. Saving Huguenots and killing dragoons."

I scratch at my cheek. "Henri branded an H on the dragoon's face."

His eyes widen. "Well, that will make for interesting conversations at the tavern."

"How did he live?" I finally turn to face Andre. "I stabbed his hand into the floor and crushed his knuckles. My boot to his temple surely damaged him beyond repair. He wasn't breathing."

"The most hateful ones seem to live the longest. It fuels them somehow."

"Andre, something happened to me that night." Goodness and kindness have evaporated and, in their place, I feel empty rage. As if Henri imparted a taste of bitterness in me before he left us.

Andre softly skims my cheek with the back of his fingers. "Your best friend was killed by the man who branded you both as children. I think there's no way you couldn't be changed."

"I need to find him. Kill him and watch him bleed. I've never felt this before."

Andre kisses the back of my hand. "I think you have."

"Explain yourself, Monsieur Boucher."

"I'm not afraid of your dark side, but I think you are." Somehow, Andre finds a smile, as if he can choose which memories he lets in. "I forgot my rage when I first looked at you. I still do."

"I don't think I can ever forget this."

"No, you won't. But I've always known you love the way you do because you will not tolerate the hate. It's a battle inside, and I'm certain good will win."

I crack my knuckles by pressing my fist against my chin. "And if it doesn't?"

"Then we will feed our rage together. And I will still love you forever."

I lean my head on his shoulder about to weep, but the memory of Henri pale and bleeding won't let me grieve. "I feel fractured. Confused."

"A warrior on a journey will meet many setbacks."

Naira's words. They will always bring me a sense of home. "Breathe and listen, then move forward with love."

Charlotte and Elizabeth join us, Charlotte's eyes red and swollen. Elizabeth hugs her and they lean their foreheads together.

"I'll check the group in the barn. It's nearly time to leave." Elizabeth opens the front door to find Tremblay sleeping on his side at the threshold. Elizabeth taps his back with her foot until he stirs awake. "Can I help you?"

We rush to Elizabeth's side, ready to fight.

His doe-like eyes are filled with red streaks. His crumpled body shows no sign of fight. "I don't want to be a dragoon."

"How did you find us?" I ask.

"I followed you. After you buried your friend." He slowly stands and wipes his hands on his thighs. "You're Huguenots, aren't you? And you certainly aren't related to Beaumont."

We don't speak or turn our gaze away.

"I want to help you," he says.

"Dragoons cannot be trusted," Andre says. "And we don't need help." He reaches to shut the door, but Tremblay thrusts his hand out to stop him.

"I'm not a dragoon." He pulls back his shoulders. "Lieutenant Louvois escaped last night. I watched him crawl from the village, burnt and bleeding."

"Why didn't you help him?" asks Elizabeth.

"Because he deserves everything you did to him." He looks at us with the kind of longing I understand. Longing for a family. I don't want to trust him, but beyond comprehension, I do.

"We don't need help," Charlotte says.

"Clearly you are all capable. But I can offer secrets." His fingers move toward his ear, but he stops himself. "I know things."

"And why would you offer those secrets?" I ask.

"You could have killed me, but you let me live. After everything we've done to your people, you spared me."

Elizabeth steps forward. "You didn't hurt us."

"But I allowed it. I'm as evil as the rest of them, just as you said. But I'd like to do something right. Help you dismantle the Dragonnades so I can return to Paris and bury myself in the bosom of a prostitute or three. Back where the world makes sense." His usual silliness has taken a reprieve, while impossibly, the real Tremblay shines through.

Andre whispers in my ear. "He knows more than we do."

"And he could kill us in our sleep."

"I slept outside all night," he says, obviously hearing our words. "If I wanted to kill you, I would have." His grimace at the word kill suggests he has never shed anyone's blood.

Charlotte reaches for a rope. "Hands out."

He looks at the rest of us but lifts his arms.

She ties his wrists together." You will be our prisoner until you prove you can be trusted. But no dragoons can ever be trusted, so you will be blindfolded and used for your secrets, until we discard you. Understood?"

"Seems fair." He holds out his hands with a bow. "I am here to serve your little party."

Charlotte ties his wrists together, crunching his bones together until he winces. "You have a chance to prove you are not a monster. Take it, Tremblay. Perhaps you won't go to hell."

"You aren't as helpless as they make you out to be," he says.

"No, we aren't," Elizabeth says with one last yank of the ropes.

"My name is Duke Edward Tremblay. Men in my family fight the king's silly wars and I plan on filling my time with art and music and nonsense."

"You're a duke?" Elizabeth asks.

Charlotte slams a pot against the duke's forehead and he crumbles to the ground. "Load him in the wagon. It's time to move."

.   .   .

Three days on the trail, we drag the tied-up duke and weary Protestant refugees between us in near-silence. Charlotte leads the way, preferring to walk in front of the wagon carrying the wounded and elderly. Her eyes look both dead and fully awake, and no one has dared try to comfort her. "Let her sit in her rage," Andre says. "Lest she take it out on us."

We arrive at another friendly home at dusk where the family greets us with relieved smiles. This is the largest group we've ever saved. They help the listless refugees to the makeshift beds in the barn. Charlotte leads Tremblay to the house where we can keep an eye on him. She isn't rough, but she isn't gentle either.

A duke as a prisoner. At least we're brave.

In the warm home, a pot of stew and jug of wine greet us which we greedily dig into. Elizabeth sits next to Tremblay on the floor, removes his blindfold, and brings a bowl to his lips. He seems to thank her with soft eyes. When he has finished, she tilts her head. "Don't take me for a fool. I can kill with much more ease than the rest of my damaged crew. I simply don't think you should go hungry."

After food and drink, Charlotte bends down in front of the duke. "We killed your entire regiment without much effort. Dragoons are ill-mannered and stupid."

"Agreed."

Resistance and disdain are the expected reactions from soldiers and thus, Charlotte doesn't know what to do with his compliance.

"Who started this Dragonnade program?" Charlotte doesn't blink.

"The intendant in Poitou. He was eager to join royal favor and encouraged by the king's minister."

"Louvois's cousin."

I think of the way Louvois ran from me to save himself and brand more innocent people. "The rich are cowards."

"Louvois is many things," the duke says. "Dangerous above all else."

"Where did Louvois go?" I ask.

"If he lived, he would have sought help from a healer. Then he'd report his experience to the Louvois and the king."

Charlotte exhales loudly. "His experience? That he tortured innocent Huguenots and killed my husband?"

"He wouldn't reveal how brutal they are. He wants the king to think they're in control of these men." The duke's eyes shift to me. "They aren't."

Heat pulses from Charlotte's red face. "You watched him brand women and children."

"Yes." He doesn't cower. Doesn't deny.

Charlotte reaches for the ladle burning off food scraps in the fire. I hope she's merely scaring him, though the look in her eyes suggests she could sear his eyeball into dust and not flinch. "You allowed unimaginable pain. You didn't stop it."

Tremblay closes his eyes. "That's what I'm doing right now. Eye for an eye. Go ahead if you must."

"Charlotte," Andre says with a warning in his voice. "Don't."

"He killed Henri."

"He didn't kill anyone," I say, pushing away her arm.

"What your people have done to him. What you've allowed." One solid finger points from her tightened fist toward the duke's nose. "He woke in screams many nights with memories of watching his father burn. He could never rest. He nearly died in the Bastille. And for what?" She slams the ladle to the tile floor next to him. "Being Protestant."

I inch closer to Charlotte, the anger in her voice rising high and trembling. She opens her white fist, presses her palm against her thigh as she contemplates her next move. Tremblay keeps his eyes shut but tears leak from his eyes. He prepares.

"You're all monsters." She lifts the ladle again, black and smoking, holding it dangerously near his face. His breath is rapid, his reddened skin beads with sweat from the heat pulsing near his cheek.

Elizabeth rests her hand on Charlotte's shoulder. "Aunt Charlotte?"

She hesitates. She wouldn't if myself or Andre spoke, but Cricket's innocent voice gives her pause.

"You taught me to be smart and focused. We can get revenge, but not like this."

Charlotte closes her eyes. Her hand shakes the ladle near Tremblay's eye. Suddenly, she drops it and we all exhale. The duke's face drains to pale.

She turns to me. "We find Louvois, and we kill him."

"I thought I did. But that bastard lived."

"Not for long, he won't," Charlotte says with steely eyes.

There have been two times in my life where vengeance seemed the only option. Once when I threw LaMarche from a cliff in the Alps, and once again when we find the man who set me on this path at the tender age of eight. He burned in me a journey that will end the moment I kill him.

At least, I hope it will end.

.   .   .

One by one we lead the feeble Huguenots across the mountains to Geneva. They're tired and hungry and hurting, but every one of them cries when Charlotte leads prayer over our Protestant Bible under the light of the midday sun.

We bring them to the Temple where volunteers organize housing. Our system is efficient now. Andre escorts Duke Tremblay to the jail where he'll be taken care of. Unlike the Catholics, we treat our prisoners humanely. Charlotte prepares to break the terrible news to Clémentine that her father is gone. We've always understood the risks, but our children shouldn't bear our burdens.

"I'll stay with her tonight," Elizabeth says. "They need me."

I nod. Andre hugs his daughter. "I'm very proud of you, Cricket."

"Don't shower me with praise yet. I'm just getting started." She flashes a smile before linking arms with Charlotte. They stare down the street in silence for a long while. Charlotte coughs back the beginnings of tears and they walk toward their house where poor Clémentine will have her world shattered.

Back at our cottage, Andre boils water so we may wash off the memories of the previous weeks of blood and loss and indescribable anger. After bathing, we collapse in our nightshirts, tangled together on our bed.

"It's getting dangerous," he says.

"It's always been dangerous."

"Yes, but now Elizabeth is involved. This is a new level of danger. Louvois knows you're the Red Fox. You've branded and injured him."

I prop on my elbow and stare into his rich, dark eyes. "I want to kill him. I tried and failed."

The way he stares at my lips suggests he wants to entice me with sweet whispers of plotting Catholic demise. "The only option is to stop the Dragonnades."

"And how will we do that, my handsome husband?"

My skin warms in the evening breeze, yet chills spread across my arms as Andre runs his eyes over my body. "We have a member of the nobility. He knows their secrets."

"I'm not certain we can trust him."

"We can't trust anyone but each other." He rakes his fingers through my curls. "But we can outsmart him. It's what you do best."

"Are you tired of this life, Andre?" I pull away from his touch. "Do you want to live a quiet life, safe in Geneva?"

"Yes."

I hate myself for asking a question I already know the answer to. If I'm honest with myself, I wanted him to lie to me and to himself. I wanted him to sooth the burns marks on my heart and allow me to carry on this trail I'm not sure I can ever turn away from.

"But not while our people are tortured and murdered," he says. "We have a calling. I promised to fight by your side every day and I meant it."

I swing my leg over him and run my hands up his stomach. "You never hold me back, though I know you want to."

"That would be stupid of me, wouldn't it?" He lifts his hands as if he will remove my shift, but settles his hands behind his head, teasing me with a smile. "You are the Red Fox. My job is to protect you. Support you." I ache for his hands on me, but he holds firm. "How will we use our prisoner to ruin the king's plans?"

This man knows how to excite me. Something that was foreign to my first husband.

I arch my back and stretch my hips, pressing into Andre's pelvis. "We use him to find Louvois. We stop the Dragonnades and keep Elizabeth safe."

"And how will we do that?" He runs his eyes over my body, his cheeks red and shining.

I remove my shift and kiss his stomach and chest. "Touch me."

"Tell me your plan, my little wolf."

I use the heat in my belly to fuel my bravery. Andre makes me feel as though I can do anything. I remove his nightshirt and kiss his neck. He groans, but his hands remain behind his head.

"We can rescue Huguenots, but the attacks will keep happening until we stop them." When I suck on his soft earlobe and lick behind his ear, fear evaporates. Insecurity drains away.

"How do we stop them?" he asks.

I hover my mouth over his, our naked bodies pulsing with need. "We go where the decisions are made." He kisses me so softly it leaves me groaning for more. "We go to the king."

Andre stares at me in disbelief, then he grabs my hips and rolls me to my back. He presses my wrists to the bed and lowers his strong body over mine. He kisses me with all the strength and passion I hunger for. The strength I need.

I have no time to question my plan. No space to worry. I'm too lost in Andre's touch.

We're going back to Paris.

CHAPTER TWELVE

The next morning, Andre paces in front of the fire, rubbing his chin. "A group of Huguenots arrive in the royal palaces aided by a potentially lying ex-dragoon, a girl who pretends to be named after your murderous ex-husband, a grieving widow with poisons, and the infamous Red Fox to stop the king from enforcing the Dragonnades?" He turns to look at me. "Have I missed anything?"

"Not a thing."

He finally stops pacing and sits next to me. "You're oddly calm about this."

"We've spent years rescuing Huguenots from France. Hundreds, maybe thousands. We could keep this up forever and I wouldn't regret it. But then they killed Henri."

Andre reaches for my hand. "He fought with bravery and pride. Naira would be proud."

Andre's wooden sculpture of a wolf still sits in our window, reminding me of a girl who refused to live in fear. It reminds me of training in the Quebec woods with the great Huron fighter who has never left my side. "Naira has been whispering in my dreams."

"What has she told you?"

I tilt my head. "You don't question that I hear her from across the world while I sleep?"

"With Naira? No. She's magic. Always has been."

Raindrops patter the windowsill in a soft, dreamy dance. "A wolf and a fox watch me from a cliff. Both with green eyes and reddish hair."

"Do they speak?"

"They don't need to. Naira trained me to be the wolf. A fighter who protects her pack. But then came the fox. She's telling me I need to be cunning and use my wits."

"You already do."

"We lost Henri. Our passion and our fight will blind us, and we'll end up just like him." I widen my eyes. "Unless we stop them."

The more disturbing parts of my dreams remain silent in my mind, far away from Andre's worry. For months, Naira has appeared in murky form in the background as I sleep, warning of my approaching death.

Andre holds out his hand, requesting mine like a prince. "My lovely wife, shall we prepare for the royal palaces of nobles and Huguenot-hating Catholics?"

"Yes, I believe it is time." His hand is soft, slightly wrinkled by time in the most comforting way.

"I've learned not to question you, Isabelle, so tell me. How do we manage this?"

"You won't like it."

Andre rubs his eyes with his thumb and forefinger. "Why do I always follow you into the fire?"

"Because you love me. And you know the path of fire is where we change the world." I can see him struggle as he considers talking me out of this plan. Standing up to me and demanding I stop this fight. He's been reaching for that strength for a while. I certainly won't help him find it.

He takes a slow, deep breath. "Yes, my darling. I do love you."

"Tremblay can discover the inner workings of the Dragonnades." I pace the room, lost in my own frantic mind swirling with grand ideas of triumph. "He'll report military plans and strategies. Officer names and towns. Methods of torture. We'll clear villages before they arrive. And we will wait for them."

"We attack them first," Andre says, poorly hiding the sadness in his eyes. I assume he knows it will never be enough bloodshed for me. I will never stop fighting.

"This marks a new world for us," I say, out of my imaginary conversation with Naira and back in the present where the world has consequences. "We will now be the aggressor. Have you thought through what this will mean for your soul?"

I've long given up on rest and peace. My loving husband has not.

"I don't need to think it through. I promised Henri I would seek justice, and that is what I plan to do." Andre kisses my cheek, sending chills up my neck. "Once we find Louvois, will you be satisfied?"

"I will never be satisfied. Not until every Huguenot is free." I don't release my gaze, challenging him to accept me as I've always been, a resistor till death.

Andre wraps his arms around me and exhales. "You really think we can trust the duke?"

"We trust no one. But he's there for the using, and he's willing. Only time will tell if we have to slice off his head for betraying us."

"You don't even flinch when you talk like that."

I bite back a smile as Elizabeth opens the door. "You two. Must you always be touching?"

Elizabeth still doesn't see how the right person can lift her to new levels of triumph. "Someday, Cricket, you'll appreciate having parents who taught you about love."

She snorts in agitation. "Cricket is a child's name. Isabelle is the Red Fox. Can't we come up with something fiercer? Lion or eagle?"

"Your name was given by Naira," Andre says. "It stays."

"Fine." She shakes her hair free from her bonnet.

"We have a plan," I tell her. "Are you ready to become one of us? A true resistance fighter?"

She puckers her lips, as if she's considering the option. "The duke's family is nobility. His father attends the royal court. If we use him to gain information, we can anticipate the route of the Dragonnades. Of course, this would involve false identities and pretending to be Catholic, but I think it's time to get ahead of them, don't you?"

Andre opens his mouth to speak but shakes his head. "You both terrify me."

"Excellent idea." I wink at Elizabeth and her face beams with pride. Cricket might become a fox yet.

•   •   •

Henri's death haunts me. My oldest friend, one of the few who understood my complicated past. He showed me trust and love and I hate to face life without him. But as painful as his loss is for me, it's worse for Charlotte. Their mischievous ways tempered each other in a strange balance of wits and power. Now, without him, I worry she's turned wild and fearless.

If Red Fox is to continue fighting, we must take out the man with the severed hand. Weakness and empathy can bleed together, and I've learned not to mistake one for the other.

Louvois must die.

Before the sun breaks over the misty Geneva morning, I step onto the moonlit dirt, wet from summer rain. Silvery flecks of light shimmer like stars under my boots. Alone with only my breath and Naira's whispers from my memory, I connect to the earth. The untamed land that sets me free. From Quebec to France to Geneva, the silent trees and creeping animals have always been my friends.

It is people I fear most.

Andre slumbers away in our warm bed while I make my way to the prison. My plan depends on one man, and I need to look into his eyes. I need to understand him.

I approach the cage where Duke Tremblay sits wide awake, staring at the slit of moonlight pouring through a window.

"You aren't sleeping," I say.

He turns to me, showing his swollen forehead from Charlotte's hit. "No, I'm not."

I step closer, nodding to the guard to leave us. "Are they treating you well?"

"As well as can be expected for being in a cage. Though I quite enjoy the break from insufferable soldiers."

I smooth my skirt. Reach into my basket and hand him a roll. "Why did you join us?"

He stands and walks closer to the cage door. He takes the bread from my hand. "I told you. I want the Dragonnades to stop. I don't want my family to continue this horrid tradition."

"What else?"

"Is that not a good enough reason?" He tears the roll with his teeth.

"I've learned a few things over the years. How to read a man's thoughts through his eyes. How to listen to what is unsaid." I tuck an unruly curl behind my ear. "You could run away. You have money, a title. Why join forces with lowly Huguenots wanted for treason?"

He licks the crumbs from his fingers. "You say it as if you didn't plan this."

I flick my eyes to him without moving my head.

"I know you're the Red Fox. And I know you let me follow you along the trail. You wanted me to join you."

"You're smarter when you're sober, Duke Tremblay."

"We all are. Drink takes away my fear and hatred. I feel less of all the things that make me hate myself when the ale flows. I feel less of everything."

I think back to my mother, how drink was the only thing that kept her breathing. How we all face the horror of this life in our own way. "I saw something in you back in the village," I say.

"What was that?" he asks with a laugh. "A failed cadet you could manipulate?"

I lean my face close to the bars, fingers slowly grasping around the door to his cage. "A young man who wants to do right but hasn't the strength yet to figure out how."

"At least you see my desire. My father only sees weakness."

With a deep inhale, I watch his light brown hair quiver in the breezy, pre-dawn darkness. Rain drips from the window in rivulets down the wall toward his feet.

"Those who question the expectations of their people face unimaginable pain," I tell him. "A life of doubt and fight. But before that, unspeakable loneliness."

"Are you speaking from experience, madame?"

I step back, to leave space between us. "You were never meant to be like them, Duke Tremblay. Perhaps you were always meant to meet the resistance."

His eyes flicker with hope when I say the word resistance. "You may call me Edward."

I lift my eyes toward him like streaks of fire. I need him to know we are not friends. "No, I may not, Duke Tremblay."

"Elizabeth saved me when she could have poisoned me." He pauses to see if I'll drop my guard. I won't. "You haven't laid a hand on me when I know how desperately you want to kill dragoons."

"I want to save Huguenots," I say. "Killing dragoons is merely an added perk."

He hasn't yet realized I know most everything about him. A scared, lonely boy who grew up without a mother. I can tell by how he respects my position and allows Charlotte to direct him. We already know his father sees him as a disappointment. Playing violin and writing poetry make him too emotional for military life. They make him too human.

His qualities make him an asset to the resistance. And to me.

"I want to believe in something so fiercely that I would die for it." He crosses his arms and tucks his damp hands under his armpits.

"We will consider your usefulness once you prove yourself."

"How do I do that?" he asks.

I reach into the basket for a cut of fur. "Use this for your head. You'll sleep more soundly on a beaver pelt."

"Where did a peasant find beaver fur?" he asks.

I rub the back of my neck, flushed warm with memories of warrior training and stealing secrets. "Quebec, New France. Another lifetime ago."

"The Red Fox came from Canada?" A smile tugs at the corner of his mouth. Is it surprise or deviousness? I must be very cunning to find out that answer. What he does with this information will tell me everything I need to know about his intentions.

"The resistance comes from everywhere, Duke Tremblay." I lift my skirts and walk to the guard who unlocks the heavy door for me.

"Thank you, Madame Beaumont," he says with a laugh. "Or whatever your name is."

My neck muscles tighten hard enough to tug on my temples. "You may call me Isabelle."

· · ·

Gathered around the lamplit map in our hidden barn, light flickers around our solemn faces. Andre's eyes reveal worry. Elizabeth's, eagerness, and Charlotte's, focus.

"Tremblay is lost," I say, pacing. "An eager soul. He doesn't yet know right from wrong or good from evil." I'm not certain we're the ones to teach him these rules, but something drastic must be done.

"Living with dragoons will do that to a person," Elizabeth says.

Charlotte leans her hands on the rough wood table. "We can't trust a noble. Don't be fooled by his sad eyes."

"I'm fooled by no one." The strength in my voice surprises me. "We have a way into the heart of the king's circle. Secrets only the nobility would know and power only people like his family can give."

Charlotte grits her teeth. "And what if he is a spy? Tracking you for Louvois?"

I can see in Andre's eyes he holds the same worry. I don't reveal one word of my true plan. If he is a spy, I'll use that to my advantage. I'll be dead within the month, anyway.

I close my eyes and shake my head to rid myself of doubts. "My instincts tell me he'll be useful. If I am wrong, then I'll take the fall for that error."

Andre rests his hand on mine. "What did you tell him?"

He knows me too well. "That he can call me Isabelle."

"Isabelle Beaumont?" Andre says, practically biting the tip of his tongue.

"He knows we aren't Beaumonts, but I did tell him I once lived in New France."

Elizabeth drops her head to the table. "This is my fault. I should never have said that name."

"No," Andre says. "You shouldn't have."

Charlotte smiles with a light laugh. "Isabelle has a plan. She always has a plan." She turns to me. "Tell me it involves poisoning the king's entire court?"

"If that's what it takes, yes."

Her eyes light like full moons. Nothing makes her sparkle like the notion of poisoning powerful men. I almost wish I had that streak of horror. I'm stuck with morality like a stone weight around my ankles.

"Charlotte, please take Elizabeth home." He rubs his palms together. "I'd like to speak with my wife."

Charlotte links arms with Elizabeth and they both stare at me with worried eyes as Charlotte clicks the door shut.

Their footsteps fade to silence. Andre rubs his forehead while he prepares his thoughts.

The quiet is too much.

He reaches for the waist of my dress with a firm tug. "If you step into the king's court again, you won't escape."

It's easy to have faith when you've glimpsed your own death. There is no changing the outcome. "You had no issue with this plan when you were disrobing me the other night."

"That is not fair." He turns away from me.

"If you think you'll talk me out of it—"

Andre whips around, presses me to the wall, low back protected by his hand. He breathes heavily into my mouth. "I can't stop you, I know that." His sweet lips graze mine, but he doesn't kiss me. He presses his hips into mine. "Please don't leave me."

I shake my head, confused by his words.

"If I am strong, you'll forgive my weak words." Tears gather in his eyes. "I cannot live without you, Isabelle. I won't."

I don't think him weak for wanting me. Or worrying about losing me. Quite the opposite. "I would die without you, Andre."

"Then you know how I feel. If I lose you, I will never recover." His arms tremble around my body.

This is not how our relationship works. He doesn't guilt me and I don't press him to fight with me. It's been a lovely arrangement I don't care to disrupt. Still, his vulnerability is soft and sweet and kind, and I can't bear the heat rising in my belly. I can't hurt him.

"Then I must not lose." I press my lips to his and run my fingers through his hair. I wrap my leg firmly around his waist, his body pulsing into mine. Desperate eyes and a hungry mouth turn his face wild, a side of him I rarely see, and desperately crave.

"Please don't leave me," he whispers into my hair. Then he lifts my skirts and presses me harder into the wall of the cabin. I remove his breeches as my eyes leak with tears. We kiss madly, desperately. We both know there is no turning back from this choice.

He presses inside me and grunts into my neck. "Don't leave me."

I don't want to, Andre, but the resistance is bigger than us both.

CHAPTER THIRTEEN

I'd like to say I'm strong. Focused on and committed to my larger purpose. But Andre's quiet desperation the other night has stayed with me. His voice has seeped into my memory, and I hear his words repeat over and over *don't leave me*.

What good is saving thousands if I hurt the only man I've ever loved?

Guilt and anger rip through me as I stomp through craggy wilderness, past lush firs and a floor of greenery. Andre thinks I'm here to chop wood, but nothing clears my mind like the remote quiet of a land where I am the only human. The ax handle burns hot in my palm as I remember Naira's training.

"You have been called to be both a wife and fighter," she once told me. "When you let your mind rule, you cannot hear the call of the warrior."

That call seems loud and desperate, burning from deep in my soul. I wish Naira were here with me now. I need her guidance.

I slam my boots into the dry ground, tighten my stomach and twist back my shoulder. With a grunt, I heave the ax through the air. It spirals, then lands with a hard thunk in the dense trunk of a pine.

Footsteps.

I ready my stance, arms up.

"It was easy to find you," Charlotte says. "I simply followed the angry marches through the dirt."

Without a word, I step to the tree, place my foot on the trunk for leverage, and wiggle the ax loose. I walk back to her and drop the ax on the ground.

"Anything on your mind?" she asks.

"Something's different." I straighten my elbows to limit the shaking. "I've changed."

"We're constantly changing," Charlotte says. "I'm a wildly different person than the annoying girl you first met at the abbey in Quebec."

That wild girl was too eager for her own good. With vengeance in her sights, she used the King's Daughters program to escape France. In Quebec, she found me, a Protestant hiding as a soldier's wife. "You've come a long way, Charlotte."

"As have you," she says. Her voice strains, but she forces a grin.

"Have I?" I close my eyes and tighten my mouth, as if I can hold these feelings inside, and maybe force them far away. "Fear still holds me back but now, I sometimes fear myself."

"That's what makes you strong, Isabelle."

"That makes no sense."

She lifts the ax from the soft greenery, stares down a trunk and throws. "Fear means you make wise decisions. Fear keeps you grounded." She wipes her hands together and flicks away the dirt residue. "I have none. It's why I poisoned Henri by accident and why my daughter has enough fear for both of us."

"Clémentine is lovely."

"And too careful. I think her one goal in life is to not live like her mother."

I place my hand on her shoulder. "I think you've given her such a lovely life she doesn't want to leave. I can't blame her."

Charlotte shrugs. "I suppose we can't change who our children are in their hearts."

Guilt gnaws at my insides, sharp enough to take my breath away.

"What's happened?" she asks.

"My focus seems so cloudy lately. I've now a fierce daughter to contend with, and a husband I don't want to hurt. I must kill a man to save myself and the taste I have for his blood makes me worried for my soul."

"You think too highly of yourself, Isabelle."

I straighten my shoulders. "Excuse me?"

Charlotte smiles as if hiding a silent laugh. "You're a brave warrior. A committed resistance fighter with a giant heart. But I hate to break this to you. Above else, you are simply human."

"I once had such clarity." I kick pebbles across the dirt, watching them tumble over a rocky hillside. "When every choice was simple and every sacrifice worth the pain."

"And now?"

"Nothing is simple."

Charlotte walks to the tree and retrieves the ax. When she returns her cheeks have reddened. "I'll never recover." She clears her throat. "Henri is gone. I've lost a piece of my soul."

"You will recover, Charlotte."

A light breeze lifts the fine blond hairs that frame her face. "But I won't be the same."

"No, you won't." I tilt my head and wait for her to make eye contact with me. "This is what it means to be human." I wink.

"You think you're so clever, don't you?"

I shrug. "Sometimes."

With a shake of her head, Charlotte flings away the remnants of emotion that bead on her skin. "I came to find you because I have news."

"Tell me."

She bites her lip and hesitates. "I saw Elizabeth sneak out of the prison this morning. I asked the guard, and she's been visiting Tremblay secretly. She brings him food and listens to his ridiculous stories."

I scratch my temple where my loose curl constantly itches my skin. "Did you ask her to collect information?"

"I think you know the answer to that." The bright sun appears behind the trees, flickering pale yellow light on Charlotte's face.

Charlotte nods. "That girl knows no patience. She'll stop at nothing to prove herself to you."

"Do you trust Tremblay?" I ask.

"I trust no one." She hands me the ax handle. "Except you. I trust you with my life."

Blind commitment. It's the Huguenot way.

．　　．　　．

"Take him with us on a rescue mission?" Andre disrupts his cleaning to scowl at me, which I find cute.

"What good is an asset who sees and knows nothing?" The candle on the table between us drips onto the pewter dish like a rhythmic clock.

Andre throws the rag to the table. "That boy can hardly find his way out of a tavern."

"Exactly. He's hungry. Maybe a little dense. We can teach him."

He leans his head against the window and taps the glass with his fingernail. "He's a Catholic noble, Isabelle. He's either a selfish young man in search of a cure for his loneliness, or he's just as evil as the rest of them. I think you know how much faith I have in Catholics."

I step up to Andre and rest my hands on his chest. His deep gold eyes flicker under the amber beams of daylight. "He's our way in."

"You really envision us draped in ridiculous costumes and bowing in front of the king in his own palace?"

"How else do you propose we kill Louvois?"

"The King has met you, Isabelle." His frustration shows on his face through reddened cheeks and a pulsing jaw.

"Yes, but only briefly. He won't remember a once-Catholic Daughter of New France."

Andre hasn't returned my touch. "Send Charlotte to poison him. We can continue our rescues."

"I could. But that would leave me with this burning hole of hate inside me. I promised Henri vengeance. And I can stop the Dragonnades. I know I can."

He stares into my eyes as if to say *no you can't*, but he knows better. He understands that if he controls me, I will only push harder. The way he rolls his eyes to the ceiling has me arm my thoughts with innumerable ways to convince him.

To my surprise, he looks at me with acceptance. "The things I do for you, my green-eyed wolf."

I glide my fingers through his thick hair and kiss him softly. "I think you do it for you too, my handsome husband."

"You make me do things I wish I could ignore."

I don't want to be responsible for his soul and mine. I want him to want this as much as I do. Alas, I know want means very little in our world. "Maybe I should take this trip without you."

He kisses me firm enough to turn my knees weak. "We fight alongside each other. Forever."

Relieved, I exhale against my tightened chest. "It's settled. Tremblay joins our next rescue. We test him. On a very short rope."

"When do we leave, madame?"

"Tonight."

. . .

Andre escorts Tremblay to the base of the Huguenot Trail. So called because thousands of people have traveled this path in search of freedom. One day, it will be nothing more than a worn line in the dirt with memories of Protestant footsteps. I can only hope those lives will never be forgotten.

Andre stops at the foot of a pine and turns to face the view of Geneva under a late summer sunset. "Here we are safe. We are not hunted or beaten. We are not the enemy."

"Am I the enemy?" Tremblay asks.

I jump from a pine branch overhead, landing with my knees on Tremblay's back where his tall, lanky body breaks my fall. I press his face into the dirt and slide my knife from my boot. I hold the blade to his cheek as Charlotte and Elizabeth each pin one of his arms to the ground.

I lean to his ear, his frantic breath whistling near my cheek. "You are only the enemy if you choose to be."

We release him, each of us encircling him with weapons in our hands.

Tremblay sits up, eyeing the blades and arrows. "Understood." He swallows with a wince.

I reach to help him up. He hesitantly takes my hand and scans the group.

"A pampered duke is no match for us," Charlotte says. "If you wrong us, we will slice your tongue in your sleep without hesitation."

"There will be no need for anything that drastic." He straightens his peasant clothing from the prison. "I quite like the movement of these clothes. Simple, yet unrestricted." He puffs out his bottom lip and nods.

I narrow my eyes to him. "Move."

Andre walks behind him, rifle pointed at his back. Elizabeth and I walk ahead with Charlotte in between.

"I know you've been visiting him," I say.

"The silly man needs a friend." She glances over her shoulder at the ridiculous dragoon who smiles hopefully. "I can't figure him out. He seems kind and simple, but with his life of privilege none of that makes sense."

"He's lost. That makes perfect sense to me." I link my arm through hers. "He will decide who he is when he comes face to face with the consequences of inaction."

"What do you mean?"

"He's survived by playing simple and dumb, but he is nothing of the sort. He hasn't participated in torture, not that we can see. He hopes to remain a good person, though by ignoring the evil around him, he might as well be the one holding the torch."

"How do you understand people so well?"

"My childhood in La Rochelle made me listen to every sound. It taught me to read someone's body before they attack. It wasn't until I met Naira that I learned I'd been listening to the whispers of thoughts. My own, God's."

"You don't speak of God often," she says. "Why?"

"I feel God in my breath and in the whistle of trees. In the faces of those we save. That's enough for me."

Charlotte trips Tremblay and we turn to watch him. He rubs his nose that is now full of dirt. "Ouch."

Charlotte shrugs. "Just making sure you're paying attention."

"Must the poor man break bones to prove himself to us?" Elizabeth asks the group.

"Don't give the blond one any ideas," he whispers. "She terrifies me."

We walk through the night without difficulty, the duke, to my surprise, does not complain once. We stop in the early morning to sleep in a clearing a few minutes off the trail. I wouldn't dare show him our safe houses.

Andre builds a fire while Tremblay watches like an intrigued child.

"You simply rub sticks together?" he asks.

"It's a bit more than that," Andre says with a head tilt. "Have you never built a fire?"

"That does make me sound rather useless." Tremblay's cheeks flush with embarrassment. "We always had servants for that sort of thing."

I hand him a jug of wine. "It's a good thing we only need your secrets. You'd be useless in the battlefield."

Elizabeth sits next to him. "You must find life to be quite a bore."

"I find people tedious." He catches himself. "Not any of you fine Huguenots, of course." Charlotte sharpens a stick to a fine point and blows the remnants toward the duke's face. Discomfort bounces across his tightened features. "Can you tell me where we're going?"

"No," I say.

"We'll be rescuing Huguenots from dragoons, yes?"

Charlotte rolls her eyes. "Are you worried about your fellow cadets?"

"No." His eye twitches. "I have no loyalty to them."

He shares wine with Elizabeth before Andre yanks it from her grasp. A light tingling brushes my skin despite not even the slightest hint of a breeze in the air.

"I've never saved anyone. It all sounds so romantic, like something out of a sonnet."

Charlotte snarls her way to a response. "There is nothing romantic about what we do, you spoiled man-child."

Movement. I feel it but see nothing. I scan the trees as birds fly overhead. I slide closer to our weapons while Charlotte berates the poor duke. She breaks her stick over her knee to watch him flinch, then returns to sharpening another point.

"I want to help," he says. "I promise I can be more useful than I currently appear."

Andre connects eyes with me.

"I will need to learn, certainly," the duke says. "But I can assure you nothing is more difficult than learning the violin. I've never fought a man. Can you believe that? Or woman or animal, for that matter. Not even a snail has met the underside of my boot. At least, not by my intention." He gasps. "Think of all the innocent snails I might have squished unknowingly!"

In one swift motion, I lift the bow and arrow and aim it at Tremblay's face. His mouth drops open as all color drains from his face. A sound grumbles from his throat, half gargle, half shriek.

"Duck."

He buries his head in his lap, hands over his head just as my arrow spirals above him. It lands in the neck of a Frenchman who drops a blade from his hand before falling lifeless into a pool of his own blood.

Andre approaches the man to ensure he's dead. We gather around his body, examining his clothing. "Too clean," Andre says. "Not a farmer."

"Could he have been lost?" Elizabeth asks.

"He approached us with a knife," I say.

The duke lifts his head, hand to his chest, on the verge of fainting. "You could have killed me," he says to me.

"But I didn't, did I?"

We examine his clothing. His shoes. The duke stumbles past the body toward the closest tree.

"What are you doing?" I ask.

"That man." He falls to his hands and knees and crawls through the dirt. He finds a bag and carries it back to us. "He looks familiar," the duke says. He holds up the linen bag to show us a symbol of the Sun King. "He's military."

We release our hands from his pockets. "Is he a dragoon?" Elizabeth asks.

"I don't know," the duke says.

"How did you know the bag was there?" I ask.

"We're taught to leave our belongings hidden when we come across an unknown threat." He opens the bag and removes a rope.

"What is a French military man doing on this side of Geneva?" Charlotte raises her eyebrows. "With a rope."

The duke coughs as he unrolls a scroll. He turns it to face us as we gasp at a drawing of me.

The illustration is surprisingly accurate, except for my nose. I do not have a big nose. "He's looking for me."

Tremblay reads from the scroll. "Wanted. The Red Fox. Huguenot sympathizer and tyrant. Reward for her safe return."

"They want you alive?" Elizabeth asks.

"So they may torture me for secrets of the resistance."

I don't react when Elizabeth covers her mouth or when the duke grimaces. But I do feel my stomach turn rigid when Andre meets my eyes. Without words, I hear his desperate pleas.

Don't leave me.

CHAPTER FOURTEEN

Charlotte leads the way as we climb the rocky mountain into France where the sun glows like gold and the rivers tumble like emeralds. Such beauty frames such wicked deeds.

"You didn't let Andre talk you out of this rescue," Charlotte says.

We stop to catch our breath and wait for the duke to scramble his way up to us.

"He didn't try to talk me out of it."

"I know he worries about you."

I stare at the bright blue sky. "Most women love to be safe and warm in their homes. They don't need danger like I do."

Charlotte takes in a deep breath of clear mountain air. "There's a reason Andre loved you the moment he met you. You both live on the edge of safety. He won't admit it, but I think your danger is one of his favorite things about you."

I hold her hand and grasp tight. "You and Henri were perfect together."

She almost breaks her icy exterior but catches her tears by the tail. "He loved you so much, Isabelle. He knew you would fight long after he was gone."

A gust of wind brushes a chill along my neck. My heart thumps so hard it's like it has feet. "I've seen so much pain but losing my best friend has left a hole in me I'm not sure I'll ever repair."

"Interesting," she says. "Losing him has focused me. I will die if I must, but I'll bring him justice."

I want to tell her to think of her daughter, but I know she needs this fight. She's absorbed Henri's wants and desires. They're part of her now.

The duke crawls his way to the top of the rock, breath wheezing like steam from a copper kettle. Elizabeth and Andre follow, looking fresh and relaxed.

"I'm fine," the duke sputters. "Just need a moment."

Elizabeth raises her eyebrows at him. "Have you never walked before?"

"Not this high."

Andre lifts him by the arm. "Come. We can rest in the field below."

Other than a few slips from the duke, we make our way without difficulty to the rolling terrain of Eastern France. We find an abandoned stone cottage and set up for the night. Andre stands guard, rifle in hand, at the opening where a door once hung.

"I don't understand," the duke asks me. "They're all looking for you. Your hair marks you as the Red Fox and you're walking right into dragoon occupied villages. Why?"

"Tremblay, what would you do if you could never play another note on your violin or write another sonnet?"

He ponders that question. "I would want it more."

I nod.

Elizabeth rolls a pebble between her palms. "You are not prepared for this, Tremblay."

He rests the back of his hand on his hip, fingers curled out. "And how do you know that?"

Elizabeth launches toward the duke as he shrieks. She slams her shoulder into his fleshy side and flattens him to the ground. He tries to roll but she grabs his hair in one hand and pulls his hand behind his back with the other.

"I don't want to hurt a woman," he says into the dirt.

She yanks his wrist farther up his spine between his shoulder blades. "That was your first mistake." He grunts, and Elizabeth releases him. "Get up. You need to learn some things."

While Charlotte and Elizabeth work with the duke on basic fighting skills, I step up behind Andre and wrap my arms around his waist. My face finds a familiar comfort in his warm neck.

"Beautiful night," Andre says to the moonlit sky.

I don't respond, enjoying the feel of his golden hair tickling my cheek.

"What's your plan for the duke?" he asks. We turn to watch him swat and Charlotte as she kicks him in the knee. "Battle doesn't appear to be his forte."

"I'll force him to look at the people we rescue. He'll watch the torture and I'll read what his heart says. All the answers will be right there in his eyes."

Andre pulls my hands to his mouth for a soft kiss before tucking them under his chin. "His first trip is a test with the Red Fox as his commander."

"He will either prove useful or we'll discard him."

He turns to face me, silver light gracing his cheek. "And you? How do we protect you?"

I place my palm to his cheek. "You don't."

"That drawing. The king has offered an award for your capture."

Warm evenings in France bring me back to an earlier version of myself, where this place was my homeland, something I didn't want to lose. That girl died a long time ago. "That reward means the king is afraid of me. That's something I've wanted for years."

The duke groans for mercy. Charlotte and Elizabeth each grasp a fistful of his hair while twisting his limbs like an old oak branch. "Merde! How do two sprightly things have this much strength?"

Andre glances at his predicament. "You aren't looking deep enough," he says with a smile. "They are sprightly in body, but monstrous in the soul."

· · ·

We arrive on the outskirts of Dijon, Duke Tremblay limping and bruised, but somehow still eager to participate in this rescue. We've traveled off the trail, mirroring its path to avoid sightings. Lying on our bellies, watching the village from a nearby hill, familiar sounds crash through the afternoon. Shrieks and cries. The crack of a skull and clank of chains. And the most sickening sound of all—laughter.

The duke gasps for breath next to me. "Are they beating them?"

"Among other things," Charlotte says. She begins to leap forward but Elizabeth stops her. "Wait."

Elizabeth's solemn focus fills me with pride. Emotion. Sympathy. Anything that makes you human is a liability out here in the resistance. I fear the horror will break her of that softness soon enough. For now, she remains calm as a windless field.

"This village looks quite different than I imagined," Tremblay says.

"What did you imagine?" Andre asks.

"Father always spoke of the land as dry and useless here. It's quite beautiful."

"Your father?" Charlotte asks.

"Yes. My family manages the land here for the king, but Father felt it was too barren to bother with."

We glance at each other, shocked at the simplicity of his statement.

"Of course," Elizabeth says. "What self-respecting noble doesn't determine the worth of an entire region?"

"Focus," I say. "We haven't much time. They've already initiated beatings."

"How do we rescue them?" Tremblay asks.

"We kill the bastards who beat them." Charlotte jumps nimbly over a rock and slides down the hill to the back of a cluster of homes.

"Now? We kill them now?" His bumbling words make me question bringing him along.

"No." Charlotte bounces through the shadows below, hiding under eaves and behind barrels. "We count them first."

Hours drip by, screams pulsing in the air at odd times. Tremblay sweats, his head in the dirt, while the rest of us stare into the torchlit village. Elizabeth begins to squirm. "Why is she taking so long?"

"Trust, Cricket."

Finally, as the sun sets into an orange burst of light beyond the horizon, Charlotte scrambles up the hill to meet us. "We must act now."

"Now?" I ask. "We need a plan first."

"No time." She reaches into her pocket to show me the empty vials. "I poisoned the Lieutenant."

"You what?" I want to shake her for her stupidity, but I remind myself she is not the impulsive girl she once was.

"I had no choice."

We load ourselves with weapons. Knives and swords and arrows. No guns. We survive by remaining quiet and lethal. "He had a little boy by the neck. He was about to beat him. A *child*. I'd rather get burned than watch a child take a beating."

"Understood," I say. "How many?"

"Five houses. Two dragoons each. She draws lines in the dirt to simulate the village. This one next to the church. This one behind the communal oven. She points to each, stabbing broken slivers of sticks into the dirt. "The rest are Catholic homes."

"How did you kill the Lieutenant?" Elizabeth asks.

"I pretended to bump into him while I poured arsenic down his neck. He instantly started itching and turning red. The child managed to wriggle away. I whispered to grab his family and run."

Andre tightens his grip around a blade. "How long until they discover he was poisoned?"

"They probably already have."

"Go." I lead each one down the hill, about to whisper to Andre when he cuts me off. "I know. I'll cover Elizabeth."

We crawl through the night, a short reprieve from screams while the military men gather in the town square, screaming of tyranny. I grab Tremblay by the shirt. "You stay close to me. Here." I hand him a sword. Too cumbersome for me, but the poor lad deserves a fighting chance.

"A sword?" He lifts his arm as if to assume a fencing position. "I am ready."

"Put that thing down. Your job is to protect me, not get us killed."

He shakes his head like a baby pinecone in the wind. A shriek pierces the relative quiet. Shrill and desperate. I lock eyes with our group, each positioned near a home Charlotte identified. The dragoons drag a young woman through the dirt to the center of the village. She kicks and fights, terror overtaking her Protestant teachings to remain calm in our moment of torture.

Elizabeth's eyes glow white through the dark.

"What are they doing to her?" Tremblay asks.

"Lashings. Burns. Depends how awful the dragoons want to be." I remain cold but inside fear bleeds into every crack in my memory. I feel her screams deep in my bones.

Tremblay chokes, trying to catch his breath. "Simply for being Protestant."

As if he needs reminders as to how hateful his people are. "Yes."

All I need is a nod from Charlotte to understand her thoughts. While the crowd of horrid soldiers gathers to watch a girl tortured, we will sneak into the empty homes and make the Huguenots flee by any means necessary.

"Scatter."

I drag the duke with me to the house near the church. We lean against the wall in the narrow alley. Dragoons yell and cheer, deciding what to do with the girl in the center of town.

"Now." I shove the duke behind me as we slip into the house and shut the door.

He freezes at the sight of bleeding foreheads and ripped clothing. The father is bruised and bloodied and swollen. Children cower. He braces himself on the wall, looking as if he might faint.

"I'm here to help, but we must leave now." I lift the children up, carrying the youngest and handing her to her mother. "We must go now."

"Who are you?" the mother asks.

"The resistance."

The family hugs quietly. "We have nowhere to go."

They always say the same thing.

"Yes, you do. With me."

The child cries and the mother buries her face in her chest to quiet her. She looks at me and nods. "Yes. We'll follow."

The duke uselessly stares at us with confused horror. "Perhaps you could open a window for us?" The duke nods. One by one we climb out the window, except the father who is hurt too badly to move. I instruct the mother and children to wait for us under the cover of trees. "When my friends come for you, follow them."

"Not without my husband," she says. I smile, understanding her completely. Without our family, where is the will to live?

The duke and I fall against the alley wall yet again as two dragoons linger around the corner. They shove each other, voices rising louder by the second.

"Drunk or simply stupid," I say.

"That describes most every dragoon I've met," the duke says. "What do we do?"

"We wait. They'll tire themselves out soon enough."

The girl resumes her screams. Through a narrow slit between homes, torches burn. I focus my gaze. They're tying her to a stake. Her voice, so strong and desperate. She sounds to be the same age as Elizabeth.

"They're gone," the duke says.

Andre creeps toward us and motions back to the group of terrified Huguenots. "We've got them all. Let's go."

"The father is still inside," the duke says.

Andre pushes past him and slips into the house. I run across to the next row of homes to get a better look at the girl. Tears streak her face. Light brown hair in a plait over her shoulder. She's just a child.

I count dragoons. Two, four, six.

The drunk ones lean along the sides of houses.

One officer.

"Isabelle." The duke's voice comes as a loud whisper, surprisingly shrill. I turn back to see Andre, his arm around the man's waist. They limp to the helpless group of Huguenots waiting to flee.

My feet won't move.

Do not sacrifice twenty for the sake of one, Isabelle.

Don't be a fool.

The girl wails. I'm brought back to La Rochelle. Screaming children. Blue faces. Blood dripping down walls. I hear nothing, stuck in that terrifying memory of the exile. My wrist branding.

Henri.

Arms wrap around me. A hand gripped over my mouth. I nearly bite the fingers off when I smell Andre. "It's me," he says. "Shh."

I pull away from him, reaching toward the girl. He holds me tight, mouth to my ear. "You can't save her."

"Try and stop me."

He turns my face to the trees. Glowing white eyeballs like the moon reflected on the sea. "*They* need us. Don't risk the entire village."

"But she's just a child."

"I know." He kisses my forehead and holds me tight. "Sacrifice. We are always in a sacrifice."

Impossible choices where the outcome is always heartache. This is our life now.

Andre drags me away, the desire to kick him off me and run to the girl stronger than anything I've felt. I've become so strategic. So planned. So emotionless. But this girl breaks loose every desperation inside me. Unspools it like a thread.

Elizabeth wraps her arm through mine. "Can we save her?" she whispers.

Andre and Charlotte push the crowd forward, instructing them to move quickly but stay silent. I stop the man we just rescued. "What is that?" I point to a stone shed behind their house.

The man sighs. "They ate all our meat. There's nothing but empty hooks and shelves now."

"You hunt?"

"I did."

The duke stays next to me, surprisingly loyal. "I don't know what you're considering, but you can't fight a dozen dragoons. *Can you?*"

"It's only six. And one officer."

I smile at Elizabeth. "I love you."

She never questions my erratic choices. In fact, I think she admires them. "I love you too."

I slip inside the shed. Weapons still in place. Those arrogant bastards only wanted the food. They never dreamed they'd need to defend themselves against helpless Huguenots. Behind me, Charlotte appears. "Are you certain, Isabelle?"

"No. But I'm doing it anyway."

Blades stuffed in my boots and a holster around my waist, I hand her a pistol. We each lift a bow and arrow. "Just like old times," she says.

The girl screams. Dragoons taunt her, tease her fear with weapons and fire.

Andre waits for me in the dark. "Don't," he whispers.

"I have to." I kiss him hard and quick. "Promise me if something happens to me, you'll still fight."

He tightens his lips and stares back at the Huguenots.

"Promise," I whisper.

He nods, deflated. "I promise."

"You're my forever, Andre." I don't wait to see his reaction. Too much at stake, so I turn away. The duke follows me like a shadow. Charlotte covers me from an opening between houses.

Elizabeth positions herself behind the church, arrow aimed at the officer's head.

The girl begs. She pleads. She screams. Then, she whimpers.

The men wave torches near her face, nearly burning her. Black soot covers her cheeks and forehead.

"What do I do?" the duke asks.

I hand him a pistol. Can you shoot?"

"Yes."

"Then do that."

A fiery ball of light shoots across the night. One of the dragoons launches for the girl, burning her hand. She releases a howling cry as the officer grabs him and shoves him to the ground. "Order!"

The dragoon seethes, breathless, almost excited to torture.

Patience, Isabelle.

A gunshot.

The duke took out the officer in one shot.

I raise my arrow and aim for the dragoon closest to the girl. Breathe. Release. The arrow spirals into his eyeball, He falls on his torch. His smoking body soon turns to flames at the girl's feet. Without a thought, I run.

Blade in hand, I scream as loud as my lungs allow. Every dragoon turns to me. I surprise one with a dagger to the face. A swift slice from his eye to his mouth and another stab to his neck. He falls to the ground, but I don't stop there. I slash the blade through his neck and chest so many times I lose memory of why I'm here. Out of my body, tears stream through cries but I don't feel them.

No remorse. No rules. Just kill.

My throat tightens so I step back and survey the damage. He didn't even attack me, and I slashed holes all through his body. Time crashes back into me.

The girl.

Flames near her feet. Arrows fly from all directions. Men scrabble. Fire grows.

All I see is the girl's face. Her braid. Her burnt hand.

Someone grabs my arm. With a swift kick behind me, I'm able to shove the man away from. I turn back and kick him squarely in the cockerel then shove my palm through his nose. Once he's down, I stab his face. Three times.

I feel nothing other than the desire to keep slashing.

Men scream and fire grows all around us. I hear gunshots and the whoosh of arrows. I kick the man on fire and roll him away, my skirt catching flames in the process. I cut the girl's ropes, sawing feverishly.

Snap.

The girl falls to the ground.

I drop with her and roll myself like a log down a hill until my dress smolders with smoke. I reach for her. Our eyes meet and I feel myself smile.

A hard thwack to my head turns everything black.

CHAPTER FIFTEEN

Is it a dream? A memory? Perhaps reality. My mind hovers somewhere unfamiliar. Somewhere dark.

Death, have we finally met?

Pain thunders through my body and my mind stutters to life.

Murmurs.

I drag my eyes open. A foggy view of a face over me. Yellow teeth. A branding iron in his hand.

Louvois.

My arm shoots into the air toward his shadowy face. My fist makes contact with his nose and the figure's head snaps back.

My eyes focus.

"Argh. You certainly like to fight." The duke holds his bloody nose.

I'm in a bed. In a home. Next to a fire.

Collapse again to blackness.

·   ·   ·

A girl holds broth to my mouth. "Please don't hit me again," she mutters.

"I can't promise anything," I want to say, but it comes out as word mush.

I manage a few swallows. *My head.*

"Gave quite a fight, you did." She holds the back of my head as broth mostly dribbles down the sides of my mouth, but she manages a drop or two in my mouth.

Round cheeks. Sweet face. Coiffe tied neatly around her chin.

"Who?" It's all I manage, but she seems to understand.

"My name is Angelique."

That was my mother's name. I think I speak, but words possibly stayed in my mind without making their way out of my mouth.

"You're awake!" The duke steps inside the kitchen where I realize my bed is. The room takes focus. Dried herbs dangle in bundles from the mantel where half a pig roasts on a turnspit. The ceiling is low and angled to a paned window with a warped view of golden fields.

The girl dabs my mouth dry and lowers my head softly then disappears from view.

"Can you speak?" Tremblay asks.

"Ouch."

"Splendid." He pulls a chair next to me with a nervous grin.

Memory floods back to me. "The girl. Did she live?" My mouth is dry, and my tongue swollen.

"Yes. There is much to report to you. But you need your rest."

I grab his sleeve and pull him close to me. "Tell me everything."

He nods. "Alright. Where to start? The girl crawled her way to the church. She had just about made it when a half-drunk soldier grabbed her by the ankles. The remaining soldiers had arrived at the square by then and it wasn't looking good for her. Charlotte ran straight for the girl with four soldiers closing in on her. Arrows and shots flew from the trees and took out two of them."

"Did she save her?"

"Charlotte fought two men. That little thing is like oil on fire. She took a few blows but grabbed a torch and burned the last one's face. Then she stabbed the drunk one. As easy and methodical as a carriage rolling over pebbles."

I swallow against a painful throat. "Where are they?"

"I dragged you back to the trees. You were out cold, so I slung you over my shoulder. I had only a few moments to speak with everyone." He loosens his cravat. "I knew you couldn't flee. I told your husband I would find somewhere to keep you safe."

"He left?" No, something doesn't make sense. He would never trust the duke.

"He said he made a promise to you. He would make sure every Huguenot arrived safely in Geneva."

I look around the room with panicked eyes. My usual iron nerves have melted while my brain fumbles around like thought soup. "Andre would never leave me alone with you."

The door clicks open. Elizabeth.

"Isabelle!" She drops a basket of mushrooms on the table and runs to me. "You're awake."

I hold her hands to my cheek and do not want to let them go. "You're safe."

"Of course I am. You don't think Papa would allow me to trek back to Geneva with the refugees, do you? Too dangerous, he said." She purses her lips. "Besides, my job right now is to make sure you recover." She jabs an elbow into the duke's arm causing him to flinch. "And to keep this man in line."

The duke clears his throat. "I'll leave you two. The lady of the house requires firewood." He bows formally and heads outside.

"He really is an odd man," Elizabeth says. "He's like a strange older brother I never wanted."

My forehead thumps like a chisel trying to break loose from inside my skull. "Where are we?"

She tears off crumbs from a roll near the bed and hands them to me. "The duke found a former manor house and demanded they take us in as we're on special instructions from the king. He offered coins." She covers her mouth in a whisper. "They believed him. Money and power can do that, I suppose."

"Are you safe?" I ask again, terrified and knowing I can't protect anyone right now.

She rests her hand on mine. "Yes. I've already threatened the duke at knifepoint several times." She waves away the thought. "Papa was so worried about you."

I made him promise to save them. He never lets me down.

Elizabeth dabs a wet cloth to my bloody forehead. "It will take weeks to reach Geneva with that damaged group. The poor families were all injured and frightened. The girl you rescued is strong. She lifted an older woman and helped her walk, even with a burnt hand."

"And Charlotte?"

"Focused as ever. Bruised face and a twisted wrist couldn't stop her."

My eyes fall closed of their own accord. I try to focus but everything turns foggy.

"Get some sleep," she says. "The duke is going to play music for us later. He's good for entertainment at least." She cleans up the kitchen as I fall in and out of sleep.

As the numbness wears off, the throb in the back of my head becomes unbearable. I fumble my hand to the back of my tender scalp. I expect an egg-shaped lump but find sharp edges. Two long sides. A rectangle.

The shape of the butt of a rifle. Exactly like the one I handed to the duke. I want to warn Elizabeth, but intractable pain swallows me once again.

.   .   .

My mind has conjured dreams of unimaginable terrors in the hours since I last spoke to Elizabeth. I shake off nightmares of burning flesh and twisted bones. Death reaching its twisted fingers into my empty eye sockets. I sit up with a gasp and feel my eyes to make sure they're still there.

A bright morning floods the kitchen in blinding light. My joints ache. I rise to sit and brace myself against the spinning room. Sickness waves through me but I manage to hold myself steady.

Wine sits by the bedside like healing juice for my parched body. I drink it slowly, letting it bathe my throat in liquid relief.

Elizabeth opens the door. She rushes to me as I attempt to stand. "You shouldn't be up." My knees falter but she holds my waist and leans her body into mine to prevent me falling.

"How long did I sleep?"

"Two days."

I fall back to the bed and bury my forehead in my palms.

"Here." She helps me sip a bowl of cold broth. "Rosemary and nutmeg to help the pain."

I smile at her. "You've become so strong and capable, Cricket."

She brushes her thumb over my swollen cheek. "I've learned from the best."

I finish the broth and lean my elbows on my knees. "Where are we?"

"An older couple lives here with two servants and a few workers to manage the farm. They keep to themselves which suits me fine. Get comfortable. We won't see Papa and Charlotte for weeks. Maybe months."

"You probably wanted to escort those families back to Geneva to watch their faces light with glee when they pass into safe territory, but you're stuck here with me. I'm sorry."

"Don't be. That village attack was the most exciting thing to happen to me since Papa said I could join the resistance."

I consider my worry and how much I want to burden her with. Tremblay isn't who he seems. No one ever is. "Cricket, did you see how I got knocked out?"

"No. I was too busy shooting arrows into dragoon's necks." Her elated sigh suggests she's hungry for more violence. She has so much still to learn, but I'm too ill to teach her. "The duke said he dragged you out after he saw you unmoving on the ground."

I nod. "That's what I thought."

She smooths back my curls as if I'm a child. "Everything's going to be okay, Isabelle."

I force a wide smile, knowing that my instincts warn of lies and danger and deceit. I just can't prove it yet.

. . .

One week of constant sleep and my head finally stopped thumping. Two, and the daily vomiting waned. Now, by week three, I resemble normal, though everything inside me rocks with unsteadiness. Every night, I hope for a dream with Naira, and every morning I wake from a nightmare, stifling screams.

As the afternoon sun lowers over the golden hills, Elizabeth glides through the fields, her silhouette backlit by an amber glow. She practices everything I've taught her, her moves sharp and focused. I watch her in awe, my own body struggling to recover in a way my younger body never did.

"I've never met women like you." The duke leans against the stone wall next to me.

"When you've had to fight for your life, you see the world in potential dangers." My stiff neck finds a way to turn toward Elizabeth moving like a dance against the setting sun.

"Those families we rescued, do you think they're safe now?"

I glance to the side but not directly at him. "Charlotte would die for their chance at freedom. So would Andre."

"When I say I've never met women like you, I don't mean your physical strength. I've never met anyone as committed to something purely for other people."

My stomach clenches, as if I need to hold in the eruption of worry that's about to release. "It isn't only for others."

He tilts his head. "Explain it to me."

I'm not sure why, but I speak plainly. Unreserved. "Fear and revenge and resistance gives me a feeling of control when I've lived so long without it."

"I would argue that every hero has a soft spot for the glory."

Elizabeth rolls and kicks and balances on her hands. The soft scent of woodsy lavender rests on the breeze. "And what about you, Duke Tremblay? What are you after?"

He scratches his neck and squints at the burst of red sky. "A purpose."

"And you thought you'd find that in the resistance of Huguenots? Interesting choice for a Catholic poet and musician."

"I certainly wasn't finding it drunk in the tavern to drown out the screams." His face drops. "And I didn't find it in Paris as the spoiled son of a noble."

"Am I to feel sorry for you?" I ask. "No joy in the business of torture and stolen property?"

His cheeks redden. "No, I need no sympathy. Only a chance to do something good."

His eye twitches and he returns to watching Elizabeth who now sits solemnly in the dirt, watching the sunset disappear into a clear gray night.

. . .

I wait until midnight when the house is quiet. Elizabeth sleeps soundly next to me. My grasp tightens around a blade handle. I thirst for blood. The need hasn't left me since Henri laid dead and cold at my feet.

I slip into the sitting room and climb the stairs. Creaks whisper under the weight of my feet. I pass empty rooms with poster beds in this unnecessarily large house. Every wall holds a framed painting, the wood freshly oiled to a high shine. Wind beats the windows as tree branches waver through shadows. The hallway's runner softens my steps until I arrive at the room at the end of the hall.

Quiet. Slow. I step into his room as soft as a whisper.

Minutes pass as I watch him. Heavy breathing and body twitches. He has no idea a Huguenot stands over him so full of rage she imagines how his blood might stain the sheets.

Finally, I move.

I grab him and yank his body to the ground, one hand over his mouth and the other holding a blade to his neck. "Don't move."

His eyes wide and his body frozen, he heaves hot, heavy breathes into my palm.

"You move any direction and I'll slice this blade through the closest body part. Right now, that's your neck."

He barely nods in understanding, blinking hard.

"I'm going to take my hand from your mouth. If you scream, I will kill you. Understand?" I slide my hand slowly from his face and wait to ensure he follows orders. "You've lied to me, Tremblay."

"I promised to protect you and that is what I've done."

I press the blade into his skin at his throat hard enough that he winces. "You knocked me out with the gun I handed you."

He tries to shake his head no but is too afraid of the sharp dagger against his windpipe. "Yes."

I'm almost impressed with his bravery. "Shall I kill you now?"

"No, wait." He swallows, a light line of blood blooming along his skin under the blade. "Just listen."

I don't let up on the knife's pressure. "I'm waiting."

"Your need for triumph blinds you."

Silence drops heavy on us broken only by the beating wind outside. "I see you need a lesson in flattery."

"Listen," he says. "You were going to save that girl. That's all you saw."

The last thing I remember is my skirt on fire. Her crawling toward the church. "You stopped me from getting to her."

"No,' he says calmly. "I stopped you from running toward the five dragoons that would have killed you."

"I didn't see any threats."

"That's because the girl's screams made you falter." His hands tremble under the weight of my knees.

I want to ram this blade through his chin, but I don't.

"Those soldiers ran in a crowd toward her. If you ran after her, they would have rammed your side with spears and torches without you ever seeing them." He exhales to relax his muscles. "I hit you over the head to save you."

"You would have let the girl die?"

"I had one job. To protect you. That is what I did. If you must kill me for that, then by all means, slice me in two right now."

Much to my surprise, I don't tear into his flesh. "I have one question." His glassy eyes have calmed. "Why haven't you attacked us yet?"

"I want to make music and poetry. Drawing blood gets me no closer to being an artist."

"You joined the resistance against your family and everyone like them. Explain." Howling wind hisses through the trees and the moonlight makes his face appear silver.

Tightened muscles relax under my hand. He exhales into a soft abdomen. "When you've lived without passion, it is nearly impossible to summon art."

My arm drops slightly, the dagger still against his skin but with no pressure. "Aren't music and poetry passion enough?"

"I've never felt love. Or disappointment, or adversity. I don't know survival or fear. I am an empty, soulless, musician with no notes to play."

My dizziness returns. The carved detailing on the bedpost suddenly ripples like the ocean.

How he's managed to find my sympathy, I'll never understand. I collapse to the floor beside him, head dropped in fatigue. "Is this why you drink, to feel?"

"No." He sits up and wipes the blood from his neck. "No. Drink does not make me feel. It makes me ignore that I can't."

"Perhaps we're more alike than I realized." I stand and drag myself to the window. He nervously rises to the bed.

"How?" he asks. "You're full of passion."

"To survive in the horrors of this world, I can't let my emotions rule as I wish I could. Screams. The smell of death. They start to feel like smoke. You swear you can see it, but when you reach to touch it, you feel nothing."

"What was it about that girl that rattled you?" he asks.

"She had fight in her eyes." I smile, despite the awful images that bubble through my mind. "When Louvois branded me, I was protecting my friend Henri. I handed that monster my arm." A clock ticks away the seconds in the corner of the room. I hadn't noticed it until now. "She knew her family needed to escape, and she offered herself up for torture."

"Create a scene so they could flee."

"Yes. I couldn't let her die. It would be like killing my own spirit."

A forced throat clearing indicates he's frightened. "Did you want to kill me tonight?" he asks.

"What I want is to resume my purpose and fall in the arms of my husband after a successful rescue."

"Why didn't you slice the blade through me?"

I hold the dagger up to the light to examine its tip, subtly shiny with a swipe of his blood. "I broke my rule in that village. I killed for the joy of watching them bleed. Yes, I wanted to save the girl, but killing the soldiers filled a hunger I've carried for years." I drop the knife into the shadows. "That feeling terrifies me."

"I didn't know anything terrified you."

I push hard into my eyes to stop any threat of tears. Once I clear my throat, I place the knife on his bedside table. "Here. Protect yourself, Tremblay. Danger is everywhere."

CHAPTER SIXTEEN

My nightmares have returned.

Stuck in this Catholic home with a restless daughter and a duke eager to prove himself, there is no air to breathe. No rescue to plan. No enemies to conquer.

I have yet to speak to the owners of this house. They throw agitated glances my way, as if they know a traitor lives among them. The duke dines with them every day and escorts the lady on short walks in the morning. Their few servants walk around me as if I'm a shadow.

It's torture here.

I've taken to spending my days in the hills, learning the terrain and practicing, pretending Naira is with me. Today, in the heat of summer, I run up a nearby hill and roll down repeatedly until I nearly retch. I haven't fully returned to normal, and my impatience is like an unbearable itch I can't reach.

Through a spinning head, I hear footsteps. When I open my eyes, the world still tumbles around like I'm rolling, but I know I'm solidly on my back with the sun beating on my face.

The steps grow closer. Faster. A shadow appears when I peek my eyes open, so I swing my arms, which just makes me cry.

It grabs me. It shakes my shoulders. All I see is blood tangled in wet hair. It drips on my face. When I wipe it away, my hand removes my skin with it.

In a panic, I scream.

It still shakes me. Deep in my mind, I hear my name. *Isabelle.* Over and over, my name coaxes me back to life. With a lurch, I land back in my body, Elizabeth yelling my name. She shakes me as I feel my cheeks to ensure my skin is still intact. Dry. No blood.

Another daytime nightmare of blood that isn't there.

"Isabelle, I'm here." Elizabeth holds me as my body shakes and trembles. I want to stand up and scream. Prove I am the wolf. But I don't. I lean into her shoulder and cry like a scared little fox.

. . .

Elizabeth brings me wine, our nook off the kitchen lit by a fire she built. "I hope you know how capable you are," I say.

She nods and nudges me to drink. "Earlier today." She tightens her brow. "What was that?"

It took a few hours to feel whole again. To stop crying. "It hasn't happened in years." I close my eyes, but the darkness shakes loose too many awful images. "I don't know what happens, but I can't feel my body, except for shaking or spinning. All I see is memories. Images from La Rochelle."

"What do you remember?"

"Blood. So much blood. Thick and pooled. Streams through water. Dead bodies of everyone I knew and loved."

"I can't imagine how devastating that would be."

"Cricket, you need to understand something." I turn to face her. "I don't remember one day of my life without struggle. My earliest memories were of loss and death and fear. Darkness and pain with little hope of daylight. Huguenots are not like anyone else. All we know is terror, and we choose to either accept it and die, or fight and die. How I'm still here, I'll never know."

"You and Papa have work to do still."

"Yes." I place my hand on her soft cheek. "We wanted you to breathe free. We never wanted you to understand this part of our past."

She leans her face into my hand with a sad smile. "It's part of you both. Of course I'd understand."

"What you saw in the hills today is what happens when you join the resistance. The unbearable horror we see bleeds into us. It changes who we are."

"Does Papa have those too?"

"No, not like mine. But your father worries. He loves us so much, he would die if anything happened."

"But—"

I shake my head to stop her. "I carry on with this torturous existence, knowing I hurt him. I don't want you to become like me." The words came from somewhere deep yet spilled out like water from a bucket. So easy and free. I hadn't realized I've been carrying that around.

"Isabelle, I already am like you."

I suddenly understand Andre. *Please don't leave me.* "I need you to stay safe. Protect your father when I'm gone."

"You aren't going anywhere. You're still in this."

"The journey I'm on ends only with my death. It will have meant nothing if you die too."

She smiles, annoyingly confident. "I'm in this with you."

My pleas don't seem to affect her. I'll have to find another way to stop her. "I hope they arrive soon. This place makes me want to scream."

"What would Naira say if she were here?"

"That dreams are the language of the soul."

"I have only one memory of my mother," Elizabeth says with a wistful glance at the sunset.

"You've never told me that."

"It's blurry, and I wasn't sure if it was real. I remember Papa staring out the window and Maman crying behind him. They were both so sad."

"Cricket, love and marriage and relationships are complicated, even in the best of situations."

"He always loved you and Maman knew it."

My instinct is to lie. Find a way to protect how she views her father. But she sees so much now. "We walked away from each other. He chose Louise and I chose James Beaumont. We tried to let go."

"James sounds like a real bastard."

I let out a deep laugh, the kind that bubbles joy through your body. "Yes, he was terrible. Weak and manipulative. Nothing like your father."

"Why did you marry him?"

"I was weak too." The Quebec winds blow through my memory. Andre and I standing under a fall burst of yellow birch trees, back when he stole my heart and I was foolish enough to believe I could move forward without it.

It took years to learn that a fight without heart is a battle never to be won.

She lays her head on my shoulder. "I think you're the only one that would ever see yourself that way."

Together, we watch the sky brighten with shades of marigold that reflect the golden hills of a land I once loved and fought for. "I needed James, and your father needed your mother. It was a different time. We were all alone. Wayward souls without families. We were each looking for something to ease our pain. For your father, a marriage where he could protect a wild girl from her own mistakes seemed like enough."

"And for you?"

I remember James so well. Every curve of his body, every ripple of anger through his jaw. His desperate need to break my spirit. "James loved me in his own troubled way. He thought if he could bring me into his Catholic world, I'd be safe and happy."

"But you were neither, were you." She fiddles with a lock of my hair, spinning her finger around the end of a curl.

"I chose loyalty over love because the way I felt about your father terrified me. Much the way my love for you does."

She sits up, face twisted. She touches her fingers to her lips. "I've made this harder for you."

I lower her hands from her face and stare into her big, soft, beautiful eyes. "You and Andre are my family. What I thought was weakness—loving someone so much I finally feared death—was actually a strength. I am no longer a soulless shell of a woman, seeking the wrong things to fill her up."

"But now you fear death."

"Yes. But I fear disappointing you both far more."

"I know the feeling."

The warm sun has faded to twilight as we hold hands. Together, we share fear, lightening the burden one heart can handle.

.   .   .

I slept soundly last night, listening to Elizabeth breathe safely next to me. This morning, I pace the grounds, kicking pebbles and missing Andre so fiercely it feels like hunger.

The duke stumbles behind me. "I don't want to surprise you," he announces. "Just here to let you know breakfast is ready."

I turn to face him. "Aren't they tired of us yet?"

"Yes." He shrugs. "But they know my father manages this land and can remove them if he so wishes."

Elizabeth runs past us. "Auntie Charlotte!"

My heart quickens. I can't believe it. "They're here."

The duke trails behind me, still afraid of Charlotte. She's tired and filthy, but she's here. I wrap my arms around her and squeeze tight. "I've missed you."

She hugs me back, squeezing my dress in her grip.

"Are you safe?" I search the hills in every direction. "Where is Andre?"

"He's behind me by a few days. Let me rest and I'll tell you everything."

The duke opens the door for her and orders the servants to warm water. Her face is caked with dirt and dried blood. "I'm fine, don't fuss over me."

"How did you find us?" I ask.

"Easy. I simply asked for the flamboyant duke who won't shut his mouth. Everyone pointed this way."

Elizabeth cleans her face, removing dirt clods and pebbles from her hair.

She glances at Elizabeth then back at me. "Elizabeth, go fetch some clean linens, please."

Charlotte waits until Elizabeth shuts the door then stares at the duke. "Tremblay, you're still here."

The duke forces a painful grin.

"He's in it with us now," I say. "Now quickly, tell me."

"We got them all to Geneva. All but one. The man with the broken bone didn't make it."

The duke clears his throat. "The one we saved from the house?"

"Yes," she snaps. "Many don't make it. We quickly turned back to France, but the trail was busy. So many Huguenots fleeing in all directions."

"That's good, right?" I ask.

"They've heard of the resistance. More and more leave their towns, hearing stories of our rescues."

I nod once. "Which means the soldiers know more about me."

She nods, rubbing her neck. "We fought off more solitary dragoons than I can count. They're all looking for the Red Fox. Money and the king's good favor make you everyone's target."

"And Andre?"

Elizabeth returns with a basket of linen scraps, noticing our silence. "What are you trying to hide from me?"

"Nothing, Cricket." I shake my head but she's too sharp.

"Lies." She throws the basket on the table. "Stop treating me like a child and tell me what's going on."

I reach for Charlotte's swollen face, but she stops me. "No, the duke will clean my wound."

"Me?" His voice cracks.

"Yes. Get over here. You must learn. You can't be a fighter when you grow pale at the sight of blood."

He takes my seat and begins to run a warm, wet cloth over her cheek. She flinches. "I'm so sorry," he says. "I didn't mean to hurt you."

Charlotte smacks his arm. "Get yourself together, Tremblay."

I kick my knee into his. "Yes, it's not like you smashed the back of her head with the butt of a gun." His eyes look like a frightened puppy. He's lucky I haven't killed him yet.

"Enough." Elizabeth bends down to Charlotte. "Tell me."

Charlotte swipes the duke's hand away. "Fine. It took twice as long to travel back into France. We stayed off the trail to avoid being seen. At the base of the mountains, we tracked a group of dragoons traveling through."

"And?" I nudge her with my widened gaze.

"They talked about the king's new weapon in the Huguenot fight. They parade Lieutenant Louvois around Paris, showing the brutality of the resistance."

"How did I not kill him?" I mutter. Though I know losing Henri and facing the man who branded me left me scared and reckless. I should have checked again for cold skin and an unmoving chest.

"You wounded him badly. His right leg and arm are contorted and unusable. You broke his face bones to where he's unrecognizable. Worst of all, Henri's branding sits prominently on his cheek. He sounds like the dead walking."

"They make *us* out to be the monsters?" Elizabeth tucks her lips in, as tightness ripples through her neck and arms. "How can they live with themselves?"

"All they know is how we resist them. We defy their king and outlast their torture. To them, we are the enemy." I've spent a lifetime trying to understand their hate. This is the closest I can find to an answer for her. I turn back to the matter at hand. "Charlotte, where is Andre?"

"He went to Paris to find Louvois."

I asked him to continue my fight. Though he longs for quiet evenings in my arms by a Geneva fire, he followed my wishes. I make him do things he wishes to walk away from. "Is he—"

I don't finish my question for fear of how it will make me feel. Luckily, Charlotte understands me without words. "This kill is for him. To protect you."

"And we'll get vengeance," I say. "For Henri."

"Yes. We will meet Andre in Paris. By then he will have tracked Louvois's movements, made note of his social circle. We'll have names and royal leaders to target." Her eyes gleam. "That part he's doing for us."

"And how will we do that when every dragoon is fighting for a chance to capture Isabelle?" the duke asks.

I cross my arms. "We stay hidden." Charlotte meets my eyes. "We leave tonight," I announce. "Prepare."

Elizabeth slaps the duke on his shoulder. "Come, I'll show you how to listen for intruders."

The duke reluctantly follows her outside.

I see how her face has fallen. How her stare steadies out the window. "What is it, Charlotte?"

She wipes the rest of her face and neck clean. "Andre made me promise to protect you."

"Of course you will. What a silly request."

"No." She throws the linen in the now blood and dirt filled water bowl. "He told me no rescues until we carry out this plan in Paris."

"We both know Andre doesn't dictate my choices."

"No." She tosses a soiled rag from her forehead into a bowl. "But I will."

I uncross my arms, sure she must be joking.

"He's right, Isabelle. If they take you, the resistance is over. We must keep you out of sight, so they think the Red Fox is no longer a threat."

"You want me to hide in the bushes when we come across a village in need, or a lost Huguenot on the trail. You can't ask me to do that."

"I'm not." She stands and exhales loudly. "I'm telling you." Her gaze tells me with certainty she would use anything at her disposal to control my moves. I don't want to know how far she'd go.

I bite into the inside fleshy softness of my bottom lip. "Andre knows me too well. He knew the orders must come from you."

"He didn't want to break your spirit."

"But you will?"

Charlotte shakes her hair free. She grabs hold of my arms. "I can no more break you than I could force the sun to stop shining."

"What am I to do? Stay in this miserable house and listen to the duke make music with his fingers? I'd sooner die."

She steadies my face so I cannot look away from her. "I'll tell you what you'll do. You make the hard choices. You stay hidden in a safe home on the trail. You let us deal with Louvois and the royal scum." She drops her hands onto her lap. "You teach your daughter what it means to survive."

I walk to the window to watch Elizabeth instruct the duke. She's so smart. So strong. But she has no idea what she's up against. Patience is not easy when all you want is to save the world as it burns around you. I close my eyes and listen, just as Naira taught me to do.

Elizabeth's laughter. The scent of Charlotte's blood soaked into her dress. Heat rising up through my belly like boiling water. Naira would tell me to listen to the call of the warrior. *The answer is always in your heart,* she would say.

A wolf must protect her pack.

Right now, my safest move is to listen to Charlotte. I'll sacrifice myself for the greater cause. And I don't mean staying hidden.

I have a plan. With any luck, my pack will get out of this alive. I can't say the same for me.

CHAPTER SEVENTEEN

At a friendly home just off the Huguenot trail, we say goodbye to Charlotte. We walked in the dark for weeks and hid during the day to arrive in the tucked away cottage in Champagne without incident. Charlotte fought one stray man, but he didn't appear to be a dragoon. All is quiet. For now.

Charlotte hugs Elizabeth. "You'll be an incredible member of the resistance, my girl."

"Just not today." Elizabeth stiffens her lips and forces a smile.

"Patience." Charlotte tucks Elizabeth's dark hair behind her ear. "Your time will come."

The duke waves at Charlotte. "Good luck."

I hold Charlotte's hand and walk her into the twilight. That magic moment of clear blue sky before darkness swallows the remnants of day. "I should be joining you," I say.

"It won't be the same without you."

"On our last trip to Paris, you were nothing more than an eager girl who made mistakes I had to clean up."

"I was young and in love and desperate to prove myself to you." She catches her breath, obviously thinking of Henri.

"Now look at you," I say. "Wise, patient. Fearless."

"I used to think courage was something I'd obtain and bask in the glow of success for the rest of my days."

"And now?" I ask.

"I realize that courage changes with the seasons. The world requires things from us, every day is different than the one before. Courage is not a reward. It's a practice."

Flashes jolt through my memory of my nightmare last night. I'd overcome this weakness, but here I am again, questioning who I am and my place in the world. I let the Catholics change me from fighter for good to woman out for vengeance.

I no longer recognize myself.

"I think you're right, Charlotte." I hug her with such intensity she gasps. "I'm so proud of you."

She lays her head on my shoulder and softens in a way she never does. She lets me hold her and smooth her hair. "I hope you find the peace you're looking for," she says.

"You as well."

She pulls away and levels her eyes at me. "I'm not looking for peace. I'm out to conquer."

Chills spread across the back of my neck. The resistance needs all kinds. I'd like to settle into the power of murder as she's done, but my faith tethers me back to the misty nights of prayer in La Rochelle, when all I had were whispered words and a hope that we all could someday breathe free.

I had those free breaths, but they mean nothing while dragoons wipe out thousands just like me.

I stiffen my posture. "Tell Andre he's my forever."

She smiles, almost childlike in her joy. "He told me to say the same to you."

"Come back to us, Charlotte. We need you."

She begins to walk away but stops herself. She turns back to me with ferocity in her eyes. "The villages have grown worse. You will hear stories and possibly even screams. Don't be fooled. They're out for you, but innocent Huguenots are the blood they use to coax you out of hiding. The royal court will stop at nothing to see you burn."

Then burn I shall.

I nod, having accepted my fate weeks ago. "Goodbye, my friend."

Without another glance, I walk inside where a strange calm has descended over me. An acceptance. Elizabeth hands me a jug of wine. "What now?" she asks.

"We wait." I decide against the wine and slide it to the center of the table. The duke stares and salivates, and I wonder what demons he's trying to fight. It's more than the need to be drunk.

"Seems ridiculous to sit here idly while people are being killed out there." Elizabeth stares out the open door to the quiet night.

"I promised your father and Charlotte I'd stay hidden."

"This isn't you," she says. "You never stop fighting."

"My needs are less important than the resistance. If they capture me, they'll be emboldened. They will kill me and build on their team of torturers. My life's efforts would have been for nothing."

"Not nothing," she begs. "We can't stop trying."

The duke slides the jug into his hands and drinks. Swallow after swallow without a breath. I used to feed Maman wine to subdue her. Maybe I've never been the good person I've seen myself as.

"Isabelle." Elizabeth's voice rings with frustration.

"Knowing when to fight is essential to the battle. So is knowing when to wait." I don't stop the duke from drinking. He drains the jug of its entire contents and hangs his head in sad relief.

Elizabeth stomps off to bed and slams the door.

Naira always kept calm and steady, even when I exasperated her. Something I can never do for myself. When I couldn't shoot an arrow, and when guilt ripped through me that I used my naked body to gain secrets from my husband. How I hurt Andre to preserve my own needs.

Every mistake I've ever made crashes through my mind like a storm.

The duke glugs more wine from the barrel. With a devious light in his eyes, he leans back in his chair and slides the jug toward me. "It will soften the ache."

I shake my head no. "And it will be that much more painful when my senses return."

He stares at his fingers as they rub the curve of the handle. "It felt good to save you." He doesn't look at me.

"When you smashed my head with the butt of a gun?"

"Yes. It felt good to know I stopped you from the attack that would surely have killed you."

I lower next to him, crouched to look into his eyes. "You must have been relieved." He pulls away but I lean closer. "Without me, you're nothing."

"What are you talking about?"

"I'm not afraid of you hurting me." Heat grows between my hands as I rub my palms together.

His chin retracts, pulling away from me. "Why not?"

A shrug and a dismissive eye roll buy me time to examine his worried gaze. His thumping chest. "Firstly, I can take you to the ground without breaking a sweat."

"And secondly?" His eyes remain wide, fixed on mine.

The time has come to corner the duke. "How will you gain your riches and land? Certainly not in the Army." I clasp my hands behind my back "No, you need me alive to deliver to the king."

Firewood pops and tumbles in the fireplace. He looks over his shoulder at the sound. "How long have you known?"

"From the moment I met you."

Forced posture. Shoulders back. "Is it so wrong? I knew I could deliver the Red Fox safely. I won't hurt you or anyone else. You have my word."

"Your word will mean nothing when the royal court gets their hands on me."

His usually smoothly combed hair falls over his eye. He throws a loose lock back with a head toss. "I haven't thought that far yet."

I swig from the wine jug and slam it down in front of him. "You don't need to. I already have."

Once again, his fingers flutter together to produce a tune only he can hear. "You're very cunning. I suppose you'll drag me into the forest and beat me? Leave me for dead?" His feverish blinks do little to focus his tremulous voice.

"No, I'm going to help you."

His lips are already stained purple, lined like crushed blueberries along the flesh of his lower lip. "Why?"

"That is our little secret. You'll find out soon enough."

"You don't want Elizabeth to know."

"No one will know but us. When Andre and Charlotte return, you and I will escape in the quiet of night. Until then, we'll protect her and keep me hidden."

"When you've accomplished your goal, will you kill me?"

I let my sigh linger long and slow. "I haven't decided yet. Goodnight, Duke Tremblay."

· · ·

I wake Elizabeth with a nudge to her shoulder, then back away while she swings her fists through the air. I've taught her to react before her eyes open.

She realizes it's me. "What is it, is something wrong?"

"Torchlights in the distance. I don't know anything more."

She jumps out of bed, fully clothed. "I'm always prepared."

"Right. Come on." As the duke snores away near the fire, we slip out into the balmy June morning. A dry, warm wind carries the scent of lemon. I forget how beautiful France is when the Catholics aren't around.

Two shadows. One torchlight. I narrow my eyes. "They aren't moving."

"Let's move closer." Elizabeth creeps through the hills toward the flickering glow while I position my bow and arrow toward the light.

Elizabeth rests her hand on my arm and pushes down. "Wait." We step toward the trail to find two girls. Barely ten, they're covered in blood. Holding a torch between them, they stumble in a haze along the dark gray trail.

They don't jump when they see us. Not even a twitch.

"What happened to you?" Elizabeth asks.

The girls stare through us, thick blood dripping from their hair onto sopping stains in their tattered dresses.

"You're hurt." Elizabeth's voice shakes, but not in weakness. In empathy.

The taller one stutters, then practically exhales the words, "Not our blood."

I move closer, hands out. "Whose blood is it?"

The girl doesn't move her eyes. She lifts her trembling hand, one finger pointed to the trail behind us. Elizabeth and I turn slowly. A young woman lies on her back, mouth open, her dress soaked with crimson blood. Sun illuminates the shadows, turning the sky a deep blue. Blood smears the trail. I swallow and step slowly toward the girl. Gashes riddle her face. Her mouth is dark and empty.

I trail my eyes down her arm. Her hand grips something as flaked blood cakes her fingernails. I curl her fingers open to find teeth.

Shiny white teeth like bone in a mess of blood and flesh.

She blinks.

"She's alive."

I lift her frail body over my shoulder and grunt into the morning with fear and anger and determination.

I stumble under her weight but force my legs to move. Elizabeth gathers the girls. All I can think of is washing this blood off them. The sharp, horrid smell of life lost. Brutality over innocents. Children too terrified to cry.

The duke hears us coming and opens the door. "What—" He can't finish his sentence. He's gone white.

"Clear the table." I push past him, leaning my cheek to hers. She's cold. Too cold. The duke swipes his arm across the table. I lay the girl on her back, noticing the gush from her exposed belly. My chest. It's slick with her blood.

"Get rags." I press on her gaping wound and scream at her to stay awake. Viscous and greasy, I wipe her blood on my dress, but her stomach keeps oozing.

The duke returns with a handful of rags but simply stares at me, mouth open. "What happened to her?"

"I don't know." I press everywhere with open skin. Everywhere her flesh has been ripped to reveal the pink organs and yellow fat underneath. Once ivory, the rags match the gory scene of the room. I press my cheek to hers. "Stay with me."

Her chest exhales.

"Please."

No rib movement. Air and life and future ripped from her by a blade. The dragoons are dark enough to tear her body with a thousand cuts but not human enough to slice once through her neck. "They wanted her to suffer." I close my eyes, the lifelessness of her body ripping my soul like claws.

"What was her crime?" the duke asks.

"Protecting us." The taller girl steps forward. She lifts her sleeve to reveal a whip mark. "They held us in the streets. This girl broke through the trio of dragoons from nowhere. She doesn't live in our village. "We've never seen her."

The smaller girl, tears in her eyes, steps to her sister. "We thought she was the Red Fox coming to rescue us."

I turn to look at her hair. Dark like a truffle freshly plucked from under a shady oak tree. "She isn't the Red Fox," I say.

"She cut us free and killed soldiers right there in front of us. "Run," she said with a smile, a strange excitement in her voice." The girl rubs her forehead. "They threw her in a crumpled heap outside town. We realized she was alive, so we dragged her into the woods with a wheelbarrow." She steps forward to examine her dead body. "She held on. Barely alive but grunting. I stole a torch, and we took to the trail until the wheelbarrow broke apart." She looks at me, choking on her words. "We dragged her, knowing she would die."

Elizabeth rests her hand on the girl's shoulder. "She saved you."

She holds her sister tight. "They killed our mother."

Tremblay falls to a chair, his knees giving way. No amount of horror can ever make him understand life as a Huguenot, but each glimpse into our torture gives the man a chance to feel regret.

"Take the girls to wash up," I say to Elizabeth. She nods and wraps her arms around the girls to lead them to the bedroom with a fresh wash basin.

I circle the ravaged body of this young girl. "Who are you?" Oddly at peace, she left this world fighting and I sense she wanted it that way. "Turn please," I say without looking at the duke. He faces the wall.

I cut her clothing with a blade as gently as my aching hands allow. Her torn body doesn't make me sick like I think it will. From blood in streams on the walls of La Rochelle, to splatters and death everywhere, I've learned to look without seeing. Touch without feeling. I lay a sheet over her body, up to her neck. I open her hand as teeth ping to the floor.

Sobs from the duke. Though he isn't looking, he sees and feels everything I do not. "Turn and look now."

He braces himself on the wall, turns to stare at the unnamed Huguenot. A member of the resistance I've never heard of. "Why did they do this to her?"

"These are your people, Tremblay. You know exactly why they do this."

"She's just a girl."

"She's dangerous. She travels village to village to rescue her people. She travels the trail to freedom and comes back for more. She is a resistor."

Elizabeth appears behind me. "She is you."

"But she got caught."

Elizabeth pours from the kettle into a bowl. The duke clears his throat. "Here." He reaches for the closest rag. He dips it in the water and squeezes it over the dead girl's hair as blood runs through her mangled locks to the wet floor. "She didn't deserve this."

"None of us do," I say.

We silently clean her body. Clear her skin of filth and memories of an unfair life. The duke cries through the process, but continues to work with us, keeping a sheet over her for privacy. We don't speak. For an hour, we scrub and clean, and I wrap her teeth back in her grip.

We wrap her in the sheet and lean over her to pray. The duke steps back, forming the cross before he says his own silent prayer which I can only assume is in Latin, and from the Catholic Church. He disappears into the hills to dig a shallow grave.

Elizabeth turns to me, tears streaking her cheeks. "How do you do this over and over again?"

"I have no choice."

"Not why," she says. "How?"

I place my hand on her cheek. "With a heavy heart full of pain."

The duke opens the door and nods. We lift her body, wrapped and clean and peaceful. This body that saved children and fought demons. Her soul now rests.

We bury her as the grateful girls watch from the window.

"May she be remembered through the lives she saved," I say.

"That's it?" the duke snaps. "She saved people and endured torture, and now her body will disintegrate in the cold dirt out here all alone?"

"All our bodies disintegrate alone in the cold dirt," Elizabeth says.

He braces his hands on his knees. Gasps for air through tears. "There is no glory. No award for this. She will be marked a heretic. A traitor to the Crown."

I grab his doublet and shake him. "We were born traitors to the Crown. If you hope to find a soul deep in that ruined life of yours, you'll find a way to defy the king too."

CHAPTER EIGHTEEN

Life without purpose is intolerable.

My body is desperate for adventure. In the quiet of the night, I miss Andre so fiercely my chest aches. The quiet girls have stayed with us. I long to escort them to Geneva, but I'm afraid to be seen. Life in hiding feels tight and small.

The girls sleep in bed with Elizabeth, and I sleep in spurts near the fire. Most nights I wander through the dark, dreaming of Louvois's face and how it will feel to slice through his heart.

This is our third morning after burying the mystery girl. Does she have family? A lover? Is she missed by anyone?

"Are you the Red Fox?" the little girl asks.

"I'm happy you believe in that fairytale. There are many people trying to save you."

Her older sister wraps her arm around her. "The soldiers will come for you. We heard them talking. Groups have headed out into the woods to find the resistance. After the dark-haired girl, they're worried there are more of you."

The duke clears his throat. "I sent two dragoons west this morning. Silly men believed everything I said."

"They'll keep coming," Elizabeth says.

"I simply have to hide until Andre and Charlotte return."

"And when is that?" Elizabeth asks. "We're only a few hours outside Paris and we have yet to see them."

"They will return." I turn from her, anger bleeding heat into my face.

"What has happened to you?" The disappointment in her voice sticks to me like honey.

I bristle but push down my reaction so far not even I can feel it. "I do not need a lecture from you on how to run the resistance."

"It appears you do."

With a clenched jaw, I remind myself how eager she is. How very inexperienced. "You know nothing of sacrifice."

"Then let me earn my way." She gulps back tears and clears her throat.

"What would you like to do, Cricket? March into the nearest village? Rescue families with two terrified children and a useless duke in tow?"

"Now that is not called for." Tremblay crosses his arms.

"I want you to fight!" Tears pour from her eyes. "I want the Isabelle who taught me to run under moonlit snowfall. Who whispered *you're strong* as I fell asleep. I want the Isabelle who made me feel like I could do anything."

"But you can't, Cricket." Her face drops but I know I'm doing the right thing. "Hundreds of men are out there looking for me, just waiting to capture me and drag me back to Paris for torture. I can't risk it."

"You're using that as an excuse."

"Excuse for what?"

"You got scared. Admit it." She steps closer to me, her eyes puffy from crying. "You nearly died saving that girl tied to the stake. We told you to leave her, but you couldn't. If it weren't for that useless duke, you'd be dead right now."

Tremblay nods, taking the compliment.

"I'm not frightened of the dragoons."

"Then what?" She slams her hands to the table.

Words stick in my throat and numb my tongue. I can't force them out. Andre understands my flaws. I understand my flaws. Elizabeth hasn't yet learned how deeply fractured my soul is. "I'm frightened of myself." Hearing the words spill from my mouth is so much worse than feeling them quietly inside.

Elizabeth stands with so much control she looks more animal than human. I can't meet her eyes.

The girls hug each other. They know nothing of us or the resistance, or my past. They simply want comfort. Safety and a home. "Girls, we'll take you to Geneva as soon as it's safe."

The older girl opens her mouth but pauses. "Geneva?"

"Yes," I say. "That's where the trail leads. You'll be safe there."

"We're not going to Geneva."

"Yes you are," I say.

The girl stands, arms at her sides. I don't even know her name. I'm about to ask her when she announces, "We aren't leaving France."

Wonderful, two willful children to contend with. "Yes, you are."

"We have cousins. We'd like to find them."

"We don't always get what we want!" The words seem to foam from my mouth, as if they're someone else's voice. Gone is the steady warrior, the focused resistance leader. All that stands in this hidden house in the woods is a weak, terrified woman who's losing control.

Tremblay gathers the girls. "Come on, I'll tell you a bedtime story."

The sisters walk with him to the bedroom, heads hung low and lips quivering.

Elizabeth sighs. "You intimidate children now?"

"Enough." I wave my hand at her, desperate to run deep into the night until my chest stings with breathlessness.

She forces past my hand and stands face to face with me. "What changed?"

I stare out the window. "I broke my rule."

"What rule?"

I rub my face hard and let my fingernails scratch down my neck. "I would never kill unless attacked. I broke that the moment I took a blade to that man's cheek. I liked it. Slicing him open fed something hungry inside me. I would have killed another one and another one, just to feel that power again. I would have killed every Catholic in that village and smiled over their dead bodies if Tremblay hadn't knocked me out."

"I don't understand. You kill dragoons. Many of them. How could you not want to hurt them after everything they've done to you? Everything they're still doing."

"I don't want to betray my ancestors." I slide down the wall to the ground and bury my face in my hands.

Elizabeth lowers next to me. "Explain."

"Protestants controlled La Rochelle. When the Catholics stripped my parents and grandparents and friends of every sliver of integrity, they held firm to their faith. They never let the hate turn them dark. They prayed. They smiled through pain. They were stronger than I could ever be."

"Nonsense."

I peek out from under my heavy eyelids. "What?"

"Letting hate-filled men beat you to death and torture your family isn't strength."

"You don't understand. Keeping goodness in your heart is the ultimate test of strength."

She loosens her braid and shakes her hair free. "If you lived as your ancestors did, we'd all be dead. That's what I admire about you. You found the will to live, and you taught it to me."

"At what cost?"

"I'm here breathing, aren't I?"

She's right. I would do anything to protect her. Even turn into the monster I've been fighting. I always pitied James, believing I was strong, and he was the weak man I manipulated. We were both broken beyond repair. I simply held on longer.

Tremblay shuts the door. "They're asleep."

"Where did you learn bedtime stories?" Elizabeth asks.

His cheeks redden. "I recited one of my poems."

He's a curious one, this duke. Sensitive and kind, but willing to overlook horror far too easily. As a soldier, and as a human.

"They won't leave France without their cousins."

I groan. "Do they even know where they are?" I shake my head. "No, it doesn't matter. They stay here until Andre returns. We all do."

Elizabeth shakes her head. "Goodnight."

After the door shuts, Tremblay fiddles his fingers at his ear.

"Must you do that? I wish you'd just speak."

"Me? No, no. I have nothing to say. I'm a useless duke." As usual, he rocks to his tiptoes and back to his heels.

I shouldn't feel sorry for him but somehow, I do. I stare at the fire and remember Maman. So frightened. So devout. She didn't know what to do with my restless spirit.

"My father would cut off his own hand to impress the king," the duke says.

"Your father sounds like a fool."

He laughs. "Aren't we all?"

I glance up at him. "Some more than others."

He stokes the fire. "I may not understand your ways, Isabelle, but I know I don't want to watch another Huguenot bleed on my hands. Ever again."

"When you turn me over to the king, that's exactly what they'll do. Bleed me for answers they'll never get."

"I'll find a way to keep you safe."

"You're doing this for you. Don't lie to yourself."

He doesn't respond because he knows I'm right. He'll hand me over to be tortured while he's showered in riches and adoration. He will be predictably weak. I'm counting on it.

· · ·

A panic dream wakes me gasping for air. A man's hand held me by the throat. As I nearly died, Naira whispered in my ear, "Watch her."

I jump to the bed. Elizabeth and the sisters are sound asleep. Everything is fine. But my heart won't stop racing. My breathing won't slow down. I lie down again, bright white visions of limestone walls in the sunshine. Blood trailing down in streams. Dead bodies. So many dead bodies. I'm frozen in La Rochelle, once again feeling the terror of exile. Swimming in the blood of my people.

"Wake up." The words garble as if underwater. The duke's face comes to focus. "Isabelle, wake up."

Tears streak down my cheeks and my voice is locked in my throat.

"What happened?" he asks.

"I don't know." The sun shines through the windows but when I laid down it was night.

He helps me to stand. "Isabelle?"

I know what he's about to say before the sentence leaves his mouth. "They're gone, aren't they? All three of them." I shake my head and walk through the house.

He follows after me. "They're not here."

"Elizabeth took the girls. She left on a solo rescue." I don't know why I thought I could tame her. Keep her in my arms where she's safe. Now she's out in the wild, unfair world of Catholic beatings and torture. It's everything I fought to protect her from, and now she's walked right into it. "Where did they go?"

"The girls told me last night they needed to rescue their cousin."

"Where does their cousin live?"

"In Paris."

I splash cool water on my face and dab my skin dry.

"How far have they gone? Will they be safe?" He growls. "Why aren't you listening to me? What do we do?"

A useless duke and a broken resistance fighter. This is not ideal in any way. "We're going to Paris."

"We can't. We'll both be attacked on the trail. Everyone is looking for you." His voice rises high. "I can't do this myself."

"You don't have to. You have me." I throw a rag at him. "And I will stop at nothing to protect Elizabeth. *Nothing*."

CHAPTER NINETEEN

"Must you move so fast?" The duke stumbles on a rock. Walking in darkness is a skill he has yet to acquire. I'm not certain he ever will.

We headed for the trail the moment the sky turned to night.

"What do we do when someone sees us? And if we make it to Paris unnoticed, what then? Do you even have a plan?"

I turn and shove him against a tree, pressing my fists into his neck. "All your blabbering will get us caught. Shut your mouth and follow me."

"But I—"

I shove harder until his eyes bulge. "If it weren't for me, you'd still be a slobbering mess at the tavern. Somehow, we both find ourselves here in need of each other. I let you pretend to take me to the king, and you do everything I say." I release my hold but keep my hands close. "Yes?"

"Seems like a fair deal."

I can't figure him out. Poets should be brooding and serious, but his humor is enough to make me want to slap the smile right off him. I don't bother to look back and see if he's following.

Hours pass without problem. I feel alive. The wind on my cheeks, the silence of night, carrying secrets only I know how to wield. It's strange, but I miss the crunch of snow under my boots. France summers are far more comfortable than icy Geneva nights, but snowfall always reminds me of Naira. Quebec may no longer be my home, but those years changed me. For the better, I think.

I wonder if the girl we buried felt the same as me.

Footsteps.

I crouch in the shadows, hand slapped across the duke's mouth. I count figures. Four. Five. They're whispering and padding along the trail as if we couldn't smell five brutes and their rotting breath before we ever saw them.

I hold my hand up to indicate we wait for them to pass.

"Shouldn't be too hard to find a red-haired woman," one says. "And oh, what we'll do to her when we find her."

One punches him in the shoulder. "No. We deliver her alive, you fool."

"Filthy Huguenot," he spits.

"Let's go back," a bony dragoon says. "Those girls know something. We can torture the truth right out of them."

I flick my eyes toward the duke.

"The older one would make a satisfying morsel."

Rage bubbles through me hot and thick. The duke holds my arm but I elbow him away. I run through the trees, a red sheen over my eyes. All I feel is hunger. The bony one lags behind, most likely drunk. I wrap my hand around his mouth and drag him into the trees. Mouth to his ear, I whisper, "Where are the girls?"

I release my hand just enough for him to speak. The fool yells out for help. I have no choice. I twist his neck in one hard snap. He crumbles right at my feet as the other four turn back towards the sound. I drag the dead dragoon into the moonlight on the path and press myself against a tree. They approach the body. Nudge him to see if he's alive.

Pounce.

My blade slices through one's neck without a breath of hesitation. Two down.

The trio approaches so I throw my dagger into one's eyeball. Three down. The final two haven't prepared for this moment, so they charge me like the fools they are.

I take one down by sliding my feet across his shins. When his face hits the ground, the heel of my boot meets his nose with a satisfying crunch. He rolls to his back, hands to his bloody face and I slam my fists into his abdomen.

The last one knocks his giant body into me. We thud to the ground. He slaps me with his fat hands, but I feel nothing behind the red hue that still covers my eyes like a swath of worn linen. I dig my fingers into his eye sockets, a favorite move of mine, and shove my knee between his legs. He grabs my coiffe and rips it away. "Red Fox." Sharp teeth salivate under his snarled lip.

All sense of rule has flown away as all I think of is Elizabeth. She needs me. I reach for the blade strapped to my ankle and slice his cheek open. From the hook of his mouth, I yank the blade back toward his ear as blood splashes onto my face. The dragoon writhes and screams but still swings at me. He lands a fist on my cheek.

His hit slows me just enough. His face gushes blood, yellow and pink flesh ripped open to expose his back teeth like a bloody, menacing grin. A gunshot rings out and no sooner does a bullet fly through the man's temple. Particles of flesh splatter on me right before he falls. Behind him, the duke stands with his pistol still pointed where the dragoon stood.

"I've... I've never killed," he says.

The last remaining dragoon groans and tries to crawl away. "Oh no you don't." I thunder my way to him and grab his hair. "Where are the girls?"

"I don't know what you're talking about."

I kick him in the back with the heel of my boot right between the shoulder blades. "How about now?"

He catches his breath, face in the dirt. "A cabin outside the city walls."

The duke aims his pistol at the dragoon, trying not to shake.

After a kick to his side, I nod. "Take us."

"No," he says with false confidence. So I throw an elbow to his cheek. He knocks me to the ground, but Tremblay thumps the butt of his pistol on the man's head. "Your signature move."

The dragoon holds his head in his hands. "Bastard."

"Let's go." I lift him by the shirt, unbothered by his stumbling. "Hurry it up."

Twenty torturous minutes later, we approach a cabin. Barely standing, cobwebs frame the busted-out windows. I run to open the door with heat in my chest. If they're hurt, I will tear out his eyeballs with my fingernails.

Empty. "Tell me where they are."

"We left them here. They were tied up."

Elizabeth can wriggle her way out of any number of restraints. They no doubt made the grave error of thinking a young woman couldn't defend herself. These imbeciles will never learn.

"You're too late," the dragoon says through a sardonic smile. "I've already sent word to Paris that the Red Fox's family is on the trail. They'll be waiting for the girls at the city gates."

Tremblay turns to me. "What now?"

I walk closer to the dragoon, staring into his dark brown eyes. "Say that again?"

"We sent a soldier back while we searched for you. The little girl told us of the woman with the red hair who was hiding out in the woods. I was hoping our paths would cross." He lunges for me, anger overtaking his face, but I twist my body, roll behind him, and jam his wrist up between his shoulder blades.

"Why did you keep them here, tied up?" He writhes but can't break free. I yank harder until he grumbles. "Why?"

He kicks backward but not before I lift my foot and throw him face first into the ground. He's got fight, I'll give him that. "Why? You thought you'd take your chances on me?"

"You would come looking for them. I wanted to watch you bleed, filthy whore that you are."

Tremblay squeaks out a warning. "You blind fool."

I lower to the dragoon's ear. "Your insults mean nothing to me. I am the keeper of secrets and the protector of goodness. The fighter you'll never conquer, and the woman you'll never break."

Tremblay aims the pistol at his face. "Shall I?"

I shake my head no. I reach for my knife and blast the handle into his temple without a speck of regret. "To Paris."

"Is he dead?"

"Perhaps." I lift my skirts and head west at a rushed pace.

"Wait."

I bite back a growl. "What is it?"

"The girls could be anywhere. Your husband and Charlotte could be dead or imprisoned. You've just killed at least four dragoons and all of Paris wants your head on a platter."

"Is there a question looming, or are you simply making sure I understand the impossible predicament we're in?"

"This is more than a predicament. Walking through those gates to Paris is a death wish."

"Do you want your reward with the king?"

"Yes," he says. "But I'd prefer not to die in the process."

"Good, we both want the same things. Now come on." I keep walking, arms steady at my sides, vision narrowed and scanning the terrain.

He carries on after me like an eager puppy. "Paris is crawling with lying, thieving charlatans. I should know, I'm the most famous of them all."

"Then we shall join the filth and lurk the streets at night." My feet move to their own rhythm as my mind plans our moves through the city.

"Do you have any idea what you're up against?" he asks.

With an exasperated sigh, I walk back, chest to chest with him. "I've broken my best friend from the Bastille, poisoned my husband, survived a Black Mass with the king's mistress, and manipulated the nastiest ragot in the slums. Do you think a few gates and prying eyes will stop me from saving my daughter?"

"I suppose not."

"And another thing." I shove my finger hard into his sternum until he winces. "If you keep complaining, I'll knock you out myself and hang your head from the entrance to Notre-Dame."

"Understood." He clears his throat. "Well, come on then. The fun awaits.

. . .

Here I am again, outside the walled gates of Paris where filth runs like a river and gangs rule the lawless streets. My skin crawls with memories of James Beaumont and then my heart speeds up when I think of Andre. They could both be here, within these walls. The husband I poisoned for his secrets, and the husband who hunts a monster because I begged him to.

"We meet again, old friend." The duke inhales the muggy filth floating in the air.

We're on our stomachs, staring at the open gates from a hill looking over the west bank. "Who do we find first, your wild daughter, your terrifying friend, or your handsome husband?"

"You talk of my life as if it's a game."

"In Paris, everything is a game." He stands and walks toward the closest gate.

"Duke, come back here!" He'll either get us killed or find us access to everything in the city.

His delicate hand swirls above his head. "Do you want my help or not?"

With my auburn curls and simple dress, I might as well expose my branding and announce the arrival of the worst Huguenot in France. I could find a tunnel and sneak into the city. Elizabeth. There's no time.

"I can see you weighing your options. Now, trusting a noble poet turned dragoon turned Huguenot sympathizer was certainly not on your hero's agenda, but right now, I'm your best chance of success. I own this city."

The duke swaggers. I haven't walked behind a man since James. I don't care for it. Not in the slightest.

He whistles at me as if I'm an unruly horse. "Come along, Pet."

"Pet?" I should take him out at the knees.

"Yes, darling. You are my new mistress."

I want to laugh, the idea is so absurd. "I am twice your age, Duke."

"Yes, well. I have an eye for mature women. Young women. Silly women. Men too. Oh, who am I kidding? I love them all!"

"Who are you?" The drunk, sniveling boy from the tavern has turned into a loud, eccentric, completely unpredictable character.

"I am the key to your plan, Isabelle. Now, hook my arm and play along. Paris nobility waits for no one. Oh, and pretend you like me. I am the most charming man you've ever met."

"I'm not an actor."

We stride to the open gate. "You better learn quickly."

The stench of city life already makes me queasy, and we've barely arrived.

"Greetings, fellow Parisians!" The duke's voice bellows, turning every eye toward us. "Clear the way. My pet deserves a grand entrance to the city of wealth and royalty."

I whisper, staring at his arm, "More like death and refuge."

"We've been on an adventure!" Who he's talking to, I'm not sure, but everyone stares dismissively.

Inside the gates, a familiar chill crawls up my arms. Trapped, at the mercy of Catholics who feast on Protestant suffering like it's a meal.

He whispers in my ear. "The best way to hide the Red Fox is in plain sight." He kisses me on the cheek, and it takes everything in me not to punch his throat. "Come along, Pet."

"Must you call me that?"

He smiles. "Yes."

"You're enjoying this far too much."

"Who will bring us a carriage?" he yells. "Whoever carries us to my chateau earns a reward from yours truly."

Several people scramble away, shoving each other with elbows. Several men approach with offers of gifts. Wine, dried flowers, handmade silver.

"They know you aren't the king, right?"

"I'm far better than the king. I am Duke Tremblay."

"And oh so modest, too."

In a few minutes, a carriage arrives, its wheels thick with muck, splattering sludge as it rolls. Its trim is gold and its body shines in lacquered black. I stop to examine a painting of the duke on the door, feathers in his hair and a ridiculous grin.

The man opens the door for us. Duke assists me inside and joins me in the carriage.

"Where have you been, your grace?" he asks.

"Here, there, everywhere. Now take us home. We are in need of proper clothing and a barrel of wine!"

After the door shuts, I stare at him, very unamused.

"What?"

"I don't know what to do with you."

He nods. "You will get along splendidly with my father then."

The horses set us on our way. "What will be our excuse for these clothes?" I ask.

"Don't you worry. Fabricating nonsense is one of my talents. I work best if I don't think too hard about it."

I wait for the cheering crowd to disperse and launch across the carriage. Sitting on top of him, I grab his shirt in my fists and press against his throat. "I have no time for your games. I must find Elizabeth and those two little girls before they're discovered."

He claws at my hands and kicks his feet, unable to speak. I'm too angry to release him. How dare he waste my time with this charade when Huguenots all around us fear for their lives. The carriage stops before I realize how long I've been holding him. I lighten my grip so he can cough, but keep my eyes narrowed right in front of him.

A servant opens the door, poorly hiding the shock on his face. "Your grace. Welcome home."

The duke clears his throat. "Just a little lovers quarrel. Come along, pet. We have work to do."

The servants open doors and smile, unbothered by our ragged, bloody clothing. "Why don't they seem surprised?"

"I once stumbled home naked, carried by a toothless prostitute. Nothing I do shocks them anymore."

The mirrored entry practically blinds me, light bouncing off crystals and gold. "If you're wasting my time, I will have your head."

"Relax, my pet. I have resources you won't find on the streets."

I ball my fists, fighting every urge to run out of this gilded mansion. We stumble down a long corridor as the duke throws open two giant creaking doors. Inside the lush parlor, his parents sip tea and preside over a feast of cakes and meats.

"Has the Army kicked you out already, Edward?" His mother doesn't even look up from her teacup.

"I survived a great attack, Maman."

"I see you brought more shame upon our house." His father stands and eyes me with disgust.

The duke waves his hand. "Now, now. Be nice. Tell the servants to draw us baths. We have a party to attend!"

The father mumbles *filth* under his breath. The duke grabs me by the arm and whisks me away to another enormous hallway before I have time to react to his father's insults.

"Don't let them win," he says. "That's the answer to survival here. Play along, act rich and mad, and do as you wish when no one is looking."

"Are you playing mad, Duke? Or are you completely unwell?"

"Yes." He wiggles his shoulders. "Now come along."

He drags me to a grand bedroom with floor to ceiling tapestries, gold clocks, and cages of colorful birds in every corner. "My mistress stays in here." He points to a molded section of the wall near his bed. A door, I presume.

"I am not your mistress, and if you keep using that word, I will brand your cheek with an F for fool."

"You know, Isabelle, I think you're starting to like my company." The duke fiddles, picking at his fingernails and pacing near the window.

"Tell me your plan now before I jump out the window and put myself out of my misery."

"Patience, darling."

"My daughter is lost somewhere in this city, and you want me to learn patience?"

The door opens and a slight, plain woman with round cheeks appears. They stare at each other, heaving with deep breaths. She leaps across the floor and throws him to the ground where she showers him with kisses. The duke grabs her face and kisses her passionately, groaning in pleasure.

"Oh, how I've missed you, my love." The duke sounds soft. Gentle.

The woman licks his lips and laughs. "What trouble are we getting into today?"

The duke turns to look at me. They both smile. "This is Isabelle. We need to find her daughter." He grimaces. "Huguenots. She came here to rescue two girls and find their Protestant cousins."

I could kill him. I just might.

"Don't look so concerned, madame," she says. "I love a challenge." She kisses the duke again, mauling him like a wild thing. She jumps off him and straightens her dress along her breasts. Her cheeks are flushed crimson, and she looks as if she could use a dowsing of cold water.

"Who are you again?" I ask.

"You may call me Anastasia. I am the duke's favorite secret." She parts her lips at him and purrs.

"If you mutter one word—"

"Don't you worry your pretty red head about it. No one here likes me. I'm Russian and not a beauty. No, no. My talents lie elsewhere." She throws her head back and laughs. "Now, let's get you cleaned up and you tell me everything I need to know." She kisses the air near the duke. "Then I'm going to tear into this delicious morsel like I have claws."

She leads me through the mistress doors with a devious laugh.

I'm beginning to think I've lost my touch for intimidation. "I hate Paris."

CHAPTER TWENTY

My skin flushes red and itchy. Back in luxurious gowns with servants fluffing my skirts and tightening my stay. It's all so absurd. I can't breathe in this hot, stuffy room. I want nothing to do with this life. I should be running wild in the dark, trudging through snow like a wolf stalking her prey.

"Out!" I yell at the women working to make me presentable. The air sits on my chest, tightening around my ribs like a leather strap. What am I doing here? I have to break free and find Elizabeth. I lift the window but find only hot air as stale as inside.

"Naira," I whisper. "It's all falling apart."

I beg her voice to find its way to me. Her guidance to settle in my heart. Being here makes me feel unsteady, like I'm still the lost girl that fled La Rochelle years ago. Blood splatters the textured walls. Droplets appear and slide down like raindrops. I want to reach for it, but the drops turn black and the wall blooms with rancid mold.

I close my eyes hard and shake my head. When I open them, the wall is clear of blood and filth. A nightmare while awake. Through the window, the courtyard bubbles with activity. The duke knocks, then carefully enters.

"Hello, Pet."

When I don't respond with a smart remark, his voice drops. "Are you alright?"

"I'm fine." I don't turn my eyes from the servants tending to the garden and the maids dumping buckets of waste below my window.

The duke steps next to me and watches the courtyard activities. "When I'm here, it's like returning to a childish version of myself. A man who drinks to keep the darkness away and seeks comfort in the arms of every man and woman I can find just so I don't have to look at who I really am."

"And who is that?"

"Weak. I am weak."

"A duke joining the Huguenot resistance. Risking his life to be part of something. A fool, yes. But weak you are not." I lean my forehead against the glass, hoping to feel something cool on my skin, but alas, it is as hot as the rest of this miserable palace.

"It's all for power, Isabelle. When I deliver you to the king, I will no longer need my father's fortune. His disapproval and beatings will be but a thing of the past."

"And what will you do with your fortune?"

"Bring music and poetry to the masses. Not just nobility. I will open a school for the arts. Paris will be the center of culture, and no one will be judged by their station. We will only be judged by our love of art and each other."

I turn to face him, his rosy cheeks faded, his jaw tight and serious. "I'm beginning to see the poet in you."

"If you can risk your life for a cause, so can I."

"You aren't just doing this for power. You don't agree with the beatings and the torture. Some rare nobles want to put something good in the world. I think that's very brave."

"Are we becoming friends?"

All I can manage is a grunt and an eye roll.

Gorgeous, wealthy people roam the yard, in and out of the mansion, oblivious to the Huguenot watching them from the mistress's quarters. Suddenly, Naira's breathy whisper sends chills up my neck. *Breathe. Listen.* But all I see are well-dressed targets ripe for the picking. A deceitful Huguenot right under their noses ready to kill them off one by one.

I tighten my fists hard enough to shake my arms. Henri's pale, lifeless face swells into my memory and it's all I can see.

Revenge is all I feel.

Anastasia tumbles into the room. "Look at you. You look like a proper Catholic Lady."

"There's no need to be rude," I say.

She laughs and throws her arms around the duke. I can't imagine how this silly woman can help us find Elizabeth.

"Anastasia is my hunter," the duke says. "Like a city fox, she creeps through Paris's dark corners. She sees things we can't and knows every thug inside the walls of this wretched city."

"That's right, my beautiful thing." She runs her finger along his lips. "I have Russian money and not the slightest interest in sharing it with a man."

"I've had enough of these games. I'm going to find my daughter." I push past them, unable to tolerate their touching and cooing for one more second.

"I know where she is," Anastasia says.

I stop at the door. "Is she safe?"

"As safe as one can be hiding in a church basement."

Images of my time in incense-filled abbeys claw at my memory. "What church?"

"Notre-Dame." She smiles with a wiggle in her hips. "She's a brave girl, your daughter."

"What is she doing there?"

"Waiting for her chance to run. Authorities reported a young girl who attacked a soldier as he left a tavern. She stole his money and left him unconscious with a swift hit to the head. Several men chased her through the dark streets, in and out of alleys and over walls. She escaped but it was night. The gates were closed. She must have slipped into one of the tunnels to hide and found herself under the most famous Catholic Church in Europe."

"Tunnels?" I ask.

"Limestone quarries," the duke says. "Medieval quays. There's an entire city underneath our feet, but only those hungry for danger venture into the depths."

"That explains how Elizabeth ended up there. Take me."

She waggles her finger. "There is one slight problem, Madame."

"What now?"

"The tunnels are guarded by the street gangs at night. They sleep there and we'd be slaughtered before we ever reach the Cathedral."

"So, we go in the morning."

"Ah, and there is the problem." Anastasia locks her hands behind her back. "Restoration is set to begin in the morning overseen by the priest and the king's engineers. When they find her, they will surely kill her."

"We had better find another way in then."

Anastasia grins, closed mouth and devious.

"As I said," the duke kisses Anastasia's cheek. "Everything in Paris is a game."

. . .

Another hot, sticky night descends over Paris. While the wealthy drink and dance and trade secrets in a chess game of nobles, the dark beings of the city's underworld crawl into the black shadows for their evil deeds.

I want nothing to do with either side of this game.

But here I am once again preparing to risk everything for the ones I love.

The duke and Anastasia sit across from me in his pristine carriage. Far in the distance laughs and screams and something resembling a gurgle fill the night air, but I focus on the horse hooves' rhythmic clopping.

"Are you certain Elizabeth is still there?" I ask.

Anastasia nods. "Yes. I have eyes all through the city. Especially at night." She growls at the duke, eliciting a bite into the air from him. "Your daughter slipped in through crumbling barricades to hide from a gang of Catholic minions who report to the king. Among other attempts to control crime, they hold a special eye for Huguenot resistance. Not sure why she would choose Notre-Dame."

"There is nowhere better for a Huguenot to hide than in the center of a Catholic church." I clear my throat to ask the question I'd been avoiding. "And the girls she was with?"

They look at each other then down at their laps.

"What happened to them?" I demand.

Anastasia's flirtatious grin has flattened. "They were caught attempting to flee and thrown in shackles this morning."

The little girl's round cheeks and pale blue eyes rest on my memory. Their resolute smiles held hopes of connecting with cousins in Paris, and my daughter walked them right into the wrong hands.

"It's a shame," the duke says. "All Elizabeth wanted was to save them."

"Instead, everyone is dead or in hiding." A desire to do good pushes us down a wicked path sometimes. I admire that she still lets love light the way. I might have lost mine somewhere along the Huguenot Trail.

"Here we are." The duke steps out first, followed by Anastasia then me. Dressed for a grand ball, yet here we stand outside The Cathédrale Notre-Dame as beggars writhe on the stone at our feet.

"What is that stench?" I ask. Far worse than any of the waste and filth of Paris summers, this odor carries the hint of death.

"Hotel-Dieu." Anastasia wrinkles her nose and points across the square. "Many who walk in never walk out. The sick share beds with the dead." She lifts her skirts. "Allons-y."

The duke stands with me at the three enormous portals. Anastasia whispers, "Not here." She scurries around the west facade to a door under a stained glass rose. I bump into the back of her as she halts.

"You must stay. No one can know of my contacts."

"My daughter is in there. Let me in."

She turns. Stands chest to chest with me. "You're playing in my city now. Here, I make the rules."

"I don't take orders from anyone."

I widen my feet and sturdy my stance, but the duke grabs my arm. "Go on, my dear. I'll wait with Isabelle."

The door creaks shut, and I stare at the duke. "Why aren't you helping me?"

"I am helping you. Anastasia is the most feared woman in Paris, and we do not want to upset her."

"Why does anyone fear a Russian aristocrat who trades in favors and gossip?" I know the most innocent appearing women can be lethal as any military man, but I need to evaluate the duke's opinion of her.

"Because her money and complete lack of social restraints allow her to flit from palace to palace, playing her favorite little games. Oh, how I adore how unpredictable she is. One minute she's throwing a statue at my head, and the next we're skipping naked through a fountain." He smiles, remembering some memory fondly. "She likes me, so she tolerates you."

"Have you not noticed that I am someone to fear as well?"

"Not like her." He points to the door with a shiver, then a smile of excitement. "She uses sex like a soldier wields a sword."

"Is she your lover?" I ask.

"One of them, yes. She is not a beauty, but she is wild, and I love that. Besides, she knows every secret. Including how to get your daughter home safely."

After her, I still have to find Charlotte and Andre, and take out Louvois and his cabinet once and for all. Then we can return to Geneva where the mountain air stays cool and life makes sense.

Anastasia slides out to the dark shadows with a head nod. "She's not here."

"You've been dragging me around this city of filth for hours, promising me we would find my daughter. Now you tell me she's gone?" I ball my fists to prevent them from any wayward strikes. "I'll find her myself."

"You could wander the streets, wasting hours and fighting thieves. Or you could listen to me and have her back within the hour." She shrugs. "Your choice, Red Fox."

She wants me to play along. She needs a game. "My life is not entertainment for you, mademoiselle. The longer my family is apart, the more innocent people will die."

Her dark copper eyes don't flinch when I approach. In fact, they twinkle with excitement. "Your brave daughter decided to follow the men who chased her through the streets. She tracked them all back to one Chateau de Louvois."

"Louvois?"

"If you truly are the Red Fox—and I'm certain you are—you won't escape this city alive, and neither will your daughter. It might be a lost cause, but I'm quite curious to see how this plays out."

The duke steps forward. I forgot he was here. "I would listen to her, Isabelle. You don't want to enrage her. I made that mistake once." He grimaces.

"If we find Elizabeth, we find Louvois. I'll kill him. End him how I failed to do the first time."

Anastasia links her arm through mine. "You know, Isabelle, I'm liking you more every minute."

"Louvois hosts nightly fêtes in his ballroom," the duke says. "He employs a host of loyal subjects who want nothing more than to kill the Huguenot who damaged their master beyond recognition."

"How damaged?" I ask, though I already know the answer. I want to hear the details again.

"His right foot drags, his arm is curled against his chest like a claw, and he drools from just under his branding."

A twinge of sympathy bites at my heart. Why couldn't he have just died? Only a fool feels sorry for a monster. He burned the skin of hundreds of Huguenot children. His henchmen chased Elizabeth through the streets. Forget sympathy. All of Paris is a game, and the Red Fox came to hunt.

"Anastasia, lead the way."

CHAPTER TWENTY-ONE

Louvois's mansion is, not surprisingly, gilded and enormous and unnecessary. In Le Marais with the rest of the nobles, his opulent chateau overflows with servants and impeccably dressed courtiers. The turrets alone rival that of Notre-Dame. I once was intimidated by this world. Now, I know how easy it is to manipulate.

"Time to find Elizabeth." I lift my skirts and straighten my shoulders. I remember these parties from my marriage to James. Wealthy, useless nobles stand around and congratulate each other on their even more useless mansions.

The duke and Anastasia link arms and lead the way under the arch and into the courtyard where harpists play. Tapered candles drip from candelabras, their flames flickering against the smooth stone walls. Hedges have been sculpted into the shape of angels and frame curved staircases like an entrance to somewhere ethereal. The harps glow like sunshine and the glass goblets overflow with champagne. Servants walk rigidly upright, their eyes never meeting those of the guests.

I lean to Anastasia's ear. "I don't see Louvois. I imagine he's hard to miss."

"I will do what I do best and create a wild diversion while you look through the mansion."

"Do I want to know what kind of diversion you'll create?"

The duke lifts a glass and toasts to the room. "To the great nobility of Paris!" The crowd lifts their goblets as laughter froths from the ugly decadence of their powdered faces. He coughs loudly and waits for the room to focus on him once again. "Music calls to me!" He practically leaps to the closest harp and bows to the young man in the seat. A courtier hands the duke a violin.

As the room hushes, a focused Duke Tremblay nestles the instrument between his shoulder and chin. He sways with eyes closed, a serious note to his features I haven't yet seen.

Anastasia nudges me with her elbow. "He plays like the heavens flow through his soul and blossom through his hands."

The weight in the air is palpable. Suspended attention and admiration. I've spent my life hiding in the shadows, yet this man transforms into something new when all eyes are on him. Gone are the awkward fumbles and insecurities. The duke becomes an artist in front of our eyes.

The violin and harp ease into a quiet melody with such control, chills skitter up my arms. The duke closes his eyes and plays without sight. Without senses at all. He sways and moves with the feel of the notes.

"Who is that man?" I ask. "Certainly, he isn't the same sniveling duke I dragged through the Rhône-Alpes."

Anastasia smiles. "He is unique in every way." She pushes me to the edge of the room near the staircase. "Go."

"What about you?"

"Oh, I'm the singer." She winks. "Happy hunting, Isabelle." She disappears through the crowd and steps proudly next to the duke. Applause breaks out and I make a move. Swiftly up the winding, glossy black staircase, I glimpse a never-ending hallway with more doors than I can count.

From below, Anastasia's voice drifts into the air, clear and bright as a spring wind. They might very well both be mad, but their music is beautiful enough to take my breath away. I stop at the landing for a moment to let her voice drift me to another place where I'm not in a fight for my life. Where heartbreaking music is enough to suspend time.

Cricket.

If I've missed her again, I'll never forgive myself. The hallway splits and wraps around the second story open to the ballroom below. I hug the wall to stay out of sight of those admiring the music below. Door after door reveals empty, lavishly decorated rooms. Up another flight. Out of view of the fête.

I nearly slam into a maid in a darkened corner with a man's hand up her skirts. "Pardon." I slip past. "I must be lost." But they don't seem to notice my presence. The servant's quarters are simple. Perhaps Elizabeth is stowed away here.

"What do you want, madame?"

I spin on my heels to find an agitated woman with disheveled hair. "Bonsoir. I seem to have misplaced my daughter. She must have been looking for an adventure. The celebration is too boring for the young ones, I'm sure. Have you seen any girl here out of the ordinary?"

She narrows her eyes. "You should leave, madame." She hurries past me but I sense she knows something, so I follow.

"Please. I need to find my daughter."

She scans her eyes up to my face and examines my hair. I can see her question if I could possibly be the Red Fox but shakes her head, realizing how ridiculous it would be for a wanted Huguenot to be dressed like a fine Catholic lady in the house of the man that has hunted her. "No, madame. You should return to the party."

In a moment of panic, I grab the woman. Press her firmly against the wall. "I see it in your eyes. You know where she is."

She freezes, her mouth open, neck trembling. "I don't know what you want."

"I want my daughter." I hope that she's a mother and has some shred of empathy left in her. A younger Isabelle would never put an innocent woman in such an awful position. The current Isabelle has a daughter to rescue. I slide my dagger from my boot and hold it to her face. "You know who I am?"

She nods, unable to speak.

"Then you know I will slide this blade through your neck without a blink of hesitation." The poor woman is frozen in a state of terror. It's amazing what we'll do to protect our children. "Are you a mother?"

She swallows then catches her breath. She nods.

"And if your child was in danger, would you kill to save them?"

We lock eyes in a fierce stare, her forgetting for a brief moment that an instrument of death rests against her neck. Her lack of response tells me I've read her correctly.

"Tell me where she is, and I will let you go."

"The basement," she croaks out.

"The basement. What's down there?"

She presses my hand away, but I don't relent. "Master is holding her there."

"Louvois knows she's here?"

"Please." She swallows with a grimace. I pull away but hold the dagger near her face. "She'll be taken for questioning tomorrow."

"What kind of questioning?"

She hesitates. "The kind no mother would want her daughter to undergo."

"And you flutter through the house, cleaning and protecting Louvois's nasty secrets."

She holds her hands up. "Master is evil. He'll torture me and my family."

"Like they're torturing mine?"

Her eyebrows tighten and she looks down. "I don't want to protect him. I have no choice."

"My mother used to tell me we always have a choice. It's consequences we are never free from." Then I slam the knife handle into the side of her head and watch her crumble to the floor. "Being a coward *is* a choice, madame." I drag her body inside a servant's room and shut the door.

To the basement.

Back down the flights of winding marble and iron scrollwork. This gown is tight and heavy, but I practice breathing as Naira taught me, with control and purpose. I pass several servants and smile as if I'm a wealthy noble lost in the beauty of Louvois's architectural masterpiece. The idea makes me want to scream.

The duke and Anastasia finish their rousing performance and send the crowd to cheers. The duke dips her, planting a kiss on her that makes all the women blush and laugh. I pause to clap for them at the base of the stairs and eye the room for another staircase leading to the basement.

I slide around the far corner and run into a guard. He stares, his face unmoving. "Not for guests," he says.

"Ah, of course." I curtsy and return to the applause.

Anastasia glides through the room blowing kisses to every man she passes. "Did you enjoy my performance, Isabelle?"

"I need your help. A guard won't let me pass to the basement. Elizabeth is down there."

"You did not answer my question. "

"Yes, fine. You were spectacular. Gorgeous, even."

"That's better." She nods with a smile and waves over the duke. "Now come on."

"Monsieur!" Anastasia shakes her hips and stumbles her way toward the guard. Her breasts flop into his chest and she leans her mouth toward his. "You're working too hard, monsieur. Perhaps these strong arms are lonely." She runs her fingers along his shoulders.

The duke and I wait behind a bronze statue where we can watch her. "Doesn't it bother you to watch this?" I ask.

He smiles. "I quite like it."

I bite back a grunt. "Nobility," I snort. "Your world will never make sense to me."

"Admit it, you're having fun."

"None of this is fun. I can't wait to be free of you both." Unfortunately, my future plans rely on this unpredictable duo.

Anastasia pulls the guard against the wall and kisses his neck. She bites his ear and shoves her hands under his doublet. "How is he not afraid she will devour him?"

"Oh, that is part of her allure. Like a wild animal tearing at your flesh. You don't know where the next bite might puncture."

I grab the duke by his neck and drag him down the stairs with surprising ease. How weak is this guard to abandon his post for an unpredictable Russian singer who may draw blood from his neck?

As if reading my thoughts, the duke says, "Like I said. Paris is the most unpredictable game in the world. And isn't it grand?"

The hot sticky air of a Paris summer settles into the underground stones like honey, no cooler or clearer than the floors above.

Another guard appears from the dark. "Get out."

The duke wiggles his fingers in the man's face. "Darling! I've been looking for you."

The guard tilts his head and snarls. He lifts his fist to hit me, assuming this wilting flower of a woman can be put in her place with a hard swipe. Fool.

Both my hands block his forearm. I wait for him to gather that I've just stopped him from striking me. Then I dig my fingers into his arm and yank him forward while driving my knee into his nose. While he's distracted, I reach for his sword and press the blade against his windpipe. I slam my knee between his legs until he groans. "Where is the girl?"

He swipes at me but I'm pressing his neck so hard, he's losing air. "Where?"

The duke crashes a vase over his head. The guard's eyes grow heavy, and he crumbles to the ground. Tremblay nods in satisfaction. "No time for these scoundrels. Come along."

We step over the guard's legs and hurry down the dimly lit hallway. "Here." He opens a door to another stairwell spiraling down into the dark depths below.

"How many rooms does one Lieutenant need?"

"Enough to hide his dirty secrets."

We creep down the stairs and a feeling of urgency floods my insides. Is Cricket hurt—or worse? I can't stop my thoughts from spinning into scenarios I never want to imagine. We arrive in what appears to be a laboratory. Glass jars and surgical instruments. Stacks of books and a giant collection of weapons.

"If they did anything to hurt her, I will tear this place apart with my fingernails. Everyone will bleed." With Elizabeth out of reach, I've lost control. Frayed at the edges, I can't summon Naira's teachings or find my balance.

A man shuffles from a storage room so we slide into an alcove. He is dressed in a black robe and carries a magnifying glass. I look over my shoulder to see a browned skull above my head, its teeth held in place with gold wire.

The duke whispers, "Medical experiments." He points to the shelves that line the walls as tall as the ceiling. "Louvois is trying to cure himself, and every other sick noble. He has an affinity for the dark arts."

The man lifts his head to examine a sound. We stand still, controlling our breathing in the shadows. My heart thumps in my throat. A young Huguenot with secrets is the perfect person to experiment on. Rage and worry take over like a wave. I step forward, ready to kill this aging alchemist and every other person who stands in my way.

The duke pulls me back by the sleeve.

Naira would tell me to find patience. Control my breath. We never discussed how to conquer your fear when your child's life is at risk. This is something I was never prepared for. It's why I've fought to keep her safe. Maybe a part of me knew what I was capable of. A mother protecting her child will go to unimaginable lengths.

Louvois has no idea how far I'll go. Truthfully, neither do I.

The old man shuffles back to his cave. The duke points to a locked door at the far end of this dark cavern where a guard stands like a sentry.

"Follow my lead." The duke creeps through the black night, rushing between candlelit shadows. We pass a table of brain slices, chillingly gray and soft, with pins stuck in the fleshy ridges. I won't let my eyes linger to discover if they're human or animal.

The duke tumbles toward the guard, pretending to be drunk.

"Merde. You again!" The guard dismisses him. "I thought you had dried out somewhere in the Army. But here you are, drunk as always."

Tremblay pats the man's shoulder and burps. "Hello, old friend."

He throws the duke's hands away. "At least you aren't asleep in a pool of your own vomit. Leave, before I force you out."

"I'd love for you to force me." The duke trails his fingers along the man's cheek. "I know you miss me."

I freeze, still hidden behind an armoire that smells oddly of rotting mushrooms. The guard hesitates. He swats the duke's hand away. "You tease me. It's unfair. Now go."

"Come, darling. Your face is far too handsome to be so cross."

It seems the duke has his hands in an immeasurable amount of drama throughout the city, and I wonder how much is for his own pleasure, and how much is for power. He whispers in the man's ear as the guard softens. They roll against the wall and disappear into a corner.

I take my chance and slide toward the door, lift the wooden bar and slip inside. A room of arches and a painted ceiling, black candles, and walls filled with bones. Hundreds of skulls and thighs and fingers are stacked like towers. In the far corner, a cell of sorts, and inside, Elizabeth.

"Isabelle?" Her teary voice nearly knocks me to the floor.

I run to her, stick my hands through the bars and hug her tight. "Are you alright? Did they hurt you?"

She shakes her head. "No. They just want to terrify me." She looks at the skeletal remains that enclose her. "It's working."

"Oh, Cricket. I'm so glad you're safe." I examine the wooden bars taller than myself, and a rigid lock and no key in sight.

She points to the corner. "I've picked that lock until my fingers bled but nothing will budge."

I look around to an empty room. Bones and candles. Nothing to crack a brass lock with. "I'll have to go back to the laboratory to find something to break you out."

She grabs my wrists. "Don't leave."

"I will never leave you. I just need a few minutes."

She yanks me back to her. "I'm sorry. I'm so sorry I lied to you."

"Never mind that now." I reach through the bars until my shoulder burns between two wooden beams. I run my hand along her hair. "All I care about is breaking you free."

"I hear them talk. Their plans." The intensity in her eyes scares me. "These bones are Huguenot remains. Trophies."

Something sour rises in my stomach. "Stop. I'll fix this."

She pulls me back, a glint in her eye. "I've seen Louvois. I've spoken to him. I act frightened and he shows me his threats. His plans."

I yank my hand from her and want to scream. How could I have missed this? "You let yourself get caught?"

"It's what you would do. I know it is."

She knows me too well. I feel around the wall of leg and arm bones. Halved pelvises and spine segments, looking for anything to help me. "I would not have allowed them to stick me in the basement." I pat my hands along the smooth crevices and bony prominences of various body parts, searching for anything I can find.

"Admit it, I saved the girls. I succeeded on my first solo mission. You should be proud." So brave. So naive. What a dangerous combination. When I don't smile or react, her eyes fall. "I *did* save them."

"No Cricket, you didn't." Her foolishness has risked us all and my anger could explode like fire. "You took it upon yourself to take them to a city you didn't know. They were captured for trying to flee. They are both dead because you didn't want to take help from those that know more than you. And now you've put us all in danger in this bone graveyard while you think you can outsmart Louvois. You can't."

Her eyes fill with tears. "They died?"

I want to find empathy for her, but I'm too filled with fear. I grab her shoulder. She winces and pulls away. "What is it?" Her face twists in pain. "Your skin is red. Are you warm? Are you ill?" My vision blurs imagining how she might respond.

Elizabeth, my brave, perfect, protected daughter, pulls down the neckline of her dress. On her shoulder, a blackened H.

"That monster burned you."

"I'm just like you now."

"No, Cricket, you're locked in a cage surrounded by remnants of Huguenot suffering. And I must find a way out before that branding turns you feverish." I can't let myself feel the grief. Not yet. "These bars aren't breakable, they're too thick. There's only one way to get you out."

"The key?"

I close my eyes to focus. "I need to steal it from Louvois."

Her eyes tear up as she covers her branding. "I only ever wanted you to be proud of me."

I realize in this very moment, I did this to her. I inspired her to stand face to face with the ugliest monsters humanity has ever created, to give our bodies and mind to a larger cause, and beg for more. We're stuck in a basement of skulls and burned flesh because of me.

CHAPTER TWENTY-TWO

Standing in Louvois's laboratory over the slices of brain matter and eyeballs floating in glass canisters of yellow fluid, I take in the reality of my current situation. I must find the man who burned myself and my daughter, steal his key before he tortures her, sneak her out of this chateau, then somehow find my husband and Charlotte lost in this miserable city. And then, I let the duke take me to the king.

All before sunrise.

I knew I couldn't hesitate when Elizabeth sat curled in the corner of her cage, face flushed and neck trembling. I wanted to crawl inside the bars and hold her, but my determination grew when she looked at me with a downturned mouth. "Get me out. I want to go home."

I search cupboards and drawers but it's nothing but odd shaped instruments and glasses of powders I wish to know nothing about. The duke stumbles out from the dark stairwell, hair disheveled and eyelids heavy.

"Greetings, my pet." He stops to catch his breath. "It is a grand night, is it not?"

I grab his crumbled doublet with both hands and shove him against the stone wall. "While you've been frolicking in someone's bed, I've been trying to rescue Elizabeth from a room of skulls." I shake him "Skulls. Do you hear me?"

"I frolicked—twice, I might add—so you could find her. Honestly, it's like you don't appreciate the things I do for you."

"He branded her, Tremblay." I drop my arms and allow him to see my frightened eyes. "He branded my daughter."

The duke nods. "We need to find the key, then."

I smooth his clothing where I crumpled it in my fists. "Yes. And quickly. She's not well."

"Perhaps I could romp with the guard again."

I hold my hands in front of his face but stop myself from clawing his cheeks. "What is the matter with you?"

"Sorry, I do my best work when I'm excited." He jumps in place and shakes his head. "Louvois is still in the chateau. We'll find him, distract him, and you steal the key."

"How will I do that?"

He continues bouncing until his breath is labored and a sheen of sweat glistens on his brow. "Anastasia." The duke stops moving and stares at me with a smile. Then he slaps himself hard against the cheek. He winks. "I like it rough."

"How did I end up here?" I'm beyond exasperated with him.

"Because you need me. Come along, my pet!"

Against all sense of logic, I follow this ridiculous man. We climb stairwells lit by dripping candles in mounds of wax, as faded moans and laughter pulse in the distance. Paris nights always feel like a fever dream. Hot, sticky air and tight clothing only worsen my rapid heartbeat. I think of Elizabeth, and I conjure an image of Naira standing in the forest, bow in hand. "Fear returns to us when we question our place in the world."

I pad behind Tremblay through lavish hallways and back into the raucous party, but my mind sits quietly with Naira. I ask her why I'm here and how I find my way back home. She smiles with her eyes, her long black hair waving in the wind. "You know the answer already." She blows a gust of cool air as my neck shivers and brings me back to the present.

At least memories of La Rochelle no longer grip me at the worst moment. Blood splatter and blue faces. Torn flesh and screams. No, those are in the past. Far away in another lifetime where Henri is alive, and I was a simple girl with dreams of triumph. In this life, I've earned my place among resistors.

"Isabelle?" Tremblay nudges me with his elbow. "Move."

Suddenly focused, I nod and play the part of a noble enthralled in midnight laughter and music. I try to ignore the notion that Elizabeth is three floors underground, locked in a cage, and my husband is nowhere to be found. "Yes, lovely evening, isn't it?" I say to a passerby. Drink is flowing through the crowd and the stench of wine turns my stomach.

Louvois is here and Charlotte and Andre are missing. I toss that worry from my mind, to obsess over at a more opportune time.

We find Anastasia having a conversation with an exotic bird on her hand, much to the delight of the people gathered around her. Tremblay nods to her and she kisses the bird on the beak. "Be gone, my feathered friend. Fly into the night and ruin a fine lady's perfectly coiffed hair!"

Anastasia prances to us and licks the duke's cheek.

"What an odd greeting," I say.

"It means she's ready for the challenge." The duke smiles, closed mouth with curled in lips, reminding me of a court jester. "We need a key for the cage the young Elizabeth is locked in. She's in the basement."

"Ah, well. Why didn't you say so? Come along." She slaps him on the derriere.

We follow her through the stench of hot, sweating, drunk nobles. She grazes cheeks and pulls on earlobes of men as we pass. "Save a dance for me, lovelies!"

We follow her upstairs and down the hall to an antechamber. A waiting room larger than my entire home in Geneva, mirrors and candelabras and painted ceilings make the room feel like daylight. Anastasia presents us to a guard at the far corner.

"Bonsoir, my handsome friend." She waves by fluttering her fingers.

The guard does not budge.

"We are here to visit with the great Lieutenant Louvois. I've brought someone he'll find very interesting."

Tremblay turns to me with a grin. A fun game, I see. If a key didn't rest somewhere on the other side of that door, I'd let my inner warrior loose on all of them. The question remains, will they turn on me? I can only assume yes.

"Who have you brought?" the guard asks, leering at me.

"I'm the woman who nearly killed him," I say. "Tell him the Red Fox is here to finish what she started."

Before he can consider his options, I've punched him in the throat. Once he's silenced, I lift my skirts and shove my heel into his fleshy lower abdomen. Curled on the ground, he's completely unable to speak, and that is when I slam a candlestick to his temple.

Anastasia stares at me, eyes wide. "I was simply going to put you inside to see how you handled yourself. It appears you can manage Paris just fine."

The duke props his fist on his hip. "Well played, madame."

"No time for games." I open the door to Louvois's bedroom where I find the man who changed me so many years ago. His face is swollen and baggy on one side. His lower eyelid hangs low, exposing bright red membrane usually covered by skin. Not ten years older than myself, he's aged to an old man since I beat him bloody.

"I knew you'd come." His words bubble from one side of his mouth.

"You have my daughter in a cage." I twirl the candlestick in my hand. "Of course I'd come for you."

The mistress on his lap covers her bare chest and waits for his approval to stand. He flings his good wrist, motioning for her to leave. A guard slides his sword from his baldric and steps toward me.

Louvois's hand is curled like an art piece rigid against his chest. He stands by leaning to one side and holding a cane. His damaged leg does a surprisingly good job preventing him from falling. "You made a grave mistake, my Red Fox. You should have never let me live back in the forests of Rouen."

"I made a calculated choice," I say. "As did you when you killed my friend and locked up my daughter."

"Your daughter is not as cunning as you." His thoughts are much clearer than I anticipated. "She has not learned to track when she's being followed."

"You brought her here to lure me."

Anastasia steps forward. "I'm sorry, madame. I didn't want to lie to you. You are so much fun."

I have no attention to give to Anastasia's games. "What do you get from him, mademoiselle?" I ask.

"What I always do. Favors."

"One guard?" I look the man up and down. "You don't have much faith in me, Lieutenant Louvois."

"A dozen more wait outside. I couldn't take the chance you'd attack me again." He slides his twisted leg behind him, painfully dragging himself toward a glass jar. "Here is the key, madame—I don't believe I know your last name."

"You have no need to know anything about me."

He wipes the drool from his chin. "I should have died several times by your hand. You've let me live. Why?"

"There is something you don't know about me, this Red Fox you've created in your mind."

"What is that?" He turns over the jar as a brass key clangs on the marble desk.

"I'm not real." Anastasia eyes us with intrigue. Excitement even. I take a step closer to Louvois. "I'm just a woman who's no longer afraid to die. And that is a difficult thing to break."

"You are Protestant. You have anger toward me." He presses his finger to the key and slides it toward me. "Your daughter came to avenge some wrong I have created. So tell me, Red Fox, where is your branding?"

I pull back my sleeve, my eyes not leaving his.

He leans to examine the scar on my forearm. The raised flesh I once hated, but now claim as proof of my strength. "The man you killed, his brand was on his calf."

"Ah, my early work. You must be from La Rochelle then?"

My stomach roils but I don't show my disgust to anyone in this room. "You no longer blacken the limbs of children?"

"No." He sniffs. "The upper body is far more damaging and painful."

I think of Elizabeth, which was his intention. He swipes the key to the ground and kicks it across the room. "Kill her."

The guard launches for me, but I round my back as the blade barely misses my belly. Anastasia kicks the key away from me. "Watch out."

I turn as the guard swings the blade through the air again, aiming to slice off my head. I duck and kick my foot to the man's knee then roll out of his way as his head cracks against the tile floor. I slam a chair onto his back, hearing a bone crunch that lifts a memory from deep in my soul.

He screams in pain, yet I'm unable to move.

Tremblay is nowhere to be found.

I'm transported from Paris to the rainy November day in La Rochelle when they exiled us from our homes. Nineteen is still a child in many ways. Before the world broke my hope for freedom. When I dreamed of safety and thought I loved a Catholic. I had saved my mother, who is huddled against the wall, her hair smeared in blood. Screams echo far away though mouths open all around me as they release strangled, silent cries. I've broken a man's back to protect Maman. He stopped moving after one thwack, yet I continued to hit him until his spinal bones crunched like shattered glass. Until I was satisfied I'd hurt him like he tried to hurt me.

The blood still slithers with the rain down limestone walls. Like a scene painted on canvas with colors that never fade, its scroll rolls out in front of my eyes. The grim scene is all I can see.

Naira whispers, "Breathe. Listen."

When I open my eyes, I see Anastasia. She watches me, all sense of humor drained from her face. I sense Louvois near me, so I throw my elbow once to his face, knocking him to the ground.

"You are not the terror I remember you as." I kneel to face him. "I am Isabelle Colette. Proud Protestant of La Rochelle. You burned my skin at eight years old and helped our enemies the LaMarches turn our world into hell on earth. And then you killed one of the most important people in my life. If he were here, Henri Reynard would slice your neck open right now and watch your evil bleed from your soulless, damaged body."

"But he is gone, Isabelle," Louvois mumbles, his crooked smile lined with bloody gums. "And your daughter will be next."

A calm settles over me. "You have no power over me, Louvois. I've left you damaged and drooling, unable to reach your own behind. That is the fate you deserve."

"Don't think you'll escape. It's too late."

I lift my boot to crunch his fingers, but I can't bring myself to do it. I'm protecting no one right now. I am only bathing in his pain. Anastasia breathes like a whistle through tightened lips.

"Why don't you kill him?" she asks. "Or me?"

I step back and whisper to her. "You helped Tremblay escape with the key. You need him to think you're on his side. I understand your ways better than you think."

"And him?" She gestures to Louvois.

"He wasn't going to kill me. He wanted to present me to the king like a hunting trophy. I won't watch him bleed to death. I won't take that opportunity away from the one who desperately needs it." Louvois's mangled legs look shriveled and useless. Charlotte will take great joy in breaking them. "Until we meet again, Louvois. And you can be certain we will."

I open the doors to the balcony and turn back to Anastasia, a steely grin on her face. "The duke knows what's next," she says. "You'd better not fall."

She reaches to unlock the door as I climb the railing and stare down the three floors to the chateau courtyard. Moonlight brightens the dark sky over this pristine garden protected from the city's filth and hate. With a jump, I reach for the thick branch of a maple tree and swing for a moment as if I'm once again in the wilds of Canada with my Huron friend, learning to listen to the wind and shoot arrows.

Once I scramble down the tree and land with a thud to the grass below, Tremblay arrives dragging a weakened, coughing Elizabeth through the manicured garden. I wrap my arms around her hot body as she cries on my chest.

"Not now, Cricket. Too much still to be done to be weighed down by tears."

Tremblay looks over his shoulder. "How did you know to trust me?"

"I didn't. But I didn't want to lose hope either."

Tremblay wraps his arm around her waist and carries her to the street. I see through the windows that the guards have disrupted the party looking for the devious fox among them.

Naira once taught me to accept my fear. She threw me to the ground so my body and mind could learn control. Choices and sacrifice will never leave the warrior. I watch Tremblay lead Elizabeth's wobbly legs out of sight and now I understand Naira in a new way.

The battle was always of the heart.

CHAPTER TWENTY-THREE

There is only one place I can think of where Charlotte would dare spend her time in this thieving city. Her original poison and potion teacher, Mademoiselle Boulais. Mistress to the king and black magic practitioner, she spends summer nights extracting blood from frogs and setting fingernails on fire, and Charlotte feels right at home.

I knock on the familiar door more frantically than I intend. Mademoiselle Boulais does not disappoint. She welcomes us, her face slick with sweat and her lips bright purple like an August berry. "Madame er-what is your name now? Boucher?"

"Yes. My daughter is ill. Please help."

"Come in." She opens the door to her home and the familiar splash of rotting vegetables and burnt animal hits my nose. The scent has never left my memory.

Tremblay lowers Elizabeth to a bed in the kitchen. She curls into a ball, teeth chattering.

Boulais removes her bloody apron and feels her forehead. "Get me the bucket and linens. Isabelle, help undress her."

We remove her layers of drenched clothing down to her shift. Her body seems so small like this. Boulais tucks wet rags under her arms and behind her neck. She rubs herbaceous oil over her hands and feet. We nearly lost her to fever as a young baby when her mother died. Does she remember the fear?

"How did she fall ill?" Boulais asks.

I gently tug back the shift to reveal her shoulder, burnt, black, and oozing a thick, oily fluid.

Boulais nods while she gathers her thoughts. "Louvois found you?"

Tremblay faces a wall away from us, examining jugs and jars.

"Yes. Where is Charlotte?"

"On an errand for me. She didn't expect you here. Neither did I."

I rub Elizabeth's hair from her face. "They wanted me to stay in hiding. My daughter had other plans."

"Did you kill him?" she asks. "That bastard deserves death."

"No. He'll surely be looking for me around Paris."

"You certainly love to stir the mischief around this city, don't you?" She winks. "I'll clean this wound and monitor her. You should get some sleep."

"Not without Andre and Charlotte. I can't rest until I have everyone I love right here with me." We need to flee this city of refuse and return to Geneva to a land of snow and secret Huguenot resistance.

"You'll have to wait a while for that," Tremblay says without turning around. "I can smell that wound from here."

"This is not how it ends." I throw a glass jar across the room. "I did not come all this way and survive more times than I should have only to fail this girl." Elizabeth opens her swollen eyes to look at me.

"I'm sorry, Isabelle."

Though I want to tell her not to apologize, I can't bring myself to say the words. She wasn't ready for any of this. I kiss her on the cheek and step back to allow Boulais to work her magic.

The stench of seared flesh fills the room. My skin beads with sweat as shadows on the wall turn to blood rivulets.

"Isabelle?" Tremblay grabs me by the arm as my knees give way.

Boulais points to a doorway. "Take her to get some air."

Through a doorway and up a winding flight of stairs, all I can think of is air, even the hot stale air of Paris. We burst through a door and find ourselves on the rooftop of Boulais's house. A small square outside an attic window where the city bubbles below like a cauldron.

"Sit." We lower to the ledge and take in the dense air. "You nearly fainted."

"I'm fine."

"Of course you are." He shrugs.

Fires burn throughout the city and smoke climbs into the night air, carrying the smell of yeast. Finally, a break from the chamber pots and river of filth.

"Why do you hate Paris?" he asks.

"What is there to like? The wealthy live in mansions, surrounded by servants, ignoring the desperate, hungry souls around them who cannot find any air to breathe."

"I can't imagine your life has been easy."

I withhold an eye roll. I don't care to divulge the depths of my suffering to this fool.

"But this is a new level of difficult, is it not?"

I wipe the sweat from my brow with the sleeve of my dress. "I've met the king before. He doesn't scare me, and neither does anyone else."

The duke tucks his hands between his knees and stretches. "Do you know why I play the part of a fool?"

"I didn't realize you were acting."

He crinkles his nose in a false laugh. "If I care about nothing, no one can hurt me."

"Do you truly care about nothing?"

"Outside of poetry and music, yes. At least, until they sent me to the Royal Army. I couldn't laugh my way out of the things I saw and heard. In Paris, I can play a game where no one wins or loses. With the dragoons, everyone loses."

Without realizing it, I've been scratching at my scar. This old habit from childhood seems to remove the layers I've built over the years. "That's why you drink."

"Yes."

"Don't think I've forgotten our purpose here. I know you'll deliver me to the king. I just ask that you wait until my family is safe and healthy."

The duke leans back and looks to the moon. "I think you're afraid."

"I let go of fear long ago. It doesn't serve me."

"Until Elizabeth joined your cause." I don't react. "Now she's branded like you are. But what's worse, now she'll never leave the cause. Just like you."

Gone is the fool and in his place now sits the philosopher. "Losing myself is a risk I've always accepted. If I lose her, all of this would be meaningless."

"Ah, to love. It must feel nice."

A slight breeze cools my neck. "You've never been in love?"

"No," he says. "Only lust."

"Perhaps you're afraid as well."

Neither of us speak. We listen to hollers and the bumping of carriages as they roll through the streets below. The unpredictable, messy, chaotic city taunts me with its Catholic extremes. I will lead Charlotte to Louvois and take my final attack on the royal family. Then I will sacrifice myself so others can live free.

I have no other choice but sacrifice.

. . .

Four hours Elizabeth has slept soundly. Despite her raw flesh and weakened body, she looks stronger than ever. Boulais and the duke have gone to sleep but I can't rest until her fever breaks.

Just as the sun rises from the horizon, the door clicks open. Charlotte appears, apron full of sticks and leaves, her eyes in disbelief. "What are you doing here?"

"Elizabeth decided to take her turn at Louvois. It didn't go well."

"Merde." She drops the items on a table and shakes out her skirts. "Is she unwell?"

I pull down the neckline of her shift where her H has begun to bubble and harden. "We escaped, but he'll be looking for us."

Charlotte closes her eyes and purses her lips. She doesn't move or speak while her face reddens like a flame. "He could have killed her."

"He enjoys torture far more."

"Oh, Isabelle." She pulls me into a hug. "I'll kill him for her, and I'll enjoy every second of it to avenge Henri."

"Will it never end?" I ask.

"No. Not in our lifetime."

We stare at Elizabeth as if she is still a child. In her face I still see the three-year-old who sat on Naira's lap while her father and I tried to ignore our love for each other. So much fight everywhere. Our daughter has become a force of bravery in the years I've tried to hold her in our cottage, attempting to protect her from the world that might take her from me. As if she is the fragile girl and I am the mother who knows better.

"Back home in La Rochelle, did you wonder why our parents didn't fight back?"

"Every second of every day," she says. "I still can't understand it."

"My mother drank and wouldn't leave the house. She warned me not to fall for James Beaumont. She taught me to save myself while she withered away in fear. Then she died."

"Much like my sister," she says. "Clémentine is at peace now, just like your mother."

"But we aren't at peace, are we?"

"Perhaps that isn't our purpose." Charlotte lifts her chin, gaze lifted to the ceiling. "We sacrifice so others will know happiness."

Elizabeth half wakes as her fingers crawl over to mine. "Good morning, Cricket. How do you feel?"

"Like the contents of a chamber pot left in the sun."

"Ah, she's one of us now." Charlotte rubs her cheek. "Welcome to the fight, my dear one."

"I've always been in it." Her eyes fall heavy and her hand collapses back to the bed.

"Where is Andre?" I ask, preparing myself for any number of difficult answers.

Charlotte bites her lip. "Oh, Andre. He's not here."

"I can see that. Subtlety does not suit you. Now tell me what I need to know."

She nods, then glances at Elizabeth as if she doesn't want her to hear. "He's discovered the secretary who oversees the dragoons. He's gone to take him out."

"Gone where?"

"Versailles. Naturally." She shrugs. "That's why I've been collecting herbs and such." She points to her haul from the streets and the hills. We need large amounts of poison."

"Charlotte, tell me now."

"Andre is pretending to be a servant for the nobility. He's gotten himself in a bit of trouble and we need to get him out."

"What trouble?"

"Oh, he's safe. He's simply stuck as a servant in the apartments of an artist. Andre's stash of poisons—enough to kill every courtier in the city—was discovered and confiscated."

"They didn't arrest him?"

"No one knew it was his. The court is conducting interviews and mistrust is everywhere. Andre listens to whispers and secrets that ripple through a hysterical court. How he hasn't slashed every one of them in their sleep, I'll never know."

"I have an injured daughter, a murdered best friend, and a husband who requires vats of poison to escape the clutches of royal eccentrics."

"But you have me," Charlotte says with a grin.

"I'm one hell of a shot with a bow and arrow." We turn to see Elizabeth, hand extended. "Don't think you'll have all this fun without me."

My instinct is to tie her to the bed and steal her back to Geneva against her will. But just as I don't drink to dull my pain, I do not force my child to ignore her calling. Much as I want to.

"Please don't hold me back any longer," she asks.

Both look at me and wait for my response. "Looks like us three women are responsible for stopping the king."

Tremblay stumbles in, hair a wild mess and drool dried in the corner of his mouth. "Good morning, fine ladies."

Charlotte sighs. "Oh, and him. We've got him."

CHAPTER TWENTY-FOUR

Two weeks of preparation has left us with a healed, strong Elizabeth, and pockets full of powders and poisons. Mademoiselle Boulais has agreed to furnish her creations. Louvois has wronged her many times and a shared enemy is the fastest way to get Boulais on our side.

We find ourselves so far from our cause that my chest aches. How many Protestants have died in the weeks we've wasted here in Paris? I keep reminding myself that Elizabeth is safe, and we have an opportunity to stop the Dragonnades at their source.

"Are you certain you're fully healed?" I ask.

Elizabeth smiles as if I am the child. "Don't you worry, Isabelle. I'm stronger than ever."

The duke has disappeared nightly to prance through Paris doing whatever the duke does. He instructed me to wear a wig and provided all three of us with lavish clothing. The duke is our way into the court of Versailles.

Mademoiselle Boulais bows. "You all look grand. Now run along and get to work." She practically kicks us out her door without so much as a smile.

"Are we ready?" Elizabeth asks.

Charlotte straightens her shoulders. "I've been ready for years."

We link arms and make our way through the streets toward our planned meeting place with Duke Tremblay. He waits for us in a gilded carriage at the Tuileries gardens, arms extended in a grand gesture. "Bonjour, my darlings!"

Elizabeth elbows him in the chest. "Have you been practicing your fighting skills?"

"I'm in the best physical form, mademoiselle."

"That means no." Elizabeth rolls her eyes. "It will be up to us, Isabelle. These soft arms will do nothing to help our fight."

We settle in the carriage as Tremblay signals his coachman to move ahead. "Who is ready for a grand party?"

We don't crack a smile.

"Oh, come now. We'll fetch Andre and poison a few people, but amid all that we'll feast on pheasant and boar and cream cakes, just as nobility should."

"Not all on one plate, I hope." Charlotte loosens her robe around her waist, forcing deep breaths against the restrictive court clothing.

Paris fades from sight as we enter the countryside west of France. Along a busy road, Parisians in all states of dress wipe sweat from their temples and wave at the glamorous carriages as they pass.

Elizabeth scans the slow-moving people. "Peasants and royals walking together?"

The duke smiles. "Yes, all manner of citizens are permitted to walk the grounds and visit the king's palace. The Sun King does love his show of power."

"What does it look like?" Elizabeth asks.

"Versailles? Well, you're about to see for yourself."

We enter through a hedge-lined grand entrance into a courtyard and garden the size of Paris itself. Peasants gawk at the statues and fountains. A man rides an elephant past us, followed by a line of what I assume to be ostriches. I've only ever seen them in paintings.

"How many people stay here?" Charlotte asks.

The duke puffs out his bottom lip. "Around ten thousand."

"I suppose that's how we can pass for nameless nobles here to admire the king's ostentatious flare." I withhold a snarl, knowing Andre must be ready to break down walls to escape this horrid display. He came here to stop the Dragonnades, but I know his intentions run deeper. To force me to retire from the resistance. To live a quiet, humble life in Geneva in his arms.

The thought makes me want to cry.

"Do we need to review protocol?" Tremblay asks.

Charlotte leans forward. "Find Louvois and poison him until his brains ooze from his nose."

"Yes. Glad we got that sorted." He loosens his collar. "Isabelle, might you wish to keep Charlotte locked away in a quiet room until her time has come? I'm afraid she might bite the nobility."

Charlotte opens her mouth wide and gnashes her teeth.

"Why do you think we brought her?" Elizabeth asks with a smile.

The girls enjoy taunting the duke, but my mind is elsewhere. I'm dressed as a Catholic among thousands of nobles here to celebrate the whims of a childish king while Protestants have their homes stolen and their bodies bruised. I don't react when the duke points to a juggler.

"Isabelle," the duke says, "It is possible to smile once in a while."

"Not for her," Elizabeth says.

A strange ache grabs at my chest. Something altogether different from fear and anger. Disappointment. I don't care for this feeling at all.

"Here we are." The duke exits first and holds our hands one at a time to help us out of the carriage. I swat him away when he reaches for me.

We step into an entrance so bright gold, I squint. The grandeur is offset by a particularly repulsive odor. We all cough and cover our mouths.

We follow the duke past servants fanning ladies and couples parading arm in arm down the longest hallway I've ever seen. Behind a statue, a lady's maid holds her madame's skirts above her head while she relieves herself.

Charlotte's eyes begin to water. "Is she—" An offensive plop hits the marble floor. "Yes, she is."

The duke places his hands on his hips. "The king is the only one with a receptacle for that sort of thing, I'm afraid. Courtiers relieve themselves in hallways and stairwells and frankly, anywhere they please."

"Who are the unlucky servants who clean these floors?" Elizabeth asks.

"They don't often clean them. Disgusting, I know, but such is life at Versailles! Come along. And watch your step."

The girls exchange looks, and I believe for the first time, Elizabeth might miss life in Geneva.

Charlotte whispers in my ear. "All these nobles ripe for the picking. Just think of how many we could kill in one night."

As deeply as I despise these people, my desire is not for retribution. Charlotte would massacre all ten thousand of these Catholics if given the opportunity. Much like Andre, if I dip into that pool inside my soul, I'm afraid I'll drown in hate.

We follow the duke to a wing of slightly improved odor. "Here we are," he says. "My apartment."

"You have an apartment here?" Charlotte asks.

"Yes. All high-ranking families do. The king likes to keep us close where he can control our lives and prevent us from conspiring against him. I do love his distrust. I find it adorable."

We step inside his lavish quarters where the furniture alone could fund hundreds of families with food for years. Copper statues frame the marble fireplace, and the walls are paneled in decorative scrolls, each painted with gold highlights. The entire place reflects light.

"You ladies may share the servant's quarters." He opens the door to a room that overlooks one of the gardens.

"What will the king think of you?" I ask. "You left your regiment and fled back to Paris to attend parties."

"He will revere me for escaping the onslaught of Protestant revolt. I am one of the few soldiers who has seen the Red Fox up close. Ragged beast that she is." He growls at me with a smile.

I ignore his teasing. "Where is Andre?"

Charlotte loosens her stay and breathes a sigh of relief. "I've always met him in the woods outside the palace, so I've never set foot inside this abhorrent place. He told me he works for a sculptor. Lorraine, I think?"

The duke blushes. "Oh, he is one of the most handsome men at court. And so wild and unpredictable. He's magnificent."

"Cool yourself, Tremblay." Charlotte begrudgingly tightens her stay. "Take us to him."

"First, we will tour his sculptures."

"Why?" I ask, exasperated. "There are Lieutenants to kill."

"Because Lorraine will not acknowledge your presence if you don't understand his artistry."

"Wonderful, more eccentric Catholics to contend with." I close my eyes and focus on my breath. "Andre has found a way to endear the man to him. I'm curious to see how."

The duke takes us through the gardens. We meander through manicured hedges and star-shaped groves, the type of gardens one could only dream of. Vines and fountains and sculptures of stone bring to life stories I've only ever read about in books and imagined in fairytales.

"Here is his most fascinating work," the duke says with a tilted head. "The man's anguish is painful. His are muscles strong and powerful, but unable to withstand heartbreak."

Elizabeth and I give the duke a moment to reflect, but Charlotte is uninterested. "White marble, naked men, lots of anguish. Understood. Now let's go."

The duke snarls. "If you don't appreciate art, you'll die a bitter, lonely woman with a heart of stone."

"Haven't you noticed, I am already that person." She lifts her skirts, and we follow, too afraid to stop her.

The duke bows and smiles to parades of people and animals, servants, maids, and peasants alike. Not even a hint of disrespect in his smile. Perhaps art does provide some form of medicinal protection to the soul. Not that I've ever been permitted to stare at such things. All Protestant figures and symbols have been demolished long before I came into this world.

Elizabeth, sensing a change to my demeanor, links her arm around mine. "I'm certain Papa is safe."

"Yes, I'm sure he is."

"You know it isn't your job to protect every Protestant in the world?"

"Of course it isn't my job. It's my destiny."

She shrugs. "I don't believe in destiny."

She's the result of a protected childhood where she was never given the impossible task of finding meaning in her own torture. I'm grateful for that, but still want her to understand strength and sacrifice.

Smarter than she should be, this girl seems to read my thoughts. "You've protected me, Isabelle. And for that, I'm so thankful. But we are at Versailles, in the presence of the Sun King and all his power and glory. Don't think I haven't been listening. It is best to attack a man when he least expects it."

Elizabeth walks away, leaving me to listen to my heels crunch the pebbles and dirt on the winding pathways of intricate, seemingly endless gardens. She can't think we're here to kill the king. Where have I given her that idea? "Cricket," I yell, "keep your wits about you. Focus on why we're here."

She nods, appearing to placate me, which both irritates and terrifies me. No one has any idea what I plan to accomplish. Charlotte will kill Louvois, Andre will find me the man responsible for the Dragonnades, and I will kill—willingly and happily. My family will escape, and the duke will bring me to the king. Hand me in for a handsome reward. For me, there was never any way out of this palace.

Bring me prison or death, for each will give me a reason to stop fighting.

"Isabelle, hurry," Charlotte says.

I follow the women I've shaped and taught, the women who'll carry on my fight long after I'm gone. Through one of the numerous wings of the palace, the duke traverses gold hallways and more piles of human waste toward a collection of grand apartments. "The great Lorraine lives here." He points to a corner door. "The best light in the palace, besides the king's quarters, of course."

"You've been in the king's quarters?" Charlotte scoffs.

"Yes, his morning ritual is open to members of esteemed royalty. We observe him, well, releasing himself on the one throne in the palace."

"He keeps an audience while he relieves himself?" Charlotte asks.

"Yes. And only the most important nobles are permitted to witness it. I was the mirror holder while he inspected his face and hair. At precisely 8:05 every morning. I only stopped because my incompetent father sent me to join The Dragonnades."

Charlotte reaches into her pockets to touch her bag of powders. "I despise every one of you."

"I know, my darling, but I do appreciate your continual reminders." The duke knocks on the door and Andre answers. He doesn't react, but I can see in his eyes how relieved he is to see his family. We rush inside and lock the door. "Look who I found sneaking around Paris," Charlotte says.

Andre pulls Elizabeth in for a tight embrace. He kisses her forehead and strokes her hair. "I'm so grateful you're safe." He turns to me, face tightened into a scowl. "And you. I instructed you to stay in hiding."

"And when have I ever taken direction from you?"

Andre wraps his arms around my waist, his touch still able to weaken my legs. "I love you, Isabelle."

We hold each other, ignoring the eager, impatient eyes around us.

The duke slaps Andre on the back. "Enough of that. Now, tell us everything you know."

Andre caresses my cheek, shooting me a look of such deep affection, every fleck of fear in me instantly evaporates. His loving gaze is stronger than words could ever be.

"Lorraine is interesting. He wanders the grounds at night and sculpts during the morning hours in his studio. I remain here to be summoned for any needs he requires. Unfortunately, that usually involves feeding him food and finding him the mistress of his choice."

"How did you get this position?" I ask.

"I lied. Told him I'd like to apprentice, and he is the greatest sculptor this country has ever known. He's taken a liking to me. When his mistress found the poisons, he assumed it was one of his jealous lovers. He forces me to spy on all the ladies he's bedded, and let me tell you, they offer more information than I could ever hear over cards and drinks with nobility."

"His mistresses aren't all nobles?" Charlotte asks.

"No, many are prostitutes. They scatter through the woods at night like wolves waiting for their next meal. They know everything about every noble in this estate. You want to bring down an empire? The women who lie naked with powerful men could demolish it in seconds."

"And what have you discovered?" Elizabeth asks.

"Louvois is merely a pawn in the game. He's an unruly brute the leaders want out of their way. The man responsible for the Dragonnades is one of the king's assigned ministers. A Secretary of War."

"Who is he?" I ask.

"I don't know, but he arrives tonight. He'll be seated next to the king at the royal dinner."

The duke props his hands on his hips. "And we shall be there to welcome him."

Charlotte pulls out her velvet bag and dangles it by strings in front of us. "Yes, we will."

I lower her hand to see her face. "You take Louvois. The minister is for me."

"How are you going to kill him?" Elizabeth asks.

"Something up close and personal. This time, I won't make it so quick or merciful. This man will feel every ounce of pain I've carried in my life."

Andre kisses my cheek. "Will this be the last of it? May we return to Geneva after your work with the minister is complete?"

His smile knocks the breath from my chest. "Yes, my love. This will be my last sacrifice."

Little does he know that they will return to Geneva without me, while I will hand the duke his future.

CHAPTER TWENTY-FIVE

The duke is off to hunt with the king's court while we meander the grounds of Versailles, listening for secrets. Andre remains in the apartments to inquire with the servants about the king's elusive minister. Charlotte and Elizabeth lead the way through throngs of Catholics as I linger behind, watching how people smile at each other and what they notice. If all of Paris is a game, Versailles is a circus.

"It's nothing but royal gossip," Charlotte says. "Engagements and affairs. Nothing of interest to us."

"We did hear that dinner won't be until eleven this evening," Elizabeth says. "After the king performs for us." She withholds a snicker.

"This place is exhausting." The sun beats down on my neck as I search for a respite and spot a chateau and pavilion. Without a word, I lead the girls to whatever ridiculousness the king has built twenty minutes away from his palace.

We step inside a courtyard filled with sounds. Bird calls and animal grunts mix with laughter. A tall, slender, pink bird taps its way in front of us. Like something out of a nightmare, its legs resemble stilts.

"It's called a flamingo," a courtier says. "Magnificent, yes?"

"No." I bring my hand to my nose.

"Ah, yes. They do have an odor. But their color, like raspberries and anemones." He notices my confused look. "The king's favorite flower?"

"Of course."

Charlotte steps forward. "What is this place?"

"The king's menagerie." He seems offended that we know so little about royal life.

"This is our first trip, monsieur." Elizabeth flutters her eyelashes. "What can you teach us about this magnificent place?"

I hate that Elizabeth uses her beauty. I'd much rather see her as a gladiator, serious and fierce. Though the way she maneuvers a man's attention is like the mademoiselle who leads her monkey across our path on a rope.

"Here we have wild ducks, cranes and eagles, all living in enclosures," he says with pride. "To replace the rather barbaric blood sport once popular at the palace, this menagerie remains civilized, and orderly. Just as the king wishes."

Charlotte, as impatient as ever, asks, "Who's the minister arriving tonight?"

The courtier ignores her completely and carries on to the balcony of the chateau where we view the animal's enclosures below. "Porcupines. Foxes. Sheep. And here we have lions, and this is called a rhinoceros."

Charlotte growls, nearly imperceptible among the rest of the animal noises. "We're wasting time," she whispers.

Elizabeth flicks a glance at us. "Monsieur, is it true there is a man who keeps a snow leopard at his bedside?"

His face lights up. "Why yes. Brave man, if you ask me."

"And the man who limps, was the menagerie his doing?"

The courtier's face drops. "The menagerie is my father's doing. I'm in charge of maintaining excellence here. Not some scheming Army man."

"Forgive me." She places her hand on her chest. "I must have heard incorrectly. I thought it was some man who was attacked. By a Protestant no less!"

All my attempts to turn her wily and calculated have been futile. It appears Elizabeth will do things her way.

"Monsieur Louvois." His top lip curls in disgust. "Sad situation."

"Yes, very sad. Have they any idea who hurt him?" She links her arm through his as they stroll.

"A woman. They call her the Red Fox. Would you like to hear about the foxes I've named? There are twenty-five."

"Oh, I'd like to know about this strange, lumpy animal."

"That is called a camel. The East India Company brought several back from their latest excursions to Africa."

Charlotte grabs my wrist. "How much time must we spend with this fool and his odorous animals?"

Charlotte holds my arm. "Let Elizabeth work. Her approach is different."

"Fascinating." Elizabeth leans forward as if she's enthralled by these animals. "You were saying, about Louvois?"

"Yes. No one cares for Louvois, unmannered man that he is. He once kicked one of my elephants. Can you even imagine? He'll be here in the theater's front row tonight." The man mutters to himself, "I'd like to be in the front row, but the animals need me, and so does the king. Only the special ones take part in the king's routine. Still, very sad he was mutilated by some woman."

Charlotte and I exchange smiles. Our targets are confirmed, and the duke will take me there.

"The Red Fox is some Huguenot peasant who leads a revolt against our monarchy," he scoffs. "I hear she breathes fire and summons the devil."

"How terrifying." Elizabeth cups her blushed cheek. How she forced her cheek to redden, I have no idea. "Will she come here?"

"To Versailles?" He releases a laugh. "She works in the hills like the wild mongrel she is."

"She sounds very dangerous."

"The king has his ways. He'll find her and bring her to Paris to have her hanged."

"Not here at Versailles?" she asks.

"Heavens no! Here we live by honor and grace. She'll be hanged in Paris along with the rest of the traitors."

Elizabeth has no idea I already know my future. I don't want to leave them, but it's always been my destiny to end like this. I shudder at the thought of losing my skills, falling old, being tortured by a dragoon in a dark forest. I will die on my terms. Here, at the king's palace, after I rain bloodshed on the ones responsible for our misery.

Just as Naira showed me in my dreams.

"Perhaps she's a legend. A fable," Elizabeth says. "Perhaps she'll never be caught."

"Speaking of fables," he says, "Would you like to see the gallery of images of our animals?"

Before he can hope for a response, we are gone. Past the monkeys and clawed birds and ostriches, back to the palace to plan our attack.

"Well done, Elizabeth," Charlotte says. "How did you learn to be so persuasive?"

"I've learned from the best." She winks. "And I add a splash of my own wily ways."

Tonight is the night. The moment years of preparation come to fruition. Decades of pain have led to this evening. As the golden sun lowers in the sky, I swallow against the ache in my chest. I must say goodbye to my child, my love, my sister, and greet my end in the ultimate test of loyalty.

This journey started with a branding on my forearm. It ends with a final act of blood. Mine, or his, or most likely both.

.   .   .

Tightened into the heaviest robe in existence, I watch twilight fade to a silver, liquid light like dewdrops on the gardens of Versailles. So many sunsets in my life have seen the end of terrible days or the onset of wicked nights. By sun or moon, a warrior answers the call, Naira would tell me.

From this balcony, the riches of the king roll out in waves in his gardens and sculptures, his animals and his courtyard of nobles. Charlotte joins me, her heels clacking against the marble floor. She's dressed in royal blue silk, a striped bow at her decollete and shoulders as puffed as bread dough. "Yes, I am aware that I look like one of the exotic birds from the menagerie."

"It's no wonder the nobility faint so much." I try to loosen my stay. "Who would want to live like this?"

"Wealthy people." She puffs out her lips.

We snicker and lean over the balcony to watch the elephants roam through the line of carriages.

"Louvois and the nameless minister are in for one surprising night," she says. "And I can't wait to see the look in their eyes right before we murder them."

"Do you ever feel guilt?" I ask.

"Guilt? For what? These monsters have killed thousands of our people. Our sisters and mothers and innocent children. All I feel is unbridled rage."

"Sometimes I wish I didn't have to kill. I wish I wanted to be the quiet wife who stayed safe and made her husband happy."

"Is this about Andre?"

"It's about me." I wipe a tear that has gathered in one eye, swiping it dry before it can fall. "I want goodness for everyone, but to gain that I must kill. Why was I given this impossible choice?"

"Naira would tell you it isn't a choice." Charlotte turns toward me. "You were given responsibility because you love so much. Every Protestant in France will be changed because of you."

"And you," I say.

She shakes her head. "No, I murder. Kill for the thirst of it. If it makes life easier for Protestants, that is a secondary benefit. I'm driven by hate. You are the leader here because you aren't."

"I've never questioned my purpose. Not for one minute." Tears pool in my eyes, but I don't bother to wipe them away this time. "But I've created a tangled web where I cannot live without this misery. Like a flame I can't stop touching. I am nothing outside the resistance."

"Isabelle, I don't know what's caused this sudden break in your confidence but stop it."

"Very helpful, thank you."

She pulls me to face her. "I mean it. As long as I've known you, your convictions have been sharp as a blade. If you let them break you now, what will it have all been for?"

A woman faints and lands in a pile of horse droppings below, soiling her ostentatious dress. "Serves her right. This entire place is a stage and I hope it burns to the ground."

She turns my chin so she's face to face with me. "Isabelle."

"You can lose that concern on your face. I haven't changed my mind."

"Are you certain? Because I can kill them all. You and Andre and Elizabeth can flee back to Geneva with no regrets."

"It's far too late for that."

The duke throws open the door, hands on his hips. "It is a grand evening." He inhales deeply, then grimaces. "Horse and human waste aside."

"Where have you been?" Charlotte shoves his shoulder.

"At the Grand Apartments." He rolls his eyes. "The king thanked me profusely for my service and questioned me about the Red Fox. His day dress is spectacular, but his problem with sweat is quite unfortunate."

I force calm, also wanting to shove the man to his backside. "What did you say?"

"She is a wild beast of a woman, larger than any soldier and meaner than any wolf." I raise my eyebrows. "Well, I couldn't exactly tell him I've been prancing around Paris with her and invited her into his palace to kill his minister."

"What is your plan, Duke Tremblay?" Charlotte asks. "After we complete the task we came here for."

"I suppose I'll continue prancing around Paris aimlessly searching for some fun."

"Where is Elizabeth?" Charlotte asks.

"I sent her to Andre," I say. "They'll plan our escape from the palace."

The duke meets my gaze. "First the theater and then the royal dinner. It should be a lovely evening for a murder."

We follow the duke, arm in arm, pretending to gawk at the extravagance. Under my false grin, my chest thumps in anticipation. I'm not accustomed to all this pageantry, and Charlotte promised to keep an eye out for any wayward red curls that escape this monstrosity of a wig.

Andre and Elizabeth will watch from the balcony as we make our way through the celebration prior to the king's dance.

A symphony of harps and violins flutters through the room as the duke introduces us as his mistresses. We refuse to smile, forcing the duke to keep levity around us. "I do like them serious. They keep their claws long and sharp." He meows at us.

I drag him away from another set of uncomfortable eyes. "You do enjoy harassing me, don't you?" I whisper.

"It gives me great joy, my pet."

Charlotte grabs our sleeves. "He's here. Louvois has arrived."

"And that means the minister is with him," the duke says. "He'll be making a grand entrance any moment then, the first to enter the theater."

I search the balcony for my family, and find them perched like owls behind a bronze statue. They both nod, a sign that they have secured a swift escape tonight. I don't let myself imagine them running into the night without me.

My attention remains wholeheartedly on my mission tonight.

The music halts and a courtier announces Lieutenant Louvois. We tuck in behind the duke so he doesn't see our faces. A servant pushes him in a chair on wheels. His body trembles, his arm tight to his side, elbow hooked at his chest. He waits for silence.

"Let this be a night of celebration." His lips pop like bubbling stew, air poorly released out of one corner of his mouth. "I will not let Protestant hate stop any of us." He wipes the drool from his chin. "We will fight to the death for The Great Sun King."

Applause and cheers erupt around us, though I'm not sure for what.

His branding gives him a ghoulish, monstrous look. Something out of nightmares.

The courtier announces, "And now, for the guest of honor at the king's celebration. The man who will ensure the king's sovereignty reigns over a Catholic France forever."

A man steps into the hall, a hat with feathers and pearls so large no one can view his face. His tall heels and stockings fit the image I imagined. The man I will kill. He removes his hat and smiles. First, I notice the wicked grin.

Second, I notice the man.

The duke whispers, "That's him. The minister in charge of the Dragonnades."

"Yes." I glance up at Andre. His face is flat, but his eyes tell me he sees what I see.

The Minister I'm here to kill is James Beaumont. The man I plan to slice through the neck is my first husband.

. . .

While the king dances his way across his royal stage dressed in layers of spun gold to symbolize the rising sun, our little group of revolters gathers behind a velvet curtain at the mezzanine. Everyone here knows what's at stake, and all eyes remain on me.

The duke breaks the silence. "Who hasn't dreamt of killing their husband? And a pompous one at that. You'll be doing a favor to France, Isabelle."

"You know he was my husband?"

"Please. I know more of everything than I let on."

Charlotte pushes the others aside. "He deserved to die thirteen years ago. But you let him free and now look at him."

Andre laces his fingers through mine. "Charlotte, take a breath."

"I don't understand," Elizabeth says. "This man lied to you. He's responsible for killing thousands of innocent Protestants. Kill him and don't look back."

I turn from them, peeking through a slit between curtains. James claps for the show, his jeweled rings dazzling on every knuckle.

Andre wraps his arm around my stomach. He pulls me close and whispers in my ear. "I know this is complicated. There are three of us who can step in for you."

I can't speak. My mind is a jumbled mess of emotions. Flashes return of my early years in La Rochelle. The man who stood up to his father and carried me to safety during our exile. The man who survived capture by thinking of my loyalty, then traveled to Canada to find me. The man I chose before Andre. The husband I spied on and cared for at the same time.

"Say something," Elizabeth says. "You always know what to do. This is no different."

Tears press into the back of my eyes. "This is very different." I release Andre's hand and step away from the applause. I need to run free and wild in the forest where life makes sense. My chest aches.

A secret I've yet to reveal to anyone has bared its teeth deep in my gut. My recurring dream tells me I'll die at a palace, James Beaumont's eyes focused on mine. Sunrise behind us as I wither to nothing.

"You hate him," Charlotte says.

"Of course I hate him."

"Then what's the problem?" she asks, teeth gritted. "I'll do it myself."

I grab her by the arm, so hard I surprise myself. "Your emotions always get in the way, Charlotte. You've sold your soul for vengeance, and I will not be responsible for cleaning up your messes any longer."

Her eyes go wide, her lips tight.

"I've had to contend with your impulsivity and your wildness too many times. I understand the difficulties of being tortured and having those you love ripped away, but I always make excuses for you." My voice grows louder. It's reckless, but I don't care. "You're no longer a child, Charlotte. Stop acting like one."

Elizabeth steps toward me but Andre holds her back. With sobs gripping my throat, I make haste toward the theater entrance. I barely make it out the gardens before regret rips through me and tears pour down my cheeks. None of this is their fault, yet I can't look at any of them. I'm barely able to breathe.

My final act of sacrifice brings me to an impossible end. Kill the man I once loved and lose everything for the same man who I now despise. It should be simple. And it would be, if this minister was a faceless man reminiscent of all the horrors we've endured. But he isn't. He's *James*.

The test on my soul is far more impossible than I could have ever imagined.

CHAPTER TWENTY-SIX

I once roasted a mouse over the fire to stay alive, and tonight the king's family begins their meal with four plates of soup and an entire pheasant, gluttonous bastards that they are. I hear the courtiers describe the king's private dinner in his antechamber and the dozens of servants who carry gold trays of food. I watched the king's chosen ones appear at his apartments at five before ten. Among them stood James Beaumont.

I pace the hallway that leads to the royal residence, willing myself not to destroy every metallic and stone statue and claw my way through every exotic rug. James Beaumont finally slithered his way into the king's circle. And he did it by ordering the torture and killing of innocent Huguenots.

James is petty and weak and awful, but he isn't a murderer. At least not the man I once held in my arms.

"I hear the Minister who ordered the Dragonnades arrived tonight." I turn to see Mademoiselle Boulais wearing a wicked smile. "You've ventured away from your laboratory. Have you come to watch the show?"

"Walk with me."

I stride next to her into the balmy summer night. We pass a crowd gathered below the king's balcony, hoping for a glimpse of the great Sun King before his bedtime ritual, as if he is some god and not merely a spoiled man in layers of silk.

"Why didn't you tell me the minister was James?" I ask.

"I wasn't certain. He changed his name once he earned his new title. He's washed away his previous association with a Daughter of the King turned Protestant resistor."

It's quite beneficial to know one of the king's mistresses. She doesn't care much for me, but she's taught Charlotte everything she knows about poisons and black magic. I don't need to be liked as long as I get what we need. "At my disposal, I have any number of potions and liquids to bleed James to death. I could slice his neck with a blade or crush his skull with one of the king's gilded statues. Or I could squeeze the air from his throat with my bare hands."

"So why are you out here telling me about it instead of planning his end?" she asks.

Her eyes are so open, so clear. Not a hint of doubt. "It seems too sad for this to be my end. I've known every side of him since I was seventeen. The good, the evil, and the downright terrifying."

"This is why I do not trust you, Madame." Boulais looks to the sky to feel the light breeze on her cheeks. "He may be your past, but the Minister has ordered the torture of your people. By killing him you will save thousands."

"Killing to me is not personal. It is immediate and necessary and should be avoided whenever possible. Otherwise, we'd all be swimming in bloodshed."

"Madame," she says with pity, "we already are."

· · ·

I meander the grounds aimlessly, needing the breeze to carry me away from this suffocating palace. The woods call to me, as if leaves whisper and limbs open their arms. But ten paces into the thicket I hear panting, grunting, and the occasional laugh. As my eyes focus, women appear along the ground, dotted like stones dropped from the sky. Some beckon, and others lie on their backs, legs open, skirts around their waists.

Men hop through the maze of trees, searching for their chosen prostitute. I turn back toward the palace grounds and knock into the duke. "Dammit. How did I not hear you?" Naira would tell me I've lost my purpose and question my place in the world. She's right.

"Are you looking for a little adventure in the woods?" He laughs, seemingly enjoying the thought.

"Don't be absurd." I push past him. "This place is a disgrace. The king has even turned nature into a den of debauchery."

"To be fair, the king has little to do with the prostitutes. It's the courtiers that pay them."

"Go find your adventure and leave me be."

He grabs my arm to stop me. "How do you walk so swiftly in that massive robe?"

I consider biting his hand.

"I followed you." He lifts his hand in surrender. "You spoke with Mademoiselle Boulais. Did she help you with a plan?"

"I don't need her help."

"You need something." I stomp back toward him with the intention of throwing him to the ground, but he doesn't move. He doesn't flinch or react. "Why are you hesitating?"

"I was once married to that man. Yes, he's horrible and deserves to die, but I don't want to be the person to decide his fate. I don't want to kill him."

"Even though he's ordered the Dragonnades?"

The desire to fight the duke melts from my core and I feel the odd sensation of wanting to cry again. "Why do you care? You can turn me into the king at any moment."

"Where is the fun in that? He plays a tune on his cheek with his fingertips. "I want to see how you'll navigate this particular debacle."

"I can't face my family. They'll wonder why I'm hesitating."

"I wonder that myself."

I rub my eyes to stop the tears. "If James wanted me arrested or killed, I'd already be dead. He's sent his troops on a wild chase for the mystical Red Fox, but he knows who I am. I could have killed him several times over the years, but I never did. We have an unspoken truce, and as ridiculous as it may seem, I'd be breaking an agreement."

"You will risk your life for any number of Protestants you've never met but you won't off the one man who endangers them?"

This suffocating robe feels like walking through mud. I yank at my neckline, finding it hard to breathe. "I didn't kill Louvois while I had the chance. I didn't kill you. When one becomes human to me, I simply can't take their life."

He flashes a mocking smile. "I think you are nothing more than a poet at heart."

"I don't know the first thing about poetry."

"Yes you do." He places his hand on my shoulder. "You see the world in emotions, and that is the very essence of art."

I don't swat his hand away. "I think I hate you."

"Of course you do, my pet. Now carry on to that delicious husband of yours. He's in his servant's quarters worried about you. I will do my very best to keep Lorraine occupied this evening. Oh, the sacrifices I make for you." He winks.

"How much time do I have before you hand me over to the king?"

He shrugs. "It sounds as if you'll be deciding that." As I walk away, he says, "You have two days to deal with the minister. His carriage will take him to The Louvre, where he plans to expand the successful Dragonnades program."

I don't look back. Two days to kill James and escape Versailles, while I execute the final step in my plan. I hadn't anticipated James Beaumont returning to my life or finding a gentle human inside the duke's frivolous exterior, yet here I am, committed to my purpose. As warriors do.

.   .   .

I watch Andre through the window before I knock. So handsome, so strong. All he wants is a quiet life in Geneva, yet he married a restless soul who's incapable of peace. Perhaps I seek destruction and chaos, unhappy unless my hands are busy with resistance.

He catches a glimpse of me and waves me inside.

Once inside the sculptor's apartment, I lean into Andre's chest and press my cheek to his beating heart. He wraps his arms around me and kisses my forehead, not a word of admonishment for my behavior earlier tonight.

Andre leads me to his servant's quarters. Small but comfortable, his room feels safe. "It's odd to be in a bedroom we don't share," I say. "Even more strange to be in Versailles with you as a servant."

"When I followed Louvois here, I had no intention of staying. But a man approached me as I was admiring a sculpture in the garden. He asked what I liked about it. Peasants are permitted to wander the gardens, so I simply said I was captivated by this sculpture. We discussed shape and form, and I pulled the wolf from my pocket. He quite liked my woodworking skills."

"You took the wolf from home?"

"No." His eyes widen. With a reluctant sigh, he removes a small carving. "I missed you so much, I made a new one."

His love knows no limits. Years I've been captivated by his smile, which only grows more handsome with smile lines curved around his mouth. "Who does Lorraine think you are?"

"He never asked. He offered me an apprenticeship if I work as his servant this summer. I'm allowed to experiment with wood and stone sculpting—when I'm not serving him wine."

I bite back a smile. "That's sweet."

"He's surprisingly kind. He tells me what he knows of the court. The only thing he loves more than art is gossip."

I turn to stare out the tiny window in the corner of the room. "I need you to understand. I don't care about James."

Andre walks up behind me. He kisses my neck soft and slow. "You are my Isabelle. I know you carry a heart so big it sometimes doesn't leave room for your brain to make decisions."

"But James has turned even more evil than I could ever have imagined. I can't accept he's strayed this far from the man I once knew."

His lips linger on my neck. "We all have allegiances that test our humanity."

"I must kill him tonight. Quietly and masterfully."

"Charlotte and Elizabeth are preparing their poisons. Perhaps we sneak some into his wine."

I turn face to face with him. Run my hand along his stubbled jaw. "We will not be doing this. I will."

"Why?"

A minister is highly guarded and the chances of escaping this are slim. I want my family long gone by the time I take the greatest risk of my life. "I need to know you and Elizabeth are safe."

He opens his mouth to protest, but I place my finger to his mouth. "Don't fight. Right now, I need your hands on my body. I need you to make me forget we're here in this palace. Press your naked body to mine and take me home for a short while."

Andre runs his lips down my neck and sternum, kissing the space between my breasts. He stares in my eyes as he removes my wig. I shake my hair free as if I've just escaped a prison cell. He unties my bodice and takes his time to remove the layers of fabric covering my body. The heat rises between us.

"Nowhere feels as safe is being in your arms," I say.

He removes his breeches and my shift so our warm bodies can press skin to skin. He runs his fingers along my spine as my back arches against his touch. He lifts me. My legs wrap around his hips, and I softly bite his neck. With a firm grip but a gentle tug, he pulls my hair in a controlled grip. The heat between my legs burns for him as tears leak from my eyes.

Andre knows me. He knows I need him to be strong right now. To let me cry and take my body to screams. He lays me down on the bed, his eyes locked on mine. He slides his hand up my thigh, the other still holding my hair so I can't look away from him. His fingers caress me in every place that makes me tremble. As I near a moan, he whispers. "I'll love you forever."

I need him now, so much my face twists into sobs. He presses inside me, moving my knee toward my chest to find just the right position. Slow at first, then harder until I'm begging for his touch all over my body. I want him forever but forever might be mere hours away. My tears drip off my cheek and onto his arm, but his gaze never wavers. With one final thrust, we both stifle screams, his hand still holding my hair, his eyes still held on mine.

Andre wipes my tears then kisses me softly. He pulls back to look at my body. "You are more than beauty, Isabelle. You are fire."

"But every fire eventually burns out."

He tilts his head to examine my expression. "What aren't you telling me?"

I don't have the words, so I don't speak. Andre lies next to me and rubs my arm, poorly hiding the concern in his knitted brows.

"Do you ever think of death, Andre?"

"All the time."

"You do?"

"Yes." He lies on his back, hands behind his head. "I ask God to take me first so I'm not alone in this life without you."

Guilt rips its way through me. Life without him would be torture.

He turns to me and rests his finger under my chin. "This must be our last trip to France. After we take care of James and Louvois, we return to Geneva and run the resistance through home."

"That sounds like an order."

"I would never demand you do as I wish." He swallows as if with difficulty. "I just hope that after this, you might want it too."

To live forever safely in a land of snow and secrets, Andre and Elizabeth at my side. It's a lovely dream. I smile until he relaxes. My fate is here at Versailles, and my end will arrive right here, in the king's palace.

CHAPTER TWENTY-SEVEN

I spend a hot, restless night in Andre's arms, taking in every curve of his body and kissing him while he sleeps. As we lie together in the warm yellow bath of morning sunlight, the door flies open. We cover ourselves and sit up.

"Today is the day, my loves!"

"Duke." I growl, ready to shove him out of the room, until I remember I'm naked. "Get out."

"Yes, of course. How rude of me to enter your bedchamber." He glances at Andre's bare chest. "Oh my. Well done, Isabelle."

Andre laughs but I want to kick the duke in his shins.

"I simply came to tell you what an exciting day we have planned."

I ball my fists. "Get on with it."

"Today is a reception. The king has announced Versailles will become the capital of the kingdom. And he intends to celebrate."

"Another party?" Andre asks.

"Not simply a party." He spreads his fingers wide and swipes the shape of an arc. "An extravaganza."

"This will only make our work more difficult," I say. "More people, more guards. Nothing is secret here."

The duke smiles. "Exactly. The game just became much more interesting."

. . .

Back in the duke's apartment, we stand over a map of the palace. Charlotte held watch over Elizabeth in the servant's room all night yet still looks fresh and focused. We've agreed to keep her close to avoid any unwanted consequences.

"Where can I kill Louvois?" Charlotte asks.

The duke raises his eyebrows. He almost laughs until he notices Charlotte's gaze. He points to the west side of the palace on the map. "Here."

"I'm ready now. Let me at him."

I hold her arm. "Wait. Louvois has servants and guards, and there are thousands of people here to celebrate. You'll not survive if we don't think this through."

"I don't care. Let me die."

I exchange glances with Andre. Charlotte's intensity now borders on erratic and there's little I can do to contain her. All I say is, "Clémentine." She flinches but regains her focus.

Andre places his hands on the table. "We need to work together, or we'll all be arrested. Do you hear me, Charlotte?"

She sniffs but nods her head yes.

"The killings must take place at the same time," Andre says. "Before they discover one and stop the other. Can we get them alone?"

The duke peers over Andre's shoulder. "The king's schedule is timed down to the minute. Right now, his bedchamber is packed with dozens of chosen courtiers watching him be washed, combed, and shaved. He'll then have his getting dressed ceremony and at ten sharp he'll pass through the gallery to be admired. Off to the Royal Chapel for mass. He'll expect both men to be in attendance. Then council will commence back in his chamber where I presume he'll be discussing The Dragonnades."

"Get me inside," I say.

"To where, his chamber? You must be mad. It's only for his ministers and chosen servants. Men only."

"Then make me a man. Charlotte, you may not kill Louvois until I hear what the council has planned. Promise me."

"Fine. I'll search for some drunk Catholic I can strangle. It won't be the same."

Elizabeth's eyes light up. "You, a wanted Protestant resistance fighter, are going to break into the king's private council where the man who branded you and your previous husband plots the demise of your people."

"Yes."

The duke smiles. "Let the games begin."

. . .

Multiple risks teeter on the unknown. One hesitation or one wrong move, and our resistance will be no longer. Versailles, where the king notices every stitch out of place, is the worst location for taking risks, but we have no choice.

Andre convinced the sculptor to request presence at the council. Working his view of self- importance, he suggested that his new ideas for garden sculptures be discussed to celebrate the king's move to Versailles. Lorraine loved this idea and insisted he would take the ministers to view the gardens and discuss his plans.

Outside the Royal Apartment, I count servants and track movements in and out. Several antechambers surround us. The king's council will meet in his study, surrounded by guards and servants. "It isn't possible," I say.

Charlotte reaches into her pocket and pulls out a glove and glass vial. "My turn now?"

"Very well."

We count ten servants in and nine servants out. Charlotte pours a clear liquid into the palm of her thick glove, turning her head to breathe. The tenth man steps through the doorway as I pretend to see someone I know. I push past him as he follows me back inside the antechamber.

"You can't be here, Madame." He grabs my arm. "Women belong downstairs."

"Isn't that the great sculptor Lorraine? I must see him."

"Get out before I have you punished."

Charlotte comes up behind him and wraps her gloved hand over his nose and mouth. He struggles, not prepared to be poisoned by two ladies of the court. He drops to the ground in a heap.

"Please tell me you didn't kill him," I say.

"No, he's just in for a very long sleep." Charlotte drags his feet into the closest quiet room. I disrobe with her help. "I wish I could walk through Versailles in my shift," I say. "It would be far more comfortable."

"No one wants comfort here. Hurry."

I do my best to don the servant's attire which is damp and smells of onion. "It's a bit large for me but I'll make it work."

"Go. I'll find somewhere to dump him."

"A naked man asleep on the floor of the king's private apartment. That won't cause any alarm, I'm sure." I reach to lift my skirts then smile, remembering I'm wearing breeches. The wig is stifling hot, but the shoes are quite easy to walk in. Everything is easier as a man.

I keep my head down and move through the apartments, avoiding anyone who might notice something amiss. No one looks at me. These poor servants aren't even visible to the nobility unless they want something. I make my way to the gallery, near the best view of the gardens. Nerves rattle through my body, knowing it's only a matter of time until someone finds the naked man.

I stand tall near a doorway, as I've seen them do. Hat low on my forehead to shade my face serves a double purpose. The hot sun beats on my skin as the seconds pulse on like a thumping heartbeat. Horse hooves clop below, while hundreds mill about. The view is expansive. I don't like feeling exposed. Here there are no trees to protect me, no nature to hide behind. No, there is only unnecessary opulence fit for the king of France.

The doors open. Two guards step into the bright midday sun. I stare ahead, ignoring the bead of sweat trailing down my temple. Lorraine arrives and overlooks the grounds. Behind him, twenty ministers and their servants yawn and sigh, but finally the king steps forward. I can tell by his stench. I remember it well from years ago. His sweating problem seems only to have worsened with age.

From the corner of my eye, I spot James. My stomach tightens and I clench my teeth together. He's mere steps from me, the man who both protects me and murders my people. I could break his neck right here and be done with it. But the duke won't get his reward and I won't ensure my family's safety. So I stand stoically while good and evil tussle in my belly. I can't be certain which will win.

"I envision gold and marble, sculpted to the Sun King's likeness. They will be enormous and detailed, each one depicting His Majesty's power and grace." Lorraine bows his head to allow the king to envision the garden full of statues, where at every turn the monarch's face will remind peasants and nobles alike, they are nothing in the shadow of the great Sun King. I withhold a snarl.

"Go on," says the king.

As Lorraine showers His Majesty in ideas, I keep my eyes on James. He taps his foot and loosens his cravat. Why so nervous, James? Can you sense your first wife nearby? She nearly killed you twice. Perhaps on the third time, she'll succeed.

James steps up, impatient. "We have much planning to do, Monsieur Lorraine."

"Ah. You are the man in charge of the Dragonnades, yes?"

James nods.

"Quite an endeavor."

"I answer the call to ensure His Majesty's safety."

Lorraine scratches at his skinny beard. "I've heard things, monsieur. Unruly dragoons with no direction. That makes for a dangerous situation."

"It's the Huguenots who are unruly, monsieur." James puffs his chest. "Why don't you stick to stone and metals and let the experienced soldiers handle the serious matters. Our military missionaries have converted entire villages. Every Frenchman will be part of the Catholic Church and it will be because of me."

Lorraine smiles as he twirls his chin hair between his first and second fingers. "And what will your *missionaries* do next? Retreat?"

"Certainly not!" James's face reddens. After all this time, he hasn't learned to control his temper. "Next, we move to the villages around Tours. We've doubled our soldiers and authorized them to use any means necessary to force conversion."

I can't stop myself. I close my eyes to bite back the disgust that threatens to break me.

Lorraine paces, seemingly taunting James. "The resistance has been unexpected, yes? I hear there is a dangerous woman who gives you trouble. The Red Fox, is it?"

"She is nothing. A myth fabricated by lower military personnel to excuse their failed missions."

"She is not a myth," Lorraine says. He steps away so the king will not hear. "What if I told you the resistance has arrived here, at Versailles?"

I don't move one muscle in my body.

"I'd say you're mad," James says. "I would know if we were under threat."

"I'd suggest you keep your wits about you, monsieur. Danger is everywhere."

The king turns to his ministers. "This garden will be a splendor of art and design. Thank you, Monsieur Lorraine, for sharing your vision with us. Now, we must return to my study for matters of state."

The king and his attendants return to his apartment but James lags behind. He grabs Lorraine's arm. "What is wrong with you?"

"I am simply the king's sculptor, monsieur. But I do listen carefully. Something I suggest you do as well." He flicks James's hand away and carries on into the palace.

James hesitates and nearly catches my eye, but I stare straight ahead, hoping my wig hides the shape of my face. He mumbles to himself, words I can't make out. Then he stands tall and shakes his head. "Stupid woman. Go back to Geneva where you are safe."

My breath catches. I think he's speaking to me, but I realize his thoughts have tumbled from his mouth without a care who hears them.

"I can't protect her forever," he growls. Then he directs himself. "Get to work, minister."

As James strides with purpose back into the apartments, I think of his fragile morality, his weakness and desperation. But I also think of his loyalty. He's protecting me, finding goodness where he can because the rest of his life demands outrageous evils.

When I'm certain no one is watching, I make my way through the apartments and back to the hallway where Charlotte points me to a servant's quarters near another apartment. On the floor lies a woman in royal servant dress, her head on a pillow.

"Must you keep poisoning people?"

Charlotte produces my robe. "She'll wake soon enough with only a headache and mild confusion. Until then, she will enjoy a lovely break from her royal duties."

I change back into the heavy, stifling dress that makes me lightheaded. "Where is the man we took clothes from?"

"I stuffed him in an empty bed with a jug of wine nearby. They will think he drank himself to sleep."

"Charlotte, we must get word to Tours. The dragoons are headed there next, and they've doubled in numbers."

"Tonight, we'll finish off Louvois and the minister. Tomorrow, we travel to Tours."

I nod, unsure if I'll make it to tomorrow.

CHAPTER TWENTY-EIGHT

For hours the palace has been in celebration with horse races, theaters, and a parade through the Great Lawn, while I've been lurking in the crowds, watching James, reminding myself of all the Protestants I'll save. To rescue thousands, I must kill one.

Charlotte practically salivates, waiting for me to approve the moment she may slice through Louvois.

The duke returns to his apartment, his face flushed and his belly full of drink. "Can't you all enjoy a celebration? Besides the blinding sun, it's joyous outside."

We ignore him and carry on with our plans. Andre describes the stables and the horses he will lead to the woods outside the palace. Elizabeth presents masks for us to wear, pilfered from a family who had an extra dozen made so they will enjoy choices at the king's grand celebration. The longer I'm at Versailles, the sicker the wealth makes me. "They won't miss them," Elizabeth says. "I watched the servants carry in trunks for hours."

"The servants will be wearing costumes tonight." I sigh with relief. "I'll get to wear breeches instead of the robe I can barely stand in."

The duke wakes himself with a loud snore. "The ballet." We turn to stare at him, assuming he's acting out a drunken dream. "The king will perform a ballet in the gardens after nightfall. Do it there, in the crowd, so no one will notice. Wait for a moment of applause."

Andre nods. "Even drunk he's helpful."

Charlotte will track Louvois, I'll track James, and Elizabeth will signal from the balcony when I indicate. Andre will gather our horses at the end of the palace grounds near Place d'Armes and we'll ride south toward Tours to clear the villages.

"The sun is lowering in the sky. Everyone to their posts." I nudge the duke to wake. He snorts then comes alive. "Yes, I'm ready."

"How will you present me to the king if you are asleep in a champagne haze?" I whisper.

He smiles and licks his dry lips. "You will try to run, I know you will."

"Is that why you told Lorraine the Red Fox is here? Spreading word so someone will catch me?"

"You don't miss anything, do you Isabelle?"

"No." I help him stand. "At least you no longer call me your pet."

"You are a sly, wily little thing. I do enjoy watching you hunt."

"Get your rest, Duke Tremblay. We are in for one wild night."

Andre winks at me from the doorway, his smile still able to send my stomach tumbling in circles. I don't tell him what Lorraine knows. No unnecessary complications. This will all be over in a few hours. I retreat to the servant's room to change into my costume. I love the freedom of breeches and sensible shoes.

"What are you planning?" Elizabeth leans against the doorway, mask in hand.

"We've spent the day discussing it. I think you know."

She steps forward, twirling her gold and blue eye covering. "With the duke. At first, I assumed he was our way into Versailles. Now, you still keep him close, and I can't understand why. You're hiding something."

"Cricket, you've grown up to be such a smart, capable woman."

She crosses her arms. "You're ignoring my question."

I run my fingers along her jaw. "Naira and your mother would be so proud." Pressure builds behind my eyes, but I withhold tears with a deep breath.

"Don't do it," she says. "Whatever's making you weepy right now is a bad idea."

Little does she know, my mind is already made up. I lift her mask to her beautiful face. "We'll talk about this later. Right now, it's time for a party."

.　.　.

Thousands of torches and lanterns light the grounds of Versailles and reflect off the Round Pool like starlight. Such beauty and grandeur for such selfish people. While most in Paris struggle for bread, these royals feast on the delights of the world, surrounded by exotic animals, beaded costumes, and champagne fountains. They laugh and dance with no idea a deadly group of resistors walks among them.

As the ballet commences, I check my face mask is secure and tuck my hair under my hat. I enjoy the freedom of breeches, and no corset to restrict breathing. From the gardens I can see Charlotte wait at the exit, searching for Louvois to appear. Above her, Elizabeth watches from the balcony, fanning her neck in the hot, sticky night.

James stands prominently in the front row, clapping as the king dances in a gold mask to violins and flutes, accompanied by prancing animals. I watch his uneasiness. He scans the crowd, as if he can sense he's being watched. Aged, his hair has silver streaks and his cheeks have thinned. He still shifts off his painful hip, rubbing his thigh, and he still desires every eye in the room on him.

I clench my eyes shut and beg Naira to speak to me. How can I kill a man I once loved? Even if he has turned dark, I know the pain he's lived through. I don't see a target. I see a broken man who's let the devil guide his choices.

I can't hear the whistle of wind above the horse's whinnies and the bear's growl. A servant elbows me "Don't just stand there," he says. "Work."

I nod. Hand behind my back, I offer refreshments to every noble in the front row. Most hardly notice me, taken with the king's footwork and a jewel-covered elephant. I stand in front of James with my tray, hoping to see a monster.

He pauses. He tilts his head and stares into my eyes with familiarity. The crowd erupts in laughter around us, but we stay locked in this moment together. Him trying to place me, and me trying to forget my memories. He opens his mouth to say something, but I duck behind a lady's servant with a pearl mask and giant flowing skirt. From behind the tree, I see Elizabeth clap above her head, a signal that Louvois is in striking distance for Charlotte. Behind me, I can make out Andre's outline, holding the reins of multiple horses near the gate.

James stands. He pushes his way through the crowd, searching for the familiar eyes. I blend in, hidden in a sea of theatrics. The duke watches me from the edge of the crowd, waiting for me to attack James. Elizabeth holds her hand up, looking over the balcony to her left. She forms a fist.

Charlotte has made a move.

I duck behind the trees as James follows me, the duke close behind. Above the grand palace, a blast of fireworks startles us all. Loud blasts light up the sky in red and yellow, with gold rain flitting onto the treetops. I lead the men to the garden maze and duck behind a bronze statue. James patters past me, getting lost in the maze of perfectly shaped greenery.

More blasts light the sky, thumping my heart with every noise. The duke chases after James, and presumably out to follow me, when I run out of the maze the way I came. Through the trees quicker than ever thanks to these clothes, I follow the direction of grunts.

Charlotte has knocked Louvois to the ground, dragging his body with one hand, her other covering his mouth. He can't kick with his twisted leg, so he screams into Charlotte's hand then bites her fingers. She doesn't let go, and his bite only enrages her.

"Your disgusting teeth do nothing to intimidate me. I gladly bleed for my people. She wraps fabric around his mouth and ties it behind his head. He struggles to lean against a tree and stares at us both. I remove my mask and Charlotte throws hers to the ground. Louvois will register our faces soon enough.

He laughs through his gag.

"I let you free once before," I say. "That was my doing. But tonight, right here, you have another price to pay. At the hands of a far more formidable opponent than I."

Charlotte kicks him in the chest. When he recovers his breath, she sneers at him. "You've damaged so many people in your life. You probably don't remember most of them, do you?"

I can barely see the balcony through the trees, and Elizbeth isn't at her post. "Charlotte, hurry."

Teeth bared, Charlotte growls at Louvois. "Do you remember my husband?"

Louvois does not respond.

"He was strong and determined. And he loved me despite what you did to my family." I touch her arm lightly, but she shoves me away. "Tonight, I will take your life. And I will do it for Henri." We exchange glances in a moment of silent remembrance for her husband and my best friend. She swallows tears. "Where is James's body?"

I turn my gaze to Louvois, unable to meet her eyes.

"You didn't do it. This isn't just about James, is it?" she asks. "What's happened to you? You've turned weak."

"Kill him. Now."

Charlotte has difficulty breathing and her eyes gloss over as if she can only see blackness. She raises her hands toward his neck, her fingers trembling. As her fingernails claw toward his skin, a knife flies between us. The blade lands in Louvois's face, lodged in his eye. He bleeds and twitches, then stops moving.

We turn to find Elizabeth steely and focused. "Time to go."

Charlotte shakes Louvois but his head rolls sideways as his trunk slides to the dirt. "Elizabeth, how could you take this from me?"

"We have no time, Aunt Charlotte. You hesitated."

"This was my last kill. He was meant to be my final revenge for Henri, and you ruined that for me." Tears streak down her face.

"I'm sorry. I was just trying to help."

"Come along, Cricket. We must go." Elizabeth steps behind me, afraid of Charlotte's wild eyes.

Charlotte steadies her heel on Louvois's chest and yanks the blade from his eye with a pop. "Charlotte, what are you doing?" I ask.

She walks past me and wipes the blood from the blade on her sleeve. "They all must die." I reach for her, but she punches me in the face. I'm so stunned, I simply watch her walk from the trees, blood smeared on her cheek and robe. She grabs the first noble she sees, turns his back to her and slashes his neck left to right as his wife watches blood gush from his neck.

She turns to face the king on stage, her blade pointed to the ground going drip drip drip with the blood of two men in two minutes. Screams take over the crowd. All eyes turn to Charlotte, who falls to her knees.

"No, Charlotte," I whisper.

Through tears, she yells, "I am The Red Fox."

Elizabeth's hand grasped in mine, we run through the trees toward the stables. Hot wind against our faces, screams rippling through the audience, we don't look back.

"What just happened?" she asks.

"Charlotte needs a kill, and she took one. My guess is she'll probably take another."

She crashes, breathless, into Andre. "I killed Louvois then Charlotte killed a man, then she said she was the Red Fox."

"Did you finish our targets?" he asks me.

"She let James free," Elizabeth says.

"Ah." Andre doesn't seem surprised. "Leave Charlotte. We must go." He grabs our arms.

"No." I pull back. "You and Elizabeth go. I won't leave her alone."

Elizabeth loops her arm through mine. "I want to stay too."

"You'll be discovered and thrown in prison with her, Cricket. I'm your father and I demand you get on this horse now."

"But, Papa—"

"Now." He points to the horse, and she responds by stomping over to meet him. "Isabelle, please come with us. Charlotte has made her choices."

"Has she?" I meet his gaze. "She didn't choose to lose Henri. She didn't ask to avenge his death. She never asked for any of this."

Andre wraps his strong arms around me. "You couldn't kill James. I understand. But it's time to leave before we're all locked in here. To Tours, back to our battle, and back to Geneva where you're both safe. You promised me." His voice shakes. He knows what will happen tonight. He's probably known this entire time.

I kiss his cheek and run my fingers through his hair. "You are everything, Andre Boucher. Everything I've ever needed."

He pulls me in for a gentle kiss, his knuckles grazing my cheekbone. "Choose me."

"What?"

"Between loving me and giving yourself to the resistance, I want you to choose me." He slides his hand from my face and steps back. "I'll wait for you in Paris. In the garden to the Louvre, where this adventure began before you were mine."

"I have always been yours, Andre."

He mounts a horse and motions for Elizabeth to follow. As they gallop toward the gates, guards gather and yell. "No one in or out. Lock the gates!"

Elizabeth looks back at me over her shoulder. I nod to encourage her to go on. They lead their horses with furious speed toward the gates as the men work to close them. At the grand entrance to Versailles, Andre slips through. At the same time, Elizabeth rolls off her horse before it runs wild into the black night.

I run to her, worried she's broken a bone with that fall, but she pops up as I approach. "Aunt Charlotte taught me how to dismount a horse in a hurry."

The gates lock shut. Andre looks at us through the gold and iron railings. Even in the dark I can sense his disappointment. "I love you, Andre. Run."

Elizabeth catches her breath. "What now?"

"What were you thinking, Cricket!" I hold her arms in my tightened fists. "You were meant to flee with your father, out there beyond the gates, where none of this horrible night will change you. You should be safe."

"I know you're angry."

"Angry? No, I'm beyond angry." I drop my arms and turn to walk away. "I'm devastated."

"I told you, I won't retreat. I'm in this with both of you and whether you realize it or not, you need me."

I shove her forward, away from the guards who closed the gate. "What if you die, Elizabeth? What if we all die and your father is left with nothing? Have you thought about that?"

"Have you?"

I can't stop to scream at her. I'm too angry and too frightened of the guards milling about. "I don't owe you an explanation of my choices."

"No, you don't." She steps in front of me. "I'm here now. You can't shake me away like a bug. Naira told me to push you and that is what I'm doing. Now tell me where Aunt Charlotte is and why she did all that tonight?"

I want to shake her. Scream at her that she's ruined my plans. I'm meant to die alone in a standoff with my soul and I can't do that with my daughter's big, beautiful eyes on me. We don't get what we want, so I force myself into acceptance. "Charlotte let herself be taken to get closer to her next target."

We duck behind the dark shadow of a nearby tree. "And who is that?" she asks.

"Knowing her—the king."

CHAPTER TWENTY-NINE

The palace sounds like a hive of frantic bees. Women shriek and men gossip, with many believing Charlotte was part of the ballet. NO one would put it past the king to perform a murder in the middle of a grand celebration.

We sit across from the duke, waiting for him to reveal secrets. "The king is safe in his apartment," he says. "But he's ordered the guards to escort her to the Bastille."

"Not that horrid place again." I rub my eyes. "I've already broken in there once. I don't care to revisit."

"Where is she now?" Elizabeth asks.

"Locked in a guarded room. They'll take her in the morning. Once the minister determines how he'd like to deal with the unruly Protestant."

Elizabeth's expectant eyes bore a hole straight through me. "How do we save her, Isabelle?"

"We'll have to break her out." I trace my finger along the gold rim of a vase. "James won't kill Charlotte."

"How many times will you make excuses for him?" Fists tight, her arms shake. "He kills Protestants for entertainment."

"I don't expect you to understand, Cricket." I turn from her and stare at my reflection in the candlelit window. "We all share a strange, twisted past."

"No." Her chest heaves up and down. "Don't treat me like a child."

"One day, when you're my age, you will understand how your choices, though justified, leave scars on your soul."

"*Now* you grow a conscience? You watched my Papa never love my mother because of you. You married a Catholic soldier and broke everyone's hearts so you could steal secrets. You poisoned your husband knowing he could die."

"That's enough." I turn to face her. The duke watches us, his eyes wide and jaw slacked. "I was young and foolish. I didn't understand love or sacrifice. All I knew was terror. Something you've been protected from."

Elizabeth's eyes well with tears. "And we've all made you happy. I stayed home when all I wanted to do was fight, and Papa lets you crush his spirits by going on these adventures, knowing you may never return home." She steps closer, her shoulders tight toward her ears. "Aunt Charlotte needs us. Your loyalty is with her, not the king's evil minister you once pretended to love."

She lifts both hands to shove my shoulders, but I duck, slip behind her, and wrap my arms around hers in a tight hug. "Stop," I whisper.

"No." She wiggles and bucks but I only pull her tighter against me.

"We're never enough for you." Her arms drop and she begins to cry. "If Charlotte dies, it's on your soul."

"She won't die."

"James Beaumont orders thousands of Huguenots to torture and death. How could you still trust him?"

I lean my cheek to hers, swallowing against the lump in my throat. "Despite all the horrible things I've seen, I still believe in kindness."

"But we kill people." her breath hitches, trying to calm her sobs.

"No, we defend the right to live. You must learn the difference."

She collapses in my arms. Buries her face in my neck. "You were going to die to save us all. You were willing to leave me and Papa."

I wipe her damp cheeks. "All the killings need to end. All the horror. If I made the final move to kill a highly guarded minister, I wouldn't make it out alive."

Charlotte looks at the duke. "You're going to hand Isabelle over to the king after she kills the men in charge of the Dragonnades, aren't you."

"How did you know?" he asks.

"I listen," she says, "to the sound of the whispers of the world I know." Naira still lives inside us. She always will. "So many secrets." She pulls away from me. "I want you to fight for us. I will kill James so you can come home to Geneva where you belong."

For the first time in many years, I question my purpose. To kill and sacrifice myself to a larger cause no longer seems simple. What will that teach Elizabeth? That life is not precious, and people can't change. That hate wins. If Huguenots survive but her soul turns dark, I can't live with that.

Saving one heart versus saving a thousand bodies. This is why I offered myself, so she never had to make that choice. "You won't kill James."

"Then who will? Because we can't leave here and allow the Dragonnades to continue."

The duke glugs from a wine jug. "They think Charlotte's the Red Fox. They'll make a statement with her."

I kiss Elizabeth's temple and wipe her dark hair from her eyes. "Everything you've learned now gets put to the test. Can you listen and trust me?"

"Only if you promise to fight for us." She looks at the duke as he drains the wine and paces the room. "Don't let him take you."

"I promise. I'll fight."

She nods. "Just look at him. The poor man wants to bring music and poetry to Paris but must betray all of us to get it."

"Did Naira speak those secrets to you?"

"No, I heard you and the duke discussing it. I've been listening closely to everything everyone says."

"Good. We'll need those skills. You take the duke to the ballroom and find out where Charlotte is."

"What are you going to do?"

"I'm going to have a word with my ex-husband. I'll either discover he isn't evil and wants a way out, or he'll reveal himself to be the monster you claim he is. And then I will kill him. Either way, we'll rescue Charlotte from Versailles and meet your father at the Louvre by sunup."

"Isabelle." Elizabeth straightens her shoulders. "I'm sorry."

"Don't be." I hold her hand. "Don't ever lose that passion. It will guide you on the right path." Our disagreements no longer matter. I'm in my last hours and Elizabeth is by my side.

Elizabeth walks to the duke. "Are you ready to find my Aunt Charlotte?"

"This certainly has been the most exciting event I've ever attended at the palace." He taps his heels together. "Shall we?"

Elizabeth motions for him to open the door. "If you make one wrong move, I'll slice through your abdomen. Not deep enough to kill you, but enough that you will bleed slowly and painfully over hours until your insides vomit out your mouth."

He nods. "I better not make a wrong move then."

"Glad we're in agreement."

. . .

James's apartment is lavish and grand, just as he's always wanted. I sit on his bed, mask on, waiting for his return, and remembering the day he arrived at the abbey in Quebec. The day I chose loyalty over love.

The door opens and James steps inside. He doesn't see me at first, but unties his cravat, revealing red blotchy skin on his neck. Nothing out of the ordinary for this royal minister, until he catches the reflection on the window of the masked servant on his bed.

He turns slowly, seemingly unafraid. "Is it really you?"

I don't respond, partly because I'm afraid to speak to him, and in part because I need to gauge his demeanor.

He steps forward, aged but still handsome. A slight limp disrupts his walk from his injured hip that has healed over time. "Don't be frightened," he says. "I won't hurt you."

"I know." I stand to face him. "I can't say the same."

James removes my mask and hat. He stares at me until he can no longer stand the view. He closes his eyes and turns from me. "Why are you here?"

"So many reasons."

"They'll kill Charlotte. They're convinced she's The Red Fox."

"But you know better."

"I've always known it was you. The red hair, the fight. The Protestant who doesn't know how to concede defeat."

"You know I live in Geneva. You know the trails I travel. If you wanted me dead, I already would be."

"How could I kill the woman I'll always love?" He reaches for my hair but I pull away. "Was there ever a part of you that wanted to love me back, or was it simply easy to use me while still in love with another man?"

How long has he carried this anger?

I shake out my hair. "You may not believe this, but I loved you as much as I was capable. You were always meant for this life, James. Versailles, the royal court, a post in the king's circle. This is who you are. I should never have expected anything different."

"We could have had this life together, you and me. Wealth, status, comfort. But you were unwilling to give up your heretic ways."

"I can no more give up being Protestant than I could cut off my own hands. You can't remove something that's part of your soul."

"That's the problem with all you people." He slams his hand to the wall. "Just step in line and do as we ask, and you'll be free. Why can't you do it?"

"There is no life without freedom, James."

"You converted. You became a Daughter of the King and married a Catholic soldier. Don't tell me you didn't have freedom."

"Don't you see? I made that choice because I was afraid and lonely and threatened with punishment. Desperation makes people do things that don't sit right with their heart. Every time we sat in church, or I tried to pray, I was nothing more than a Protestant wearing a Catholic cloak. It wasn't part of me, it was fabric that covered me and kept me from breathing. Is that really how you wanted me?"

"I simply wanted you near me. I wanted to love you. Since the day you bumped into me in La Rochelle, I've wanted you. I still do, even though you hurt me over and over again. I will always want you."

How I want to tear out of this palace and never look back. I think of Andre's arms, his soft touch. The way he loves me. "You kill and torture my people. You wouldn't do that if you loved me."

"I'm following the king's orders, but I make sure you and your little gang of resistors stay safe. I do nothing to hurt you."

"If you help hurt my people, it's the same as taking a blade to my chest."

He drinks more wine and wipes his nose. His eyes swell with redness as he looks away from me. "You live with Andre in Geneva and run the resistance. Are you happy?"

"Do you want me to be happy?"

"Sometimes, yes. Others, no, I want you to hurt like I hurt. You broke our marriage contract, Isabelle. You used me for information. And yet, I still can't bear the idea of a world where you aren't out there somewhere."

He wants to chase me. To believe I will still return his love someday.

"At the moment, I hate you," he says. "It's a short trip from love to hate, and I travel back and forth on this matter daily."

"You had Antoinette. You were perfect for each other. She wanted this life as much as you."

"Don't you see?" He turns to me, his hands near my face. "You're the only one that ever wanted *me*." He hits his fist on his chest. "Not my money, not my status, not my name. I bed so many women at court and none of them ever make my body feel the way you did when you touched me. When you looked at me."

I won't entertain his delusions. "You understand I came here to kill the minister and stop the Dragonnades? I'm here to murder you."

"But here you stand, looking into my eyes, knowing you won't hurt me."

"Take me to Charlotte, and I'll let you live."

He digs his knuckles into his hip, rubbing in a circle. "You won't save her. She's under guard watch."

I gesture around the room. "So were you."

He realizes he's rubbing his weak hip. "I don't want any of this, Isabelle. I simply relay orders from the king to military personnel. It was never meant to get this far."

He's ignoring me. A familiar tightness ripples through my body as I remember the voiceless liar I was with him. I only knew how to manipulate and control. We brought out the very worst in each other in some dark battle of wills. "You aren't answering me."

"You know I can't save Charlotte. They think she's The Red Fox."

He can help me, but he chooses not to. I search his face. The coward still rules inside him. He'll prolong Charlotte's capture to keep me close. "All the Huguenots stabbed and burned. I fall asleep to the sounds of bones breaking and images of bloodshed." I grab his shirt and ball the linen in my fists.

His eyes gaze down my neck. I assume he wants to bite me.

"We lost Henri, and my daughter thinks I'm a traitor because I don't want to kill you." I shove him away. "Why can't I hate you?"

"We have a twisted relationship, Isabelle. We admire each other. We need the other to remain alive and hunted."

Our bodies this close does something to me. What used to drive me to attraction now turns my stomach. The heat of anger no longer excites me. It simply makes me sad. "I need nothing of the sort. You're sick." I approach the window, not entirely sure where I will go as the grounds are crawling with guards.

"They're going for resistors now. They haven't discovered the trail, but when they do, you and your family and every person who has helped will be dead. I won't be able to protect you."

"You keep saying *they*. As if you aren't the king's minister in charge of the Dragonnades. You are doing this."

"I don't want this. I want to return to an easy life in Paris where I trade favors and money. I'll never be an honest man, Isabelle, but I don't want to live hunting you."

"We killed Louvois. You were next."

"If you wanted me dead, I already would be."

"Keep your eyes open, James. You never know when the resistance will take you in their grasp." I jump out the window and crawl along the dark edges of the palace, ready to do anything to save Charlotte.

CHAPTER THIRTY

The palace is alive with news of The Red Fox. I return to the duke's apartment to find Elizabeth teaching him how to break an opponent's nose.

"I do love the thrill of fighting," the duke says. "Though I will faint at the sight of blood."

I remove my mask. "That does limit your effectiveness."

"Did you see the minister? What happened?" Elizabeth's face turns serious, waiting for my update.

"Yes, I saw him."

"I can tell from your voice he's still alive." Disappointed as she may be, I feel no guilt.

"Cricket, please." I shake out my hair and scratch my scalp.

"No. We had a plan. That man has ordered the murder of thousands of Huguenots. I don't care that you once called him your husband. If you don't kill him, I will."

"We are here because you were caught. You escape on your own over and over while I risk everything to rescue you."

She throws her hands up. "No one can live up to your expectations, Isabelle. Not me or Charlotte, not even Father, but we're out here trying to prove ourselves to you. James deserves to die, and I can't understand how you could be so selfish."

The duke steps between us. "I see we have a family situation happening here. I don't understand such things. My parents never speak to me. I'm not certain they know I still live with them." He shrugs. "Can we rescue Charlotte and leave the minister alone?"

"He'll continue the Dragonnades, Edward." Elizabeth rubs her temples. "This is our chance to save thousands."

"Yes, but if you kill him, the king will find a new minister, Isabelle will spend the rest of her life saddled with guilt, and the killings will continue. I agree with her, Elizabeth. This is very complicated."

I never expected the Catholic duke we rescued drunk from a tavern would understand me more than my family would.

"I don't care what you think." She crosses her arms and suddenly, she's a child again. She storms off to the bedroom and slams the door.

"I'm very grateful to not have children," the duke says.

"She's just confused. It's an overwhelming life we live."

"Charlotte is being kept in the attic of the Grand Commun. The clergy prays over her while guards question her."

"I wouldn't worry about her. Catholic prayers will only strengthen her resolve. What is the Grand Commun?"

"Still being built, it's meant to house the kitchens and servants. It's empty and not yet complete, making it an ideal place to guard her away from the eyes of the court."

I pace the room. "None of this is ideal."

Once again, his fingers play a tune near his cheek that only he can hear. "I can't tell you how exciting it is to watch this unfold. You must rescue Charlotte from a building not yet complete, prevent her from killing the king, and bypass dozens of guards who all want her dead."

"You'll forgive me if I don't share your enthusiasm." I may die in the next few hours, but I'll go out in a fight until my last breath. "Where did Charlotte store her poisons?"

"In her skirt." Elizabeth appears in the doorway, eyes red and glassy. "But I kept one vial. It's arsenic and alcohol."

"I need you to help poison the guards. Can you do that?"

"I've been ready for years."

. . .

The view from the south wing rooftop affords us a sweeping look at the Grand Commun. The square building is crawling with guards. Brick walls open to the sky, where open chambers are stacked like a maze and men mill about like ants inside.

"The top floor has no roof," I say. "We can clearly see she isn't there. The first floor has tall ceilings and is most likely already being used as apartments. She's on the second or third floor, in the corner where guards can watch her from two sides."

"You can see all that from here?" Elizabeth squints through the darkness.

"We've been captured more times than I care to remember. All guards strategize the same and aren't witty enough to think like their opponent."

"The duke has organized a celebration in the Ballroom Grove. Those fools will join anyone for a party."

I pat my ankle where knives are nestled in my boots. With a bag of poison tucked in my pocket and nails hammered through the toes of my boots, I close my eyes to prepare for the fight of my life.

"Isabelle, you've never looked nervous."

"I've never been at Versailles."

"This ridiculous palace is no different than the Huguenot trail. Our purpose remains the same, to rescue a Protestant from vile Catholics."

I think back to Naira's words in my dream. I will die in a grand palace, dressed in breeches, surrounded by nobility on a rainy summer night. James will watch. "I'd prefer to fight in a land of snow where I hold all the secrets, but alas, we are here. I'm ready." We crawl through the tiny door to the attic and don our masks. "At least the duke has made himself useful."

Elizabeth reaches for my arm. "Isabelle—"

I place my hand on her cheek. "I know." Yes, I'd like to spare her the torture of apologizing, but I need our last moments to be happy. I want her to remember me as strong, noble, and unstoppable.

Many in the palace are asleep, including the king. His rigid schedule will not be disrupted for anything, not even the Red Fox. A surprising number of people are undeterred by the earlier murder in the gardens, going so far as to tie a red strip of fabric around their necks.

"These people are mad." Elizabeth sneers at the group jumping through the night. "Can you imagine death being entertainment?"

I'm certain Charlotte can. All this talk of death causes my head to spin. "Walk with the crowd," I tell her. "And look as if you are excited for a midnight ball."

The duke leads a parade of drunk royals with their mistresses and servants down the steps toward the Grand Canal. He's led them in cheers of "A Red Fox will know her fate. Sun King forever."

"Wear your masks, my friends." The duke cues everyone to don their costumes. "We will celebrate tonight with drink and dance!"

Our cue to move to the Grand Commun. The duke holds the crowd at the fountains, singing and laughing as he provides a speech about The Red Fox and Huguenots while we break away. Two guards flank each entrance. I motion for Elizabeth to move to the south side closest to the trees. There, we spot two young men looking quite bored.

I reach for a blade, but Elizabeth touches my arm. "Wait." She lifts her skirts and approaches the two. "Pardon, I'd like to view my future apartment."

He laughs. "King's orders. No one in or out."

Elizabeth flashes her bright smile. "It's just me and my family servant. I've had a bit to drink and I'm so eager to see the inside." She steps up to him, stumbles, and falls against his chest.

The man looks at the other guard. "She seems harmless."

He yawns. "I'm certain these two aren't staging a Protestant rescue."

Elizabeth laughs. "Please, I can hardly make my way up steps in this gown without fainting."

"The king ordered no one in the building, but he said nothing of the courtyard. You may view the window from below. It's the best I can offer."

"You are too kind, monsieur." She tilts her head. "And handsome too."

The young guard blushes. "Perhaps later—"

"Perhaps." Her eyelashes flutter like butterfly wings. Of all the things I've taught her, being a coquette is not one of them. That she developed all on her own. We step under an arcade and pretend to view the fountain being built in the center of the courtyard. "Men can be so predictable. Why does a smile and a suggestion work on them every time?"

"You got that from your mother. Louise could charm anyone."

"Hurry." She points to an unguarded doorway of an unfinished wing. Vaulted ceilings and arched entryways have been framed but the rooms remain empty and dusty. We step over bricks, past a fireplace to find the first staircase. Above, footsteps track back and forth in a slow, rhythmic pattern. "One guard?" Elizabeth whispers.

We step slowly up the stairs where I glimpse his breeches through the balustrades. I look at Elizabeth and nod. "One chance," I whisper. "Stop at nothing."

Focused, Elizabeth marches up the stairs. "Bonsoir."

"Mademoiselle, you cannot be here. Go!"

I swiftly climb the stairs behind her, hiding behind her giant skirt. They are good for something, I suppose. "But monsieur, I've lost my way." She steps toward him as I crouch behind her and wait to make my move.

He grabs her arms hard enough that she whimpers. The sound ignites something in me. With all the force I can muster, I lift my arm and drive my elbow into the man's neck, followed by a swift kick to the ribs. The man chokes, gasping for air. Blood trickles from his chest. "My shoes." I had forgotten about the nails. I stare at him, wishing I had smashed his temple like I usually do. Now the man has a bleeding chest and possibly a punctured lung.

Elizabeth swipes his blade from his holster and knocks the handle into his forehead. "Is everything alright?"

His unmoving body turns black before my eyes. I blink but it changes nothing. Upturned toes. Blue mouth. Blood trickles down the wall in front of me. Stifled screams rattle my chest, but I can't summon any noise.

"Isabelle." Elizabeth shakes me back from my memories. I am not in La Rochelle. I'm in Versailles to save Charlotte. I seem to flit between my nightmares and my body as easily as a blink. After a hard head shake, I nod and lead the way through the completed apartments. A room of guards sit around a table discussing the party this evening.

"We must be close," I whisper. We maneuver our backs along the wall opposite the door through the darkened hallways through slices of silver moonlight. Elizabeth trips over a brick. I grab her, throwing us both into a salon where we hide under a desk.

Two guards come to check the scene. Thankfully there are no lit candles or fireplaces here and we remain frozen in the dark corner, waiting for them. They kick the loose brick. "Just a fallen piece of stone."

"Check the surrounding rooms," one says. We back against the wall, hoping no one thinks to look under the table in the dark corner.

"There's nothing. Come on."

The man walks the perimeter of the salon, his boots tapping the wood floor as slow as the sweet water drip from a Quebec maple. My eyes remain locked on Elizabeth as we both lift our hands in preparation for a fight. The clear, bright whites of her eyes shine like glass. His steps halt near us. He leans on the table, as its joints squeak under his weight. Elizabeth flinches, but I hold up my hand, noting his stare out the window above us.

"Ridiculous," he mutters at the raucous, drunk crowd dancing in the gardens. "Fools." He takes one step back where I can see his torso, then his shoulders. Just as a lump forms in my throat, the other guard whistles to beckon him.

"Follow them." I nudge Elizabeth.

We pad through salon after salon, backs against the unfinished walls. Feet shuffle on the floor above us. The untitled surfaces make for a hollow echo with every shift. I motion to the staircase. "Where are the guards?"

The eerie quiet fills me with dread. No screams, no fighting—just silence.

Elizabeth moves ahead as I examine blood splatter on the steps. Droplets, not smears.

Someone walked down the stairs actively bleeding.

"Isabelle?" Her voice cracks. I brace myself on the wall, unprepared to face a dead Charlotte, killed for my actions. We fought like sisters and loved one another despite our differences. I don't want to lose her. I can't.

My shaky knees carry me up the stairs. She died on her terms, just as we all wish to do, I tell myself. She's with Henri. But I was meant to die, not her. Before I turn the corner, I shut my eyes and hold back tears. I can't look. "Give me a second," I say.

Once I've summoned a thread of strength, I step into the room.

In the center of the salon, Elizabeth stands next to an empty chair with ropes. She's surrounded by lifeless bodies. All men. At least a dozen guards are scattered on the floor like dead flies. But no Charlotte.

"She must have escaped," Elizabeth says.

A wave of relief flows through me, followed quickly by realization. "Hurry, we need to find her." I head back toward the stairs, Elizabeth on my heels. "It's only a matter of hours before someone discovers these dead guards and locks down the palace to find her, and anyone associated with her."

We make our way through the empty corridors and salons, out to the courtyard, where a pile of men lay stacked in the empty fountain, one of them the young man that let us in.

"Where is she?" Elizabeth asks.

"She's out to kill the king."

"Would it be so awful if she succeeded? Look at this waste." She motions around her.

"If she kills the Monarch, it will wage a holy war the likes of which we've never seen. Every Huguenot in France will be murdered, including us. The resistance isn't big enough to handle that. I have to stop her."

"I've never seen anyone stop Charlotte from anything once she's set her mind to it."

"If I have to bind her feet and drag her out of here myself, I'll stop her." I peer through the arched opening toward the south wing of the palace.

"What if she's already done it?"

"Then we are in big trouble."

CHAPTER THIRTY-ONE

With nearly fifteen guards dead on the palace grounds, Versailles seems disordered and wild. The duke continues his nighttime party in the groves. We hear the faint bubble of laughter and song far into the trees, while we approach the king's apartment, knowing the sun will soon rise. Sometime, in the remaining hours of darkness, I will face off with James, save Charlotte and Elizabeth, and I will die.

A night of enchantment has turned into an early morning of chaos. It seems no one has slept, other than the king and his entourage. Nobles practically prance through the halls, as couples sneak behind statues and painted screens for a tryst.

"What's gotten into this place?" Elizabeth asks.

"A royal frenzy. The king held a grand theater, a man was murdered under fireworks, and the Red Fox was captured. I can't imagine life at court is ever this thrilling."

Guards stand firm outside the entrance to the king's apartment, and presumably more of them stand guard in the antechamber. We peer at the door from behind a marble statue. "If Charlotte made it inside, those men would be lying in a pool of blood."

Elizabeth grabs my arm. "The terrace. I noticed blood smeared on the pillars when we walked up."

The terrace overlooks the fountain and gardens, connecting the space between the king and queen's apartments. Only one floor from the steps, it would be easy enough to climb. Especially if you're as determined as Charlotte. We stand on the steps looking over the arch to the tiled terrace. "There's a gold fountain in the middle, and entrances on either side."

"I can't climb," she says. "Not in this robe."

I reach for her skirts and tear the silk along a seam. I keep ripping to create one long, red strip of material from the bulbous shoulders and velvet sleeves. Elizabeth looks down at her torn robe. She reaches into my boot and with the blade, slices through her corset and stomacher to release the pressure. "Better."

She tucks her skirt between her legs, props her hands on her hips and nods. "You go."

Memories flash through my mind of Naira swinging from a tree branch and jumping from rocks. She taught me everything I could need to know and here I am, about to scale the palace of Versailles to save the king and rescue this capable young woman who I adore more than life itself.

A drunk noble stumbles by, eating an orange. He rubs his eyes and looks at Elizabeth in horror. "Goodness, child. What have you done to yourself?"

Without responding, She punches his nose. His head wobbles and he spins, falling face first into the dirt, right on top of his half-eaten orange. "Sorry," she says to him. "No time to explain." Elizabeth climbs the stairs and crouches, hands on her knees. "Go on," she says to me. "Please don't impale me with the nails in your boots."

"I promise." Without hesitation, I run across the marble floor and leap onto Elizabeth's back, my foot landing at the highest curve of her back. As I straighten my knee, she lifts her back. I push my weight up higher until my fingers reach the molding above the arch. I hang there for a moment, checking the scene. Another man approaches, muttering something about fetching a guard. Elizabeth smashes her elbow into his cheek and her knee to his groin. He crumbles with a grunt, and I return to my current situation.

I close my eyes and remember training in Quebec. How did she climb? My fingers begin to sweat and cramp. I examine the wall under the arch, and I see notches as if a chisel has created claw marks. "Charlotte, that little fighter." I slide my hands one then another along the molding to reach the wall.

"Hurry, Isabelle, I hear men approaching."

The tip of my boot with the nail claws into one of the broken notches. It's stable enough to support me while I push up to the railing on the terrace. My other foot finds another notch but when I slip my foot into the groove, the stone breaks loose. My legs dangle so I throw my body over the railing, knocking the wind from my chest.

"What is that man doing?" I hear below.

Elizabeth approaches the onlookers. "See those two men in the dirt? One is groaning, the other is unconscious. If you don't leave me now, you will be next."

The men laugh. I hear them approach just as my ribs pull hard into an expansive breath. I throw my body to the terrace and look down in enough time to see Elizabeth knock their heads together. They crumble like breadcrumbs. "I must say, this is much more thrilling than caring for children back in Geneva." She wipes her hands on her torn skirt. "Go on." She motions to the apartment. "I'll keep watch."

A door opens so I throw myself to the black and white tile and roll until I'm laying next to the fountain, in its dark shadow. A servant walks with purpose past me, from the king's doorway toward the queen's at the south side of the terrace. Once she passes, I run for the door and slip into the antechamber adorned with marble floors and frescoed ceilings. A scuffle occurs at the opposite end of the room, where a grunt leads to a whimper, then a gurgle.

A sound thumps behind me so I have no choice but to move toward the sound.

Across the antechamber and through to the salon, I find Charlotte, staring into the king's bedchamber, a knife in her hand dripping blood. She stares at the covered bed with the sovereign asleep inside the fabric walls. Her face is bruised and bleeding, her bottom lip swollen like she holds a rock in her mouth. She stares with purpose at the bedchamber, her breathing controlled and slow.

I approach slowly, but jump behind her and cover her mouth. Knowing how she moves, I anticipate her elbow, block her jab as I whisper in her ear. "Charlotte."

She stops fighting when she realizes it's me. I slide my hand from her mouth and move in front of her. "You can't kill the king," I whisper.

"He's ordered us all dead. He stole our home."

"Yes, he did."

"The horrid, hateful man deserves to die."

I nod and stare at the sleeping king with her. "Someone will catch us. We only have a few minutes."

"I must kill him. For Henri."

I hold my breath to stop the tears. "You must kill him for all of us."

An acceptance settles in her gaze. "You aren't going to stop me."

"I know."

Charlotte watches the king sleep soundly in his bed, not knowing he'll wake in a few hours to find most of his staff has been poisoned by an escaped prisoner, or wake to his own screams in a few moments at the hands of a very angry Protestant. "You know this will leave you with a war on your hands."

"I do."

She tightens her grip on the blade's handle, sweat dripping from her hairline. "Why didn't you kill James? We had a plan."

"Something in my soul wouldn't let me."

Her breath trembles. "He's ordered our deaths too."

"He's very troubled." My gaze falls to the slumbering king. "The thirst for power seems to corrupt most men."

"Only men with the wrong ambitions."

"Yes. But when we want something so fiercely, it can be difficult to see the effects of our choices. Revenge and betrayal. Even love colors our view. Unsure where my survival instincts end and my convictions begin, all I have to rely on is my heart."

Her eyes fill with thick tears. Her breath hitches.

"If we kill for enjoyment, we are no better than them."

Quiet swells in the room, enough to cause my ears to ring.

"Henri is gone." She grabs my hand and squeezes. "I'm so lost without him."

I keep my voice steady and calm. "Then let us guide you home."

The king grumbles in his sleep. "I want to watch him bleed."

I turn to look into her eyes. "I want Henri back, and I want Elizabeth nowhere near this ridiculous palace." Some things we cannot have. "If we don't flee this palace soon, none of us will see Geneva ever again."

She takes a deep breath, her blond hair stuck to her robe with dried blood. "Let's find Cricket and leave this wretched palace."

Instead of words, I squeeze her hand firmly to remind her I love her.

We return to the antechamber, hurrying to beat the arrival of his morning entourage. Around the corner, we come face to face with James.

"Please tell me you didn't hurt the king."

"What if we did?" Charlotte asks.

"Then I will be forced to kill you both."

CHAPTER THIRTY-TWO

James never saw it coming. We knocked him out with little effort.

Two women in torn clothing, both accused of running the evil Protestant resistance. I've evaded entire companies of soldiers and broken into the king's apartment. I've killed dragoons so often I can't remember them all. And yet, he still views me as the simple young Protestant he knew, scared and hopeless.

"You could have let us leave," I say.

He mutters something which I can't make out. I remove his mouth binding. "Again."

He clenches his jaw. "I will protect the king. Forever."

"I'm curious why you're so loyal to him," Charlotte asks. "He's just a man."

"Wrong. He's the leader of our country. Gifted to us by God as the head of the Catholic Church."

"Idealism has always misguided him," I say.

James looks at me, eyes pleading to release him. We hit his head and dragged him back to Lorraine's studio. Luckily, the artist was out enjoying the festivities. Our fallback plan orchestrated by the duke, for events such as this.

"You won't kill me, not after all we've been through," he says.

Charlotte kicks him. "But I will."

Wrists bound, James lies on his side and coughs. He looks quite pathetic like this.

"What were you doing in the king's apartment?" Charlotte asks.

"I could ask you the same thing."

I bend down to move closer to his face. "Tell me."

"I've been following you tonight. You snuck into the Grand Commune then chased Charlotte back to the palace."

He didn't stop me from rescuing her. That says something. "Why did you follow me?"

"I wanted to protect you."

Charlotte rubs her palm along a patch of dried blood on her jaw. "Neither one of us needs your protection, Beaumont. Or whatever your name is now."

Elizabeth sneaks into the studio where shadows crawl along the white tile slabs. "I moved those men into the gardens. They'll wake soon." She tilts her head when she notices James. "So, you're Monsieur Beaumont."

"I'm not as horrible as you've presumably heard."

She kneels down to stare at him, expressionless. "You've ordered the Dragonnades. I'm guessing you're even worse than I could've imagined." Elizabeth drags him to sit. She leans his back against a column then paces in front of him. "We've seen bodies burned, and bones shattered. We've heard screams that turned our stomachs. What have these people done to deserve this? They're Protestant."

James's hair has come loose, hanging over his right eye. "I've tried to stop the program."

Elizabeth smacks him across the cheek. "Don't lie to me."

James stretches his jaw and blinks until he can focus. "You're Louise's daughter, aren't you? You have her hair and her eyes."

"I am just as much Andre Boucher's daughter. Possibly more. He raised me to fight for what I believe in."

"The Huguenots are passive. They don't fight back. It makes for an easy target. The king believes the entire country can be one under the Catholic Church."

"The king is wrong."

James looks at me. "The dragoons will move to Tours next."

"We already know that."

His clear eyes haven't changed. Bright and round, they reflect the silky light of dawn. "How can I prove to you I'm not the man I once was?"

Charlotte grabs his hair. "Call off the billeting of troops in Protestant homes."

"I can't." He stares up at her, wincing. "It's in the king's hands now."

She shoves his head away. "I should have bludgeoned him when I had the chance."

"Enough." I hold up my hands. "We're wasting time. There are dead bodies all over this place and the sun is nearly up. "We have to go."

Elizabeth walks over to whisper to me. "You have to kill him. There can be no trust."

"Oh, I don't trust him. Never did." His hair has darkened from copper to chestnut over the years, speckled with gray. The lines in the corner of his eyes and thickened jaw have softened him. We've all aged. We're no longer the young, hungry fighters we once were. In his place, I see a lonely man who never found the father's approval he so desperately wanted.

"Don't bother," Charlotte says to Elizabeth. "Once Isabelle has made up her mind, she won't change. Can I slice him across the neck?" she asks me.

"No."

The door flies open. Lorraine, clad in a velvet robe, raises his eyebrows. "What is all this?"

James, to my surprise, doesn't plead for the sculptor's help.

Lorraine steps toward us, a disapproving scowl on his face. "Minister, did I not warn you?"

"The resistance and I go far back. All the way to La Rochelle." He glances at me.

Lorraine turns his back to James and looks at me. "Your husband must leave Paris before sunup."

"How do you know who my husband is?"

He motions for me to walk to the far corner of the studio. Chunks of slivered stone and wood lay in various states of sculpture. Lorraine reaches for a large sheet of linen. He slides it away to reveal a life size marble sculpture.

"That's me." I run my fingers along the smooth stone, along the curls that float from the shoulders in a breeze and the eyes staring straight ahead with resolve. On her wrist, a branded H.

"Monsieur Boucher is incredibly talented. It's why I protected him when I discovered the poisons."

I don't bother trying to argue my way out of this. He knows Andre's heart, and once you do, there is no escaping.

"I think it's his pain that makes him sculpt with such passion. The Protestant resistance and his love for you cause an immense struggle inside him."

"He told you of the resistance?"

"No, madame. I am an artist. I'm trained to see what is not said."

"She is beautiful." I bite back tears.

"Yes, she is." He places his hand on my shoulder. "I've protected him all I can. They've discovered the poisons and traced them back to my apprentice. All of you must leave Paris immediately."

"Gladly." I take one more painful look at the sculpture, knowing Andre's hands carved this while he thought of me, wishing we were together, safe in Geneva, where he is enough for me.

"Truth is there to see if we only care to look," he says. "That is what artists think."

Tears fill my eyes. I'm ready to go home. I walk to James and pull my knife from my boot. Holding the blade in front of him so he can see, I cut the ties binding his feet and hands.

The girls don't speak.

James stands on wobbly legs. "Why did you free me?"

"I can only hope you remember me right here in this moment, giving you compassion despite everything you've done."

"Do you forgive me?"

He'll never escape his need for me. "I let you live. That is enough."

A grumble rolls through the sky. I walk to the window to see droplets patter on the glass. "It's raining." I turn to Charlotte. "A summer storm."

CHAPTER THIRTY-THREE

I didn't look back at James as the door shut. I don't know if I did the right thing, letting him live. But I can't tolerate any more guilt in my heart. We step into the drizzle of summer rain, the smell of greenery and moss thickening the hot air.

Charlotte limps behind us, pain setting in to her bruised leg. I wrap my arm around her waist and help her down the steps to the gardens. "How did you scale a wall with an injured leg?"

She looks at her feet as if she forgot she's injured. "It's amazing what we can do when we want something."

"We honored Henri's memory. He'd be very proud." Although I didn't kill James, I know, deep down, that Henri understands. Before this world twisted and broke him, his heart was more fragile than mine.

She leans her cheek on my shoulder. "I miss him so much my chest hurts."

"Me too. I'll always remember the day he showed up in Quebec and asked me to spy on my husband. It's because of him I joined the resistance."

"I can't believe you didn't kill him."

"Perhaps I've grown soft in my older years, but I think I believe people can change." I've changed. I feel it deep in my bones. My arms ache for Andre and my taste for fighting has waned. If I can soften, anyone can.

Charlotte gains her footing and stretches her sore hip where I assume they beat her. "I hope you're right." We stand in front of the Latona Fountain, with its marble goddess and gilded frogs and lizards as rain tinkles on the pool of water. "Why must they live with such opulence?" Charlotte shakes her head. "Someday, this country will revolt, I'm certain of it."

Elizabeth, looking back to grimace at us, holds her hand up. "We have a problem."

Guards swarm the grounds from behind, fanning out in all directions. "Did the king report us?"

Charlotte's eyes grow wide. "Those guards in the Grand Commun? I didn't poison them. I only gave them sleeping powder. They must have woken up and reported me missing."

"You're soft now too." I smile, despite the dozens of men with swords approaching. Perhaps this night has changed us all.

"We need to make it to the Apollo fountain." Elizabeth guides us to the foot of a broad avenue flanked by trees, a statue of Apollo on a chariot far in the distance. "Beyond there is the Grand Canal, and hopefully, a way out of this place."

Men descend onto the avenue from the pathways. They haven't noticed us yet, so I form a plan. "South into the gardens. It's the only way."

Charlotte forces her sore leg to hobble toward the Ballroom Grove. "We head into a maze of greenery and fountains with dozens of guards after us like bloodhounds. Nothing can go wrong here."

"No other choice." I yank her arm forward.

We dip into the cut hedges to follow the winding path toward the amphitheater. When we arrive in the center, we find an island surrounded by cascading waterfalls and marble bridges. Gilded vases flank the sprouting fountains and steps of greenery lead up to a steep incline toward the trees. An ethereal display that no doubt took hundreds of men, thousands of hours, and pumped water from who knows where. All so the king could occasionally look upon it from his terrace.

"Up. Into the trees." Elizabeth climbs the slick staircase, and we follow. Wet from moss and fountain spray, we fall to our hands to crawl our way up. Rain pelts our faces, but we are too busy scaling this slippery stone to wipe the raindrops from our eyes. If we thought hot, stale air was uncomfortable, sticky wetness under the heat of the sun is far worse.

We reach the trees, so tightly packed they've grown together like a wall. We tuck into the protection of greenery and listen as steps approach.

Two men enter the grove and stand in the center of the island, examining the circular garden. "No one here," one says. "Check the trees."

The other guard scales the steps without difficulty. He approaches the trees and peers into the darkness, wiping his eyes clear of rainwater. He doesn't see us, so we stand still as stone. An unexpected bolt of lightning lights the sky, illuminating the gaze between us and him. I meet his eyes. Before I can act, Elizabeth has picked up a stone and hurls the orange-sized rock at the man's face. It lands on the center of his forehead and sends him stumbling backward, where he teeters on the top step of the cascading fountain. He slips and he tumbles down the steep wall along with the water.

"This way." I lead them over the boxwood hedges, neatly trimmed to form flat top squares. We roll over them as their branches poke my ribs and legs. After a few grunts and skin punctures, I land on the pathway just outside the Ballroom Grove, the Bacchus Fountain in my sights to the west. I help the girls roll to the ground and we stop to catch our breath.

"Keep moving west," Elizabeth says.

Guards appear from the shadows, moving toward the fountain and toward us. We have no choice but to move south into the Labyrinth Grove, through the entrance with cupid on the left and Aesop on the right. A true maze, hedges twice as tall as us block our view of anyone in front of or behind us. We hit dead ends and backtrack through the plain pathways, only distinguished from each other by metal animal sculptures spitting water. Fashioned after Aesop's Fables, each fountain and statue is decorated with ornate gold detailing.

"The king loves his fountains," Charlotte mutters. "What a waste."

A loud clap of thunder makes Charlotte jump. Her usual focus is rattled after this difficult night. We turn the corner to a cross path, where we can move in any direction. We stop momentarily, held in by the walls of greenery.

From behind a metal fox, a guard launches at Charlotte. He knocks her to the ground, face into the stone. I reach my hand around his mouth so he cannot scream while Elizabeth slams her foot on his arm. I hear a crunch as his wrist shatters like splinters. I wince, growing to hate that sound.

"He'll scream if we don't kill him." I hold his head tight against my chest.

"Let him," Charlotte says. She rolls out from underneath him. "We'll run to the west while the guards descend on this grove."

The man writhes and whimpers. Loud enough that guilt eats away at me like a mouse nibbling on cheese. "Dammit. Let him live. Go, now."

The girls run down the long narrow passageway. I watch them for as long as I can, holding the man still. I wait, hoping they find the nearest corner exit. After a painfully long two minutes, I hear a whistle. I let go of the guard and he instantly screams in pain. "We didn't want to hurt you," I whisper.

I run down the pathway after the whistle, turning in a full circle and hitting two fountain-clad corners, before finding an exit where the girls hide in a narrow alley between two tall hedges. The man still bellows screams that echo through the early morning chaos.

"They're swarming the Spring Grove," Elizabeth says. "We have to backtrack through the Girandole Grove."

"How do you know all these names?" I ask.

"While you were spying, I was memorizing the layout of the gardens. So many dark corners to hide in, with fountains and statues for cover. I know every crook and curve of these grounds."

A man appears from inside a shrub and stabs Charlotte through the shoulder with a knife. He aimed to kill, but she ducked in time to save her neck. "Red Fox," he says through a snarl. "You're mine."

Charlotte drops to the ground, holding her shoulder to limit the blood flow while I face the man with teeth so yellow, they glimmer like firelight. The storm has lightened but the air fizzles with heat. Arms out, I drop my chin and stare at him through the upper portion of my gaze.

"I don't want to hurt you," I tell him.

"A woman dressed in servant's clothes?" He laughs, which teases my inner rage. "I'll kill all three of you." He peers past my shoulder to Elizabeth. "On second thought, perhaps I'll keep the young one for myself."

Once bottled nicely in my belly, the anger I've always summoned so easily bursts forth when his eyes fall on my daughter. I may be soft now, but I'd still chop him into pieces to save Elizabeth. And I wouldn't lose one wink of sleep.

I kick his shins with the nail in my boot. He screams but recovers with a thrust of his blade toward my belly. I avoid his attempts by spinning to the right and coming up behind him with my arm around his throat. I reach for the blade with my other hand while Elizabeth slides her legs against his feet to knock him on his side.

Stronger than he appears, he maintains control of the blade. I hold him tight from behind as he throws his body weight and lands on top of me. I try to maneuver, but I've lost my edge. He slams his elbow into my side, eliciting a sharp, stabbing shock through my ribs. Still, I don't release my grasp around his chest and neck. Elizabeth attempts to kick his face but he grabs her ankle, twists, and throws her to the ground next to him. He arches his back and slams me against the puddled ground.

Charlotte watches in horror, too afraid to remove her hand from her bleeding shoulder. I'm distracted by Charlotte's despondent gaze when the guard knocks my forehead with the back of his skull. In a fuzzy-headed spin, I try to focus but can't summon my body to move. Elizabeth fights him as I've shown her, but he lands a few hits, which pull my attention back to the moment. As sound returns to my ears, raindrops stream down my cheeks, and the mother in me fights her way through the fog.

A deep, wild, roar escapes my lips, my arms spread wide, fingers like claws. I don't care who hears and how many guards come running. All I can see is Elizabeth using every tool we've taught her and still getting punched and bruised.

The sight of blood spurting from her mouth sends me feral. I don't use my hands or my legs, or even my nail-tipped shoes. I summon my mouth.

I clamp my teeth around his ear and slam my jaw shut. The tearing sensation as my teeth rip his lobe from his cartilage feels akin to tough mutton gristle. Metallic blood fills my mouth and with one hard yank, I pull a section of skin and flesh from his ear.

His screams are shrill and desperate, seemingly unwilling to believe a woman has hurt him. I spit the bloody flesh to the ground and splash water from the nearest fountain into my mouth. After a wipe to dry my lips, I step over the screaming man to help up Elizabeth.

"What are you?" he yells between cries.

"I am the Red Fox."

Charlotte stands, tears streaming down her face. "Leave me. I'll hold you back. Just go."

I wrap my arm around her waist, noting her pale face and heavy eyes. Another flash of lightning sears through the early morning sky. "Whatever happens to us will happen together. We don't leave each other. Understood?"

"But I hesitated. I thought of Henri and sadness gripped me so hard I wished to die so I could be with him. I didn't help you."

I turn back to the man in excruciating pain. "We handled it just fine without you. Now, Elizabeth. Are you alright?"

She stretches her neck and spits a clot of blood to the ground. "Yeah. I'll remember that ear bite for another time." Footsteps thunder through the groves and alleys, approaching the screams. "There's no time to waste. We run straight through the Ancient Gallery and out to Apollo, then along the Grand Canal to freedom."

I nudge them both forward. "Together."

We fan out to separate alleys moving west. The ancient sculptures on pedestals in my sites, I run faster as the canal appears behind a gilded fountain. Our alleys merge at the center island surrounded by sculptures. A museum under the stormy sky that shimmers with pools of rainwater. It's quite beautiful here.

"Hurry," I say as I enter the circular island. I find Elizabeth and Charlotte, both held by guards, with knives to their necks. I plant my feet in the puddle beneath me and raise my arms to stop my momentum. How did I let this happen?

The guards don't move, holding blades to the girls' necks with steely focus. I meet Elizabeth's eyes. She slides a glance to the fountain behind me. I spin while pulling the blade from my boot. Standing tall and motionless, is James.

"I ordered them to follow the girl," he says. "She would lead us to you, and you'd be distracted by trying to protect her."

I hold the knife in a firm grip, knowing I'm fast enough to slice his neck before he could fight back. But the guards would take out my family before I could save them, so here I stand, at James's mercy.

Rainwater pours down my face, the sound of tinkling drops on Carrera marble statues high-pitched and light. A stormy night, in front of James at a palace, me in breeches. Killed by the man I let free less than an hour ago. I anticipated this. I didn't count on my girls getting killed too. They should be long gone by now.

"This woman right here is the true Red Fox," James says to the guards. "My wife once was a Daughter of the King. A converted Huguenot, and incredible lover, she never ceases to amaze me."

His eyes look calm, even a touch sad. "This isn't you," I say.

He laughs. "You don't know me, Isabelle. No one does."

"Not true. You saved me during the exile of La Rochelle. You fell in love with a Huguenot, despite your family's hatred for my people. You survived war and torture to travel to Canada and find me. You are a good person who's lost his way."

His jaw pulses as he closes his eyes. "I tried everything to make you love me."

I drop my blade and take a step closer.

"Isabelle, don't believe him," Elizabeth says.

"Your sister once told me you are a good person who needed approval so badly, it forced you to make terrible decisions. I didn't understand at the time, but now I do." I face him with firm shoulders and heavy eyes. "I see who you really are, James."

He purses his lips, but his eyes grow red as if he's holding back tears.

Charlotte grunts and falls to the ground. The guard looks to James for direction. "She's bleeding, James. The guards beat her and stabbed her. She will die if we don't get her help."

James blinks several times. "Why can't you just go away?" His breathing speeds up. "Go back to Geneva and never return."

"See that girl there?" I point to Elizabeth. "I made a promise long ago to protect her. I would die a thousand deaths before I'd allow anyone to hurt her. I tried to hold her in Geneva where I could control her and never allow her to experience the trauma of life as a Huguenot. What I didn't anticipate, is that she would surpass me in wit and strength, and even commitment. I'm tired, James. So much bloodshed and pain. I can't tolerate it anymore."

"We never had children," he says. "I wanted that. I wanted you."

"You wanted a version of me that never existed." I turn my back to him and lean against his chest. Knife in my hand, I wrap his hand around my fist and bring the blade to my neck.

"Isabelle, don't." Elizabeth's voice quivers.

I smile at Elizabeth, no longer afraid or sad. "Let them go, James, and you can have me. Kill me or torture me, I don't care. Just save them."

James's hand trembles, but he closes his fingers tight around mine. The cool, metal blade touches my skin. Thunder rumbles overhead. "You're willing to die," he mumbles. "Right here in my arms?"

"It's always been my fate," I say. "Perhaps we are connected for life."

He wraps his hand around my waist to hold me close. "Let them go," he says.

The guards look at each other.

"You heard me. This is the Red Fox. We have who we want." The men step back from the girls, and I breathe a sigh of relief. "Go," James says. "Leave Versailles right now. If either of you come back for her, all three of you will die."

"Please, go," I say.

Elizabeth hesitates. "I'm not leaving you, Maman."

My heart nearly cracks in two, but I look at Charlotte in a desperate plea. She knows I'd rather die than risk either of them. Charlotte stumbles to standing and nods to me. "Come, Elizabeth. This is what Isabelle wants." Her knees buckle again. "I need help."

I mouth I love you, but no words escape my lips. Charlotte grabs Elizabeth's arm and Cricket nods hesitantly. "I love you, Isabelle."

They stumble toward the fountain, the long walk of the canal ahead of them. I wonder if Charlotte will survive.

James holds me. He directs the guards to gather the remaining men from the palace. Once they're gone, he speaks to me, as if a knife isn't at my throat. "I sent them to the minister's wing to give me time to find you."

"And now you have me." I soften my body and accept what has transpired.

"You aren't fighting," he says.

I look up to the sky as the slightest hint of dawn illuminates the morning. Rain drops plunk on my forehead. "I've anticipated this moment for a long time. I suppose this is always how it would end."

"If you wanted to fight back, you could."

I lay the back of my head on his shoulder and breathe in the damp, cool air. "I hear doors open in the distance. They'll surround us in a few minutes. Wouldn't you like to be the one to kill me?" I let go of the knife and slide it into his hand. My arms relaxed at my sides, I think of Andre. My mother. Naira. Charlotte, and Cricket. I think of Henri, smiling from above, waiting for me with a hand reached for another earthly being who's stolen her last breath.

"Fight to live," he says. "This isn't you."

"I've known great love in my life from incredible people. Something your king will never accept, is that love and kindness cannot be eradicated, regardless of how many of us you kill."

James could slice my neck at any moment. I close my eyes and wait, trying not to cry. This is why I came here. It's what Naira taught me all those years ago. Answer the call of the warrior. "I'm finished."

His hand shakes. He smells the same as he always did. In so many ways he's still the young man with bright freckles who could have been a good person. He's inside him somewhere hidden under the rubble of many, many wrong choices. He shoves me away, heaving for breath. "I won't hurt you. I can't."

"Yes you can." My heartbeat quickens. This is my destiny. I have nothing beyond this moment. "I've said my goodbyes and prayed for forgiveness for all the men I've hurt. I have nothing left."

"You have a husband who loves you. A daughter you'd die for. And a brave friend who might not make it to see daylight this morning. That's more than I can say. I'm alone. I always have been." His eyes redden with a sheen of tears. "I'm sorry about Henri. Louvois was difficult to control."

"You protected me all this time. Why?"

"Although the feeling is not shared, you are the great love of my life. I failed you so many times. Perhaps now, I can die knowing I've said my apologies."

Tears rush to my eyes at the idea I could possibly live past sunrise. James lifts his hand, and all sound leaves my ears. His hand gripping the knife, he launches it at me. I don't duck or swerve. I close my eyes and welcome my final moments.

The wet thwack of torn flesh wakes me from numbness. James's face reveals horror and regret. He drops the knife to the ground and weeps.

I hear a groan.

I turn behind me to see a man with a knife in his eye. He wobbles, and lilts to the ground like a fallen leaf.

I run my hand along my chest and neck, checking for blood. There is none. James grabs me and shoves me into an alcove curved by perfectly trimmed hedges. He forces me to the tile behind a fountain.

Guards arrive, their frantic feet thumping into the grove. "Where is she?" one yells.

"She ran north. To the Star Grove. Hurry!"

The men yell, a thunderous call for blood and revenge for all the hurt I've caused. James extends his hand to help me up. I take it without hesitation.

"Come." He guides me out through the final grove, past Apollo's fountain. "Run along this path. Follow the canal but stay out of sight. The full force of the king's guards are out to find you."

I look back toward the man dead on the island of the serene open-air museum. "You killed one of your officers."

"No. *You* killed him." He cracks a smile. "Now go, before I have to save you again."

I step to him and place my hands on his chest. I lay a soft kiss on his cheek. "Thank you."

"I can't promise I'll stop the Dragonnades. But I will try to find bravery where I can. Just as you do."

"Goodbye, James." I dip into the trees without looking back. The sun crests the horizon and I know I've survived. I live to fight another day.

Warm, golden light fills the morning air, a cloudless sky shining bright sun on the rain-soaked gardens of the most magnificent palace France has ever seen. Goodbye, Versailles. I hope to never encounter your marble statues and stuffy rituals ever again.

A smile creeps to my face when out of the trees, five men arise from all directions. They approach me like sharks in the ocean eyeing their target. I back up to the middle of the canal where the giant waterway forms a cross. I could swim but they'd catch me. I can't fight off five.

Everyone is gone. It's just me and the guards, and my last grasp at freedom.

They smile while raising their swords and knives. "Nowhere to run now, Red Fox," one says.

I swallow hard. If I die, I will do it fighting like a warrior. "I'm ready. Come for me."

A swoosh flies past my head. An arrow lands in one man's neck, followed by another into a man's chest. Two down. Three to go. I look over my shoulder as a gondola glides through the canal, led by a man dressed in a striped outfit and hollering something in Italian. He's laughing like a madman.

Good gracious, it's the duke. Next to him I see Cricket, arrow drawn. She lets two more arrows fly as the last guard grabs me by the shoulders. He moves his blade to slash my neck but I lift my hand to stop him. He cuts my pinky finger clean to the bone.

I use my foot to take him out at the knees, then wind my leg back to kick him with my nail boot. A hand stops me. I turn to see the duke. Disguised as a gondolier, he says, "Allow me." He leaps like a ballerina as he swings his oar overhead. With a pirouette, the duke winds his arm and slams the wood oar into the guard's head. Then he bows to me. "Everything with a flourish."

"You stole a gondola?"

"Only the best for my pet." He winks. A crowd of men thunder toward us, splitting around either side of the Apollo fountain, running with screams along either side of the canal. "Time to flee!" He lifts me by the waist and launches me to the gondola.

"You're surprisingly strong," I say. "You'd make a good warrior."

He rests his palm on his chest. "Alas, I am a lover and a poet."

Elizabeth lifts my injured hand. "You might lose that finger."

"Yes." I examine the blood gushing from my pinky. I wrap my hand around the finger and squeeze, feeling the pain more intensely than I could imagine. "Is Charlotte, um—"

"We don't know." Elizabeth glances at the duke. "I recruited him to help us save you and he took Charlotte to a village healer." She grabs my arm. "I'm glad you're safe."

"With any luck, we'll never see Paris again."

A blissful, crimson sunset spreads over Versailles, lighting the trees in raspberry warmth.

"Thank you for returning for me," I say without looking at her.

"Papa would be absolutely insufferable without you. And I'd be lost. I need you."

The duke pushes us with ease west along the canal. Elizabeth and I stand arm in arm to watch the sun rise over the palace as the men fade into the distance.

"Here we are. Little Venice." The duke leaps from the gondola. He reaches his hand for Elizabeth to help her ashore. I follow. We run into the trees and through a break in the fence into the road outside the palace. "This way." I follow them toward the village, the sun already drying my wet clothes.

At the door to a stone cottage in the trees, Elizabeth takes a breath. "We'll discover Aunt Charlotte's fate." She steps inside and the duke follows, but I hold him back.

"It's quiet. That's not a good sign," he says.

"I'm here. You saved me. Now it is my turn to uphold the bargain."

"Ah." He looks down at his tapping feet. "The king."

"I'm worth much more now." I can't help but smile. "You can fund an entire orchestra."

"Right." He scratches his temple. "But there's a shortage of decent people in this world, Isabelle. It would be a shame to lose one. Besides, I can't leave your handsome husband alone without you. I'm not that cruel."

"Thank you," I clear my throat, "Edward."

His smile, filled with deep gratitude, is enough to throw me off balance. Elizabeth creeps through the door, tears in her eyes.

"No," I whisper. "Charlotte."

. . .

One Year Later

With snow crunch under my feet and a cover of frosty birch trees overhead, my heart settles into a calm beat. The trail is still visible at the onset of winter, but I know this path by heart. I've been gone for two weeks, eager to step into our warm home.

My breath clouds the crisp air. My cheeks sting from the cold. And I've never felt more alive.

When I open the door to our cottage, Elizabeth leaps to me, arms out. She wraps me in an embrace, which I happily welcome. She steps aside so Andre can see me. "Hello, love," he says.

That's what he said to me that morning in Paris, after I survived Versailles. When I arrived at the gardens of The Louvre, bleeding and exhausted, he wrapped me in his arms and kissed my forehead. "Hello, love. Let's go home." We never discussed the events that transpired, which is just as I prefer it. Andre knows me too well.

After a soft kiss hello, I take in his handsome face and the warmth of our home. I place my hand on the Geneva Bible and thank God I've made it this far. Once again, I return home from France unharmed, and full of secrets.

Elizabeth pulls up a chair. "What's next for the Dragonnades?"

I roll out a map and mark the cities targeted for attacks. "Here, here, and here."

"That's too much ground to cover," Andre says. "The resistance can't manage it all."

The door opens and in walks Charlotte. "I'm ready to fight," she says. "Where to, my friends?"

Charlotte died back in Versailles but refused to stay dead long. Stubborn fighter she is, she rose like a miracle as we prayed over her pale body. She gasped, causing the duke to faint. I laughed, knowing God would kick her back if she had any fight left.

"Don't think I'm done," she said before going unconscious again. We let her sleep. And here she is, a dedicated fighter with all her wits, who's triumphed over great loss to find her purpose.

"Anything else we should know?" Charlotte asks.

"Edward will await your arrival. He's managed a meeting with the king's new minister and will be eager to share his findings."

"We're lucky to have someone on the inside," Andre says.

"Yes, we are."

Elizabeth and Charlotte stand. We all join hands and close our eyes in prayer. In unison, we recite, "For Henri."

Our mission is clear, each with our role to play. The Dragonnades march on and our people still die. I fear it will never end, but all I must remember is how James saved me and I feel hope for the future. One person at a time, the hatred against Huguenots will quiet, and our people will someday live free.

"We have much planning to do." Charlotte tightens her cape. "Isabelle, welcome home."

She opens the door and waits for Elizabeth to don her cape and hat. Elizabeth stops at the door. "Isabelle, are you coming?"

"No, darling. This is your show now."

She lifts her chin. "I've learned from the best. Naira would be proud, wouldn't she?"

"Yes, I believe she is. Somewhere in Canada, she's probably mixing tea and smiling, knowing her wolves are across the world fighting for what's right."

"I love you both."

"Love you always," Andre says.

She shuts the door and I rest my head on Andre's chest. He never asked me to step aside, but after seeing how Elizabeth handled herself in Versailles, I could see she was ready.

"Naira was right," I say. "I did die that rainy morning in the Ancient Gallery. The old me in a battle to prove myself and assuage my guilt. That Isabelle is gone."

Andre twirls my hair between his fingers. "You'll never stop fighting, Isabelle. It's one of the reasons I love you."

Gone are the days of broken bones and nightmares and chases through Paris streets. I've replaced them with quiet resistance, where I travel the Huguenot trails between Geneva and France, doing as my heart guides me.

I am no longer a Daughter of the King. I am now a Daughter of Snow and Secrets, safe in Geneva, just as fate intended.

THE END

ABOUT THE AUTHOR

This trilogy has changed my life in ways I could have never imagined. I've learned to research by looking for untold, hidden, and forgotten stories. This series ignited my love for women's history with a focus on power and survival.

I needed three books to tell Isabelle's story and her search for freedom. She needed to grow and fail and learn. She needed to make mistakes and fall in love. I wanted to write an epic love story with tons of adventure, and no character could have fulfilled that dream like Isabelle has. She's fierce and good, the kind of protector we all want in our lives.

I am eternally grateful to Black Rose Writing for seeing the potential in this book and supporting me during the last few years as this trilogy came to life.

To my writing circle of incredible women authors: Lisa, Sayword, Jen, Caitlin, Naomi, Brigette, Sheila, and my friends at The Eleventh Chapter, you've made this journey one of the best experiences of my life. Thank you to the Women's Fiction Writers Association for the unbelievable resources and support.

And thank you to Mike, my best friend and favorite travel partner.

To every reader who has picked up Isabelle's story, you've made my author dreams possible. Thank you.

ABOUT THE AUTHOR

Kerry Chaput is an award-winning historical fiction author. She believes in the power of stories that highlight young women and found families. Born and raised in California, she now lives in the beautiful Pacific Northwest, where she can be found on hiking trails and in coffee shops.

Connect with her at www.kerrywrites.com.

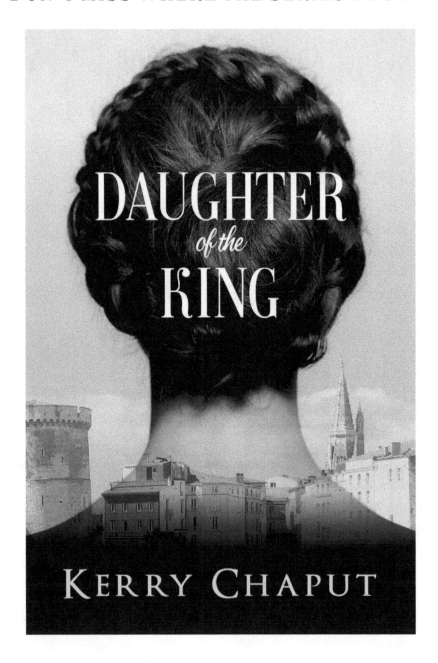

DAUGHTER
of the
KING

KERRY CHAPUT

NOTE FROM KERRY CHAPUT

Word-of-mouth is crucial for any author to succeed. If you enjoyed *Daughter of Snow and Secrets*, please leave a review online—anywhere you are able. Even if it's just a sentence or two. It would make all the difference and would be very much appreciated.

Thanks!
Kerry Chaput

We hope you enjoyed reading this title from:

BLACK ROSE
writing™

www.blackrosewriting.com

Subscribe to our mailing list – *The Rosevine* – and receive **FREE** books, daily deals, and stay current with news about upcoming releases and our hottest authors.
Scan the QR code below to sign up.

Already a subscriber? Please accept a sincere thank you for being a fan of Black Rose Writing authors.

View other Black Rose Writing titles at
www.blackrosewriting.com/books and use promo code
PRINT to receive a **20% discount** when purchasing.

Printed in the USA
CPSIA information can be obtained
at www.ICGtesting.com
LVHW040729290924
792424LV00031B/288